The Firelings

The

CAROL KENDALL

Firelings

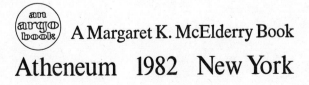 A Margaret K. McElderry Book

Atheneum 1982 New York

LIBRARY OF CONGRESS CATALOGING IN PUBLICATION DATA

Kendall, Carol
  The firelings.

  (An Argo Book)
  "A Margaret K. McElderry book."
  Summary: The Firelings, who live precariously on the edge of the
volcano Belcher, must offer the volcano a sacrificial victim or escape
through the secret Way of the Goat.
  [1. Fantasy. 2. Volcanoes—Fictional] I. Title.
PZ7.K33Fi   [Fic]   81–8096
ISBN 0–689–50226–5   AACR2

Composition by American–Stratford Graphic Services, Inc.,
Brattleboro, Vermont
Manufactured by Fairfield Graphics,
Fairfield, Pennsylvania
Map and illustrations by Felicia Bond
First American Edition

For Callie and Gillian,
and Tick

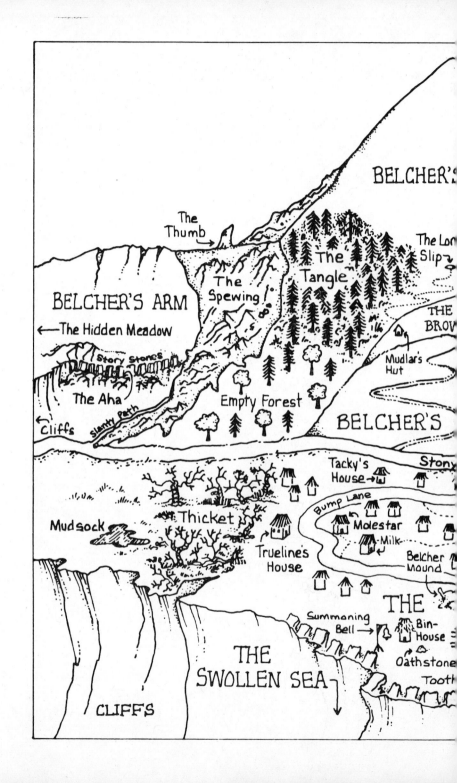

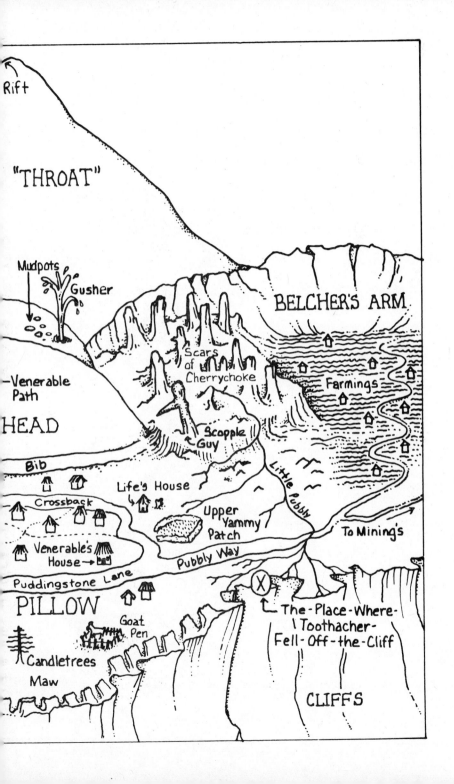

The Firelings

Long ago, as the Firelings' Story Stones tell,
Belcher, then a blundering sky-creature, put his
foot right through the sky and went falling into a
sea of his own brine. Deep in Belcher's Belly inner
fires still kindled, and to appease his rumbling
appetite hapless victims had occasionally to be sac-
rificed down what was called the Long Slip. This
had not happened for some time, but when Belcher
again developed a bellyache and gave voice to his
discomfort with cantankerous grumblings and
growlings, the Firelings began to whisper among
themselves that the time had come for another victim to be sent the way of the Long Slip . . .

1

High on Belcher's Arm,
Where the gawk birds soar,
The Story Stones tell
Of the time that went before.
(And Truth is in the Telling, for Belcher wrote
    it there.)

—Trueline, "Stone the First," from *Songchant of
the Twelve Story Stones*

The Firelings, who were no bigger than Firelings were
meant to be, dwelt high above the sea on a bumpy piece of
land they called Belcher's Body. They called it that because
it had, in fact, the shape of a body sprawled on its back.
There were head and shoulders, two vast outflung arms,
and a long throat and chest that rose up to a fine high
prominence known familiarly as Belcher's Belly, but more
nicely, albeit vaguely, referred to as Belcher's "Throat."
Clouds often swathed the heights—clouds and the smoke
from Belcher's inner fires. There were said to be legs to the
Body as well, but they lay useless far beyond the Firelings'
ken, and were known only through the tales of the Story
Stones.

There were but twelve Story Stones in all, so the pictured
tales were short enough. Belcher had started life as a sky-
creature who stamped a hole in the sky-boards from dancing too exultantly, gashing himself on the jagged edge.
Fortunately, his juices had dribbled out, and so provided a
vast puddly sea for him to fall into, else he would still be
falling straight into tomorrow. And there he lay until his
sky-brothers sent lightning flashes to rekindle his vital fires;

3

then he made things out of his inner being to keep himself company. Sun and moon and star splinters he made; trees and grass and flowers; fish and goat and gawk bird; and finally he made Firelings, but there was not enough substance left to make the Firelings as high as a grown goat or to cover them with fur or feathers or to give them more than two spindly legs. Belcher had just enough strength left to tumble these skimpy beings hugger-mugger out of his Rift, and they rolled down his chest to his head and came to rest on his Brow, where they dwelt peaceably for long years—until the time came when they tried to leave . . .

They were overwhelmed by the Spewing at the very moment of their attempted escape. Only five Firelings crawled out of the ashes of that time to find, in place of their houses on the Brow, a waterspout and five circles of bubbling pink mud. One of the five Firelings read messages in the mud and so became the Very First MudLar; the other four climbed down Belcher's pate to a bigger ledge and set up house there. And multiplied.

And that was the gist of eleven of the twelve Story Stones.

Most of the Firelings now lived on that same tuck of land—the Pillow—just below Belcher's Head. The Pillow was all built over with tussock-roofed cottages and black-rock fences; and its far edge, overhanging the sea, was rimmed with natural upright stones—for all the world like teeth jutting from a lower jaw. That part of the village was known as Toothy Maw. The summoning bell hung there, with the binhouse and the speaking bench on either side of it; the village goat pen was near the track leading to the outlying yammy patch; and the big Belcher Mound marked the roadway where Bump Lane and Puddingstone Lane rounded into each other. Candletrees grew fatly in the middle of the Maw, and saltlime trees grew scantly against the outer tooth-stones.

Below Toothy Maw roared the ocean, but so far below

4

that no Fireling ever got his feet wet in it—except for Very Old Toothacher, who some years before had fallen from his cliff-top rock and got very wet all over. Falling in was the only way a Fireling knew to reach the sea, and there was no climbing back to Belcher's Body. Very Old Toothacher had sunk beneath the waves, an ending he must have embraced most happily, for he was one who loved to study the constant wash of the Swollen Sea. It was said that on quiet nights he could still be heard counting the waves and troughs.

Besides the Firelings on the Pillow, there were Firelings who farmed and Firelings who mined. They lived and worked in the direction of Belcher's outflung right arm and seldom visited the Pillow except on festival days. A "solitary" might wander into the village now and again, but nobody knew—or much cared—where such hermits dwelt. They weren't given to washing themselves and were rather too rank for clean-living Firelings.

Those were all the Firelings there were, except, of course, for MudLar and his apprentice Skarra, who lived to themselves on Belcher's Brow far above the Pillow (but still far below the Rift) and tended the mudpots. They never came to the village at all.

As for the half beings said to inhabit the black corsa of the Spewing—those ghosts of ancient Firelings who had sought the fabled Way of the Goat and found death instead under molten rock—why they were seldom seen for the good reason that Firelings stayed away from that side of Belcher's Head. There had been a time when a journey to the Aha to read the tales of the Story Stones meant picnics and jollity, but all that had changed after Tacky-obbie's parents were swallowed by the Spewing for daring to set up a potting-oven in the side of the corsa. A scant ten years was not long enough to make Firelings forget the happenings of that frightening time.

And that was the way of it for the Firelings who dwelt on Belcher's sprawling Body, "like fleas on a goat," as Potter Ott was fond of saying.

He was saying it, in fact, on the very night that Belcher gave the first tentative lick of his red tongue against the black sky.

Potter Ott and his nephew Tacky-obbie were in their cottage at the head of Bump Lane, whiling away the hour before bedtime, like any Fireling family, in stories and talk, when Ott took up his favorite subject.

". . . like fleas on a goat," Potter Ott said. When he had got his own considerable stomach comfortable and his pipe of cherrychoke going well, he went on: "It's no easy thing to live on another's body. Just consider for a moment the plight of the flea on the goat's back. Tacky-obbie, are you attending?"

Tacky turned a yawn into a cough, and nodded his head. The flea again. Could there really have been a time when he begged his uncle to tell the flea story over and over? Resigned, he gave up poking the coals in the firepit and sat straighter on his tipstool.

"Yes, now suppose the flea in a fit of exuberance leaps too high from the goat's back, and while he is joyfully snicking his legs in the air, the goat suddenly veers and goes bounding off in another direction entirely? Why, then, Tacky-obbie, need I say that the flea is in grave danger of coming down on nothing-at-all?"

Tacky swallowed another yawn in his throat. "Yes. I mean no. No need. No. Nothing-at-all."

"Thus is the body-dweller at the mercy of the body it dwells on." Potter Ott huffed a ring of smoke into the air and sent another ring through it. An early midgin circling Ott's head wavered in its flight, staggered, and finally spiraled to the stone flagging, where it feebly kicked its last.

Ott pointed to it and shook his head. "Even that poor

6

creature, who but wished a spick of my blood, has had to pay the pipe, so to say. What I am getting around to, Tacky-obbie . . ."

Tacky knew, back-to-front, what his uncle was getting around to. In a moment now he would say, "And so it is with us Firelings . . ."

"And so," said Potter Ott, "it is with us Firelings. Forever at the mercy of Hollow Belly up there!!" and he flung his hand toward the window set high under the cottage rooftree.

Framed in the three-cornered window, Belcher's Throat stood in serene outline against the night sky. If the Hollow One heard Ott's blasphemy, he gave no sign of taking vengeance. Not that Belcher could ever run out from under them like a goat, no matter how high Firelings leaped into the air or how often Potter Ott called him "Hollow Belly" or "Afflictor" or "Old Tormentor." Belcher might give Firelings a good shaking-up from time to time, but run away he could not. He had lain supine in the Swollen Sea for so long that he was all sand and rock and soil—and a plume of smoke at the top to tell which way the wind blew.

Tacky swallowed a big yawn—and hoped his uncle wasn't in one of his fiercer moods. It had been a long day of fetching clay from the Mudsock for Ott's potting wheel.

"Ever since . . ." said Potter Ott weightily, having sucked his pipe into renewed life . . . "ever since that great blundering oafish sky-creature Belcher put his foot through the sky and . . ."

His uncle *was* in one of his fiercer moods. Resigned, Tacky stole another look at Belcher's shrouded peak through the high window, but the fallen sky-creature didn't so much as blow a smoke ring. Potter Ott shifted his ponderous weight on the creaking tipstool and launched into an attack on Fireling notions about their beginnings.

Before long Ott had reached the delicate subject of Belcher's body content. "Inner being!" he roared now.

7

"Well, what is *in* the inners of beings? Gizzards, that's what! Gizzards, that's what Old Bellyful made stuff out of to keep himself company. Plain ordinary gizzard, Tacky-obbie. Don't forget it!"

"I won't," Tacky promised with a gulp. "Ahmmm . . . gizzard."

The tirade spun out and the night grew long. Tacky felt his eyes closing and was powerless to open them again . . .

". . . the Spewing!"

Tacky jerked awake.

His uncle glared at him fiercely. "Jealousy! Nothing more than petty jealousy dressed up to look like vengeance! Mark this, Tacky—Firelings wanted to find another Body to live on, and Belcher flew into a rage. That's what came spilling out of his old gizzard-sack! Jealous rage!" He shook his pipe at Tacky and sparks flew. "Gouting out of his middlings it came . . . sucking and slurruping . . ." He made a frightful engorging sound and smacked his lips with relish . . . "gobbling up stone, bush, tree, Fireling—everything! Ever-y-body!"

Tacky hugged himself to keep from shivering. He knew the Spewing all too well—that giant lumpy black tongue of corsa naked of so much as a hair of grass. Didn't he have to pass it every time he went to the Mudsock to dig clay!

"Aaaah, but . . . !" and Potter Ott pushed his finger into one jowly cheek and looked wise. That meant it was MudLar's turn . . .

"The MudLar! Hah! The real beginning of Fireling troubles. Ashes and fire are nothing next to a MudLar. He and his messages from Belcher! I want to know, Tacky, if Belcher were to speak, would he do it in mud? 'Move off the Brow,' says the Very First MudLar, 'because the Mud speaks,' he says. 'Do all that I tell you,' he says, 'because the Mud is talking again.' Pfahp! is what *I* say! He only wanted the Brow to himself, with a village full of folk down below to sing to his tune!"

8

There was more—on and on—but Tacky closed his ears and kept an eye on the three-cornered window and told himself that if Belcher *were* offended, he would long since have shaken the house down, or . . .

He almost didn't see it—a sudden candle of flame standing above the Rift. It lived no longer than a single moment; in the next it was snuffed out. Rigid, Tacky stared at the spot. A tiny point of light, like a warning . . . ?

Ott was coming to the end of his anger for the night and was punctuating his words with gaping yawns and gigantic upheavals of his chest. ". . . and Belcher wrote it there? Thumb and nonsense! Have you ever tried to write something on the far side of your own arm?" He yawned mightily, a great *hoo-hawh*, and talked through the tail-end of it. "It's the MudNoses, one after the other, that scratch the pictures on the Stones—and that MudNose up there on the Brow right now has the muddiest beak of all . . . !"

Tacky shuddered at the new scurrility. Belcher paid no attention.

It was Potter Ott's boast that he exercised his tongue regularly instead of keeping it sneaked away like a mole in a hole. He had little care who heard him at his exercising. Fortunately, most folk chose to laugh—uncomfortably—and declare the ideas from his head to be as skewed as the pots from his awkward hands.

But there *was* that dark affair of years ago, put aside, yet never down-under forgotten: the time when poor Hulin of the webbed toes—the Crumplin, he was called by the village chidlings in their games—had been sent down the Long Slip to appease Belcher's still-rumbling appetite. There had been murmurings then against Potter Ott for "thwarting and flummoxing" MudLar's demand for a suitable Morsel, but these complaints had long since ceased to be heard. Nobody liked to talk about Hulin's end, for it brought guilt back to Fireling minds. Further, the occasion had made of the time-honored Long Slip a place of shame and fear instead of a warm, welcome return to Belcher for those who died naturally.

No, the tale of Hulin's end was not a popular one, though it was etched clear on the Twelfth and last Story Stone. Whether it had been put there by a double-jointed Belcher or by the present MudLar with stone chisel and mallet really made no difference. The Story Stones were there, had always been there, and that was enough for a proper Fireling to know.

2

What is it comes
Shrinking through the crannies,
And cringing down the cracks,
Stealing out of silence,
To go crawling down your backs?

—An ancient riddle

Belcher had a bellyache.

The long low grumble of pain came just before sunup on the day of the Sky, in the season of Shivery Rains, in that eleventh year of the Gawk, and was at first put down to thunder.

Venerable, whose skinny old shanks always rested uneasy at the joints, heard the rumbling and creaked out of bed to look anxiously at the weather, for today was the Festival of Inviting Showers, and rain would spoil the festivities. The gawk birds were just sweeping away the darkness with their noisy flappings and shrill cries of *"Yih-yih."* Venerable in his nightgown dithered into the garden to peer at the graying sky, until his sharp-nosed goodwife ordered him inside lest he be seen by an early passerby.

"How can it possibly rain at the Festival of Inviting Showers, Old Foolishness!" she said tartly, her tongue being as sharp as her nose. "For if it rained, where would be the need of inviting it?"

As usual Ven Ida's logic was impeccable. At its appointed time the sun bobbed out of the Swollen Sea and brought to life the Scars of Cherrychoke that stood in the nest of Belcher's collarbone high above the village. One by one, like a procession of elders, the angular shafts of rock cast their shadows against Belcher's right shoulder: Old Crank and Wotkin; then Ashlar with the long-tailed rat on his head; obsequious Sadiron bowing and scraping to Toplady; several minor figures known as dworkins; and last of all and most important, Skopple Guy of the Hand. It was said that as long as Skopple Guy extended his arm above the Pillow, so long would Firelings endure.

By the time the sun's rays stabbed through the snaggled stones that rimmed Toothy Maw, the green was already a-swarm. The racket and *baa*-bble of the goats in their stone pen echoed the rattle and gabble of Firelings in the binhouse as they drew extra savory and spice against the day's boilings and bakings. Chidlings streamed across the grass in festival spirits and festival clothes—reds and oranges, greens and yellows and purples, and even, woven in here and there, a few threads of wistful blue, though it was a color out of favor in the village since the shameful Hulin incident. Once a charmed color for children, it had turned unlucky, unsafe, as though the drawing of attention to any child was to mark him for the Long Slip before his time.

Only the Stone Hulin, that mute creation of Chipstone's chisels, fully dared the color, but then he stood in no danger of becoming a Morsel for Belcher's appetite. Today he was dressed in a new blue tunic, for Joke Eye, Hulin's mother, kept her young one alive in her heart. Stone Hulin, forever in his third year, stood smiling endlessly in his stone grotto at the top of Puddingstone Lane, and Joke Eye sat talking endlessly into his stone ear. Inside the house, Chipstone was supposed to be filling paste puffs for the festival, but he kept wool-gathering and would stand with spoon in air as still as Stone Hulin or any other of his carved stone figures. Then his daughter Life would impatiently take the spoon from him and go on with the dabbings and pinchings and shapings.

Life made a lot of irritable sounds as she worked, but her dar didn't seem to hear them any more than her domma ever did. They were both off in some sort of dream with her departed brother.

"There will come a day," Life muttered into the puffs, "when I shall leave this house . . ." Dab, splotch, pinch . . . "have a house of my own . . ." Dab, splot . . . "up on the Scars or . . . or somewhere, and they'll never find me. They'll look and look, and dar Chipstone will have to carve a statue of *me!*"

But dar Chipstone continued to regard the air, and outside, domma Joke Eye's voice flowed on monotonously in her one-way conversation with Life's stone brother.

"Someday . . ." Life left off her dabbing and pinching to stare at her own dream. "Someday," she said softly, "I shall go where the sun goes, to see what is there . . ." She looked up, then, at the three-cornered window framing Belcher's smoking top, and smiled. "And I shall go beyond you, too," she said. "Oh, *way* beyond . . . Someday I shall walk along your legs the other side of . . ."

Her mother's querulous voice made its way into her fancying, and with a sigh she thrust the spoon back into her father's limp hand and went outside.

"See?" Her mother held up the two halves of a small bowl. "It simply fell apart. Really, Starm and Frail are growing quite careless in their potting! You must take it back to them and get another. Thank you, daughter."

Life opened her mouth and shut it again. It was wasted breath to tell her domma that Starm and Frail had been dead for long years. She took the two parts of the bowl and went out the gate.

The village bulged with sound and sang with color, and now new tints were added as folk from the farmings and minings arrived in their festive blues and golds. Their decorated carts creaked in steady procession from Pubbly Way into Lower Puddingstone Lane and Toothy Maw. Seeing them made Life feel almost cheerful, and she set off along Crossback Lane to Potter Ott's house at the other end.

13

She pushed open the gate and was halfway along the path when the door of the house burst open and smoke came billowing out. In the midst of the billow was Tacky-obbie, holding at arm's length an iron skivver dotted with blackened lumps.

He blundered to a stop. "Oh," he said, and looked ruefully from her down to the skivver. "Seedcakes. Rainbow seedcakes. For the festival."

"No thanks." Deliberately misunderstanding, she gave a disdainful sniff. "I've come for a new bowl. This one came apart—like all the others."

"Oh." Tacky looked round vaguely for a place to put the hot skivver, absently plunked it down on top of the small Belcher mound by the doorstep.

"That's bad luck," said Life severely. *"Especially* if Venerable sees it."

"Oh." Tacky removed the skivver to the doorsill. Then, motioning to her to follow, he led the way round the house to the oven yard at the back.

On the other side of the yard wall the Stony Bib stretched neatly to the forested crown of Belcher's Head, but here in the oven yard all was clutter. The kiln looked like a load of old bricks flung in a heap; stacked all round the yard walls were the products of Potter Ott's poor art. Tacky went to a pile of small bowls and began to sort through them in that irritating, meek way of his. The trouble with Tacky was that he had no . . . no push.

Life stalked over to him. "Any will do," she said. "One's as bad as the next. Your uncle makes very bad pots."

Tacky nodded humbly. "I know. I'm sorry. Here's the best one." He handed the bowl to her without looking up.

Truckler, Life thought. "Truckler," she said, and turned on her heel.

"What?"

"You truckle. When I said your uncle makes bad pots, you should have stood up for him. Denied it."

14

"I can't," said Tacky. "He does. Most of them don't even come out of the oven in one piece."

"Then . . . Then . . ." Life stopped, confused under Tacky's suddenly steady gaze.

"Then I hope the new bowl stays in one piece," he said. "But don't count on it."

She stood, uncertainly, watching him renest the tottering bowls, but he didn't look at her again, so she left. Tacky-obbie may have been named for the cheerful *tack-tack* call of the windsong bird, but that was the end of the likeness. Too serious, he was. Solemn. Grim.

Having found a convenient niche for him, she thrust Tacky into it and dismissed him from mind.

It became a morning of errands. Joke Eye needed a speck of red thread for her loom and Life had to leave off painting her dance mask—the colors had run into a grisly smirk in any case—to borrow some, "just enough for a gully bird's eye." Grey Gammer, down the lane, usually had something of everything, but today there wasn't so much as a thumbnail's length of red in her basket. No more was domma Kirtle able to oblige, or domma Anner, and finally Life was driven to throwing herself on Trueline's generosity. Of course Trueline had not one, but several, lengths of red, in varying shades, and annoyingly she tried to press all of them into Life's hand.

"No thank you," Life had to keep saying firmly. Even in the turbulence of a festival day, Trueline's every shining hair was in place and her pinover had neither spot nor stain on it, though she had just baked a trayful of cunningly shaped doughfolk. Of course she would win the prize; she always did.

"Then have one of these," Trueline urged, holding out the tray of dough babies. "Any of them but the special Belcherboy—the one with the hole in the middle. That's for Skarra, of course."

Startled, Life drew her hand back. "For *Skarra* . . . !"

Trueline laughed. "Oh I don't actually give it to him, but I always make one for him. Poor Skarra. No festivals, ever, and it can't be much fun to live all alone with a MudLar. Nobody to play with, no games . . ."

Walking back home nibbling the doughboy, Life looked up at the Brow. There was nothing to see, really, except for an outcrop of rocks that marked the ledge. Trees grew thickly all round it and beyond—farther up the mountain of Belcher's Throat. She wondered if Skarra could look down at the village, or if he could see Skopple Guy's shadow from the Brow.

Idly, too, she wondered what Trueline *did* with the Belcherboy tart. Probably sneaked it herself, Life decided darkly, and felt oddly cheered by the thought.

By the hour of the Lizard, when the sun had topped the sky, Toothy Maw was ready to Invite Showers. Bright rain banners stretched along the snaggle-toothed rocks on the seaward side of the Maw; near at hand, more pennons flapped above the binhouse and the speaking bench, and even the goat pen had its partly munched flags. The Belcher Mound was decked with early primlips, and chidlings tumbled about on the long grassy barrows that were the Belcher mound's legs.

In the very center of Toothy Maw the ancient candletrees were festooned with woven swings flying out in all directions as short legs pumped the ground and backs arched to make the swings go high and higher. Goat carts stuffed with children rattled round the outer track. Everywhere tables spraddled under the weight of honeyed cakes and jammy tarts and all the other bakings and boilings and fryings and frizzlings and saltings and preservings that Fireling was capable of imagining. Such a buzz and clapper of voices rose from all sides that the lazy wash of the Swollen Sea far below Toothy Maw for once in a way was drowned.

Venerable, a-steam with the heat of his stiff ceremonial robe, whanged the big summoning bell to mark the beginning of festivities, and Flaw plucked the opening strings of the first dance, the "Coaxing of the Clouds." Then Potter Ott let himself be clapped into the "Growling Thunder" dance, the while Overshot whomped away on the drum to the shakings of Ott's ponderous stomach.

One by one the rest of the dars and dommas joined the dancing, until the circle was a whirl of colored cloth and glinting beads, and the jaw of rocks that bordered the cliff-drop threw back the laughter and the beat of sandaled feet.

The music suddenly changed, and it was the turn of the maskers. They came solemnly stepping from the doorway of the binhouse—toe-this, toe-that, step-step-step—the bright headmasks unwavering on their straight shoulders, the beads at their ankles jingling to the rhythm of the music. They were of all sizes and dress—skimpy smocks next to long-sleeved hubbards; plain bright tabards laced over gaily figured garbens. The youngest were scarcely able to toddle; the oldest was Bitterlick from the minings, said to be as old as Grey Gammer, but still shy of the Oathstone, as the saying went, for he had never got round to finding a wife.

Gradually Overshot speeded up the beat, and Flaw's punkshell coaxed the dancers faster and faster. Dardommas clapped time on their knees and started the ancient chant of no words:

Rmmm-ah, Rmmm-ah, Rmmmh Rmmmh Rmmmh
Kmmm-ah, Kmmm-ah, Kmmmh Kmmmh Kmmmh

Winter dust spurted under the maskers' quick toe-this, toe-that, step-step-step, round and round. Here and there a mask gave a bobble, and the bobbler had to drop out of the circle while the rest of the maskers danced on, round and round and round. The music grew still faster; more bobblers left the circle, and more, till at last there were only five dancers left: Milk and Mole Star, whose arms and legs were like flying echoes of each other; then Life; then Tacky-obbie; and the fifth, of course, was Trueline, who never put a foot wrong. The excitement of the contest took hold of the audience; folk began spurring on their favorites.

"Not one of *them* will give up!" Oldest Gar shouted at his neighbor. "We'll be here till the rats start gnawing!"

"What?"

"I said 'twill be a draw with *those* five!"

"Can't hear you!"

"I *said* . . ."

Belcher intervened. In the midst of the music and the clapping, the laughter, the chanting and encouraging shouts, there came an ear-cracking *pop!*, as though a stopper had been sucked from a gigantic cask of fermenting curd.

The music stopped like a snapped string; laughter froze; Oldest Gar's words stuck tight in his throat.

"Look!" Venerable pointed a shaking finger, and every eye traveled up the wooded incline of Belcher's Head, leaped over the Brow, went moving on up the bulge of the broad throat and chest toward that familiar Rift in the fallen sky-creature's Belly . . .

It was blotted out in a thick pall of smoke.

As Firelings watched, open-mouthed, a red flame danced suddenly against the blackened sky and was gone. A belching roar—and black chunks hurtled high against the sky, to fall again into smoke and new flame.

A thin sifting of ash drifted down to their upraised faces.

Belcher spoke no more that day, but the festivities were spoiled. The maskers' dance was declared a draw, the rest of the dances forgotten. Firelings tasted at the delicacies of the feast, but they might as well have chewed grit. In an effort to cheer their long faces, Venerable rang the summoning bell for attention and pointed dramatically at the Scars of Cherrychoke.

"Look to Skopple Guy!" he cried. "He still holds out his

hand in greeting! So long as he stands with his arm stretched out to us, Firelings will endure!"

But there was only half-hearted applause, for the sun was too high to cast shadows on the slice of mountain wall behind the Scars, and without his imposing shadow Skopple Guy was only a tall, skinny thrust of stone with a splayed top.

Long before the sun dropped behind Belcher's smoking Rift, Toothy Maw was deserted of all save the penned goats, who butted against their stone walls and bleated pitifully in the silting ash. That night Firelings huddled close inside their four walls. The worm of fear, shriveled to a thread in the years since the hapless Hulin went down the Long Slip, had begun to swell once more.

The shivery rains arrived as usual the following morning, even though the Festival of Inviting them had never been properly concluded. Venerable, who normally spent the season with his feet in a pan of hot water, climbed the steep path to the Brow to get advice and comfort from MudLar —and came back empty-mouthed. MudLar had a cold in the head and his Skarra—that feeble apprentice!—could find no Seth, no message from Belcher, in the mudpots that day.

Belcher continued cantankerous all through the season of Shivery Rains and well into Singing Grass, grumbling and growling and glowing pinkly at night. Festivals were forgotten, even the joyous Hunting-the-Balefire day when the mythic blade, the Chopper of Piercing Virtue known as Balefire, was celebrated. Nobody wanted to be reminded that the white heat of Belcher's Belly had forged the blade that was fabled to stand taller than the candletrees on Toothy Maw.

Firelings tried to make light of the small tremblings that shook the Pillow from time to time. "Bad bellyache," they told each other with false cheer. Or, "It's the damps in his poor old legs," domma Kirtle would declare, full of faith that sympathy was the salve that would heal all.

But nobody dared give voice to the fearworm's gnawing message: *Belcher is hungry again.*

They thought it, and they drew away from each other to nurse their fears. Day after day, through wet and dry, Venerable forced his aching bones up the steep path to the Brow, but each time he returned with nothing to report to the questioning faces that awaited him on Toothy Maw.

Once roused, the fearworm swelled and lengthened and crawled farther within its hosts, driving them to action. Firelings set to work refurbishing their household Belcher mounds and sent their chidlings onto the Stony Bib for smooth, bright fortune stones to rim the images' rifts. Dars climbed up on roofs and hung over the peaks to swab the stone framings of the three-cornered windows: soot and dirt might offend Belcher. Dommas kept their chidlings close, examining them from top to toe for defects, for they remembered it was Hulin's webbed toes that had marked him for the Long Slip. They put binding caps on the heads of chidlings whose ears stuck out overmuch, tied off warts, poulticed boils in secret, fattened up the skinny, and all the while searched their own minds for a reason to point to another chidling—not theirs, never theirs!—to be sent the way of the Long Slip.

It would never happen again, they had promised each other after Hulin's going, and it wouldn't happen again, they promised each other now. Morsel-giving belonged to the past-and-gone time when Firelings were brutish beings cowering in fright at every shake and rumble. The giving up of Hulin to Belcher had been a sliding-back to those old ways, a sorry mistake; but it had served to put them on guard against another lapse. These days Belcher wouldn't dare ask for a Morsel, and if he did, MudLar wouldn't dare tell the Seth to Venerable, and if he did, Venerable wouldn't dare carry it out, and if he did, they would hide their chidlings away, for hadn't Potter Ott done just that the other time!

No, of course it couldn't happen again; but all the same, when dar and domma met domma and dar, they whispered names back and forth, and after a while one name was whispered more than any other . . .

3

The small dream creeps
With the Stealthy Rat
And skitters away
With the Drowsing Bat.
But the long dream brought
—By the wind's wild roar
Wakes from its sleep
The Fearworm of yore.

—An Old Chant

It was late in the season of Singing Grass, between the days of Salt and Seed, in the black hours given over to the Rat, when Belcher gave a tremendous heave that rocked every mite and speck on the Pillow.

Houses shook and jigged. Bits of stone popped out of walls; ridgepoles and rooftrees bounced; Firelings were thrown from their quaking beds; and all the things that had been up were suddenly down.

In Bump Lane, young Milk leaped from bed straight out of his window and found Mole Star already in the walkway between their houses. Bracing each other, they staggered into the tilting lane. Trueline, running to join them from across the road, was spanked flat by her lurching garden gate. On the other side of the village, at the top of Pudding-stone Lane, Joke Eye stumbled into the courtyard to see that Stone Hulin was safe, with Life and Chipstone floun-dering after her to see that *she* was safe; and at the bottom of the lane Venerable and Ven Ida clutched bony hand to skinny arm and ran across the road to fling themselves down in the shelter of the Belcher Mound on Toothy Maw.

High above the village, the Skarra clung to his thin pallet in terror while the hut danced about him, and the rolls of goatskins tumbled out of their niche onto his head. Against the other wall MudLar, his face pallid in the red light, stared gauntly at nothing. Skarra dared not disturb him.

One moment Tacky-obbie was sound asleep, and the next he was spinning through the air. He landed jarringly on the stone floor and skidded twice his length. All round him were crashings and smashings, dust and splinters; coals leaped high in the firepit; overhead the rooftree groaned.

Belcher heaved again, and Tacky scrabbled helplessly for a handhold on the slagstones. He was lifted and slammed down like a bundle of millen against the threshing floor, the breath whumped out of him.

In that instant a picture snapped through his head. It was gone with the gasping return of breath, but it left a stirring in his mind—of memory? Not real remembering; rather a sinking unease that this had happened to him before, in another time.

The floor went on lurching, but now there was a new sound: a snorting, or a guggling, a gargling, and it came from . . . from—Tacky went limp with sudden relief—from across the room. His uncle Ott, wedged by his great girth into his bedframe and still full of fumed cherrychoke dreams, had begun to snore.

In shock after shock the quakes came, but the smashings inside the four walls finally stopped. Everything that could fall off the shelves had already fallen. Overhead the three-cornered window glowed red, and angry red pulsed through the lattices of the lower windows, staining the room with Belcher's fiery warning.

Tacky cautiously pulled his arms and legs together into

a ready crouch and, between two of Belcher's wallops, pitched himself toward Potter Ott's comforting snores. Rolling and tumbling, he came up against the solidness of his uncle's bed. The fleece wadding pouched down over the side, and he dived under it, scrunching small as his legs would allow and huddling the soft folds around him to blot out the pulsing light—and the confused stirring in his head. *The second jolt remembers the first.* But he didn't want to remember the first—it had a bad feeling. He huddled closer in the cave he had made for himself by his uncle's bed, clutching the wadding tighter. A cave . . . ? There had once been a cave, a snug, good place. He could almost remember . . .

. . . he was crouching small in the dark hiding place, hugging himself with the delight of finding it—a big, up-sloping rock cave with a chimney of light high up, at the very back of it . . . and outside, voices calling gaily to him in a game of Finders, and then . . . and then his own voice answering to guide them. There had been the delighted shivering of about-to-be-found; the fear that the voices would move away; finally, when he could be still no longer, the joyous shout that brought them—two of them—running. He saw their faces happy and amazed and wondering and loving—all those things together, familiar and unknown at the same time . . . and the one's voice bubbling clear . . . "But it's a perfect pot-ting oven he's found! Look, Starm, look at Tacky-obbie's cave! . . . chimney . . . feel the updraft . . ." Her eyes shining down, the warm clasp of her arms holding him snugly close. "Tacky's Cave, because Tacky found it!"

He could feel the memory beginning to slip away, and he clung desperately to it, for he knew the earlier feeling, the bad one, lurked just the other side. He stuffed the wadding tighter around his eyes and ears to keep the memory from leaking away, but at that moment Belcher gave one last big heave that knocked him against the bed frame and scattered the dream like raindrops on a rock.

When Tacky came shivering and groping back to himself, the cottage was dark except for a pinkish glow through the lattices. He was cold. Even his teeth felt cold. Holding his throbbing head, he got himself on to his feet and stumbled to the firepit.

Not all of the oil had spilled from the oilwick pot, and he struck a light to it. The house was a-shamble, the floor littered with shards of fallen pots and dust and yammy flour and silt and runny beans and one stunned mouse. Water had leaked a sloshy path from the broken water jar to the firepit. The fire had gone out.

His teeth chattering in his head, Tacky swept the wet charcoal from the firepit and lit dry firesticks, but the small blaze did nothing to dispel a foreboding that crouched on the frightened fringes of his mind. Jumping up, he set to grubbing out the savables from the rubbish-strewn floor. He gathered up the scattered runny beans, blew off the dust, and laid them on the food shelf. A morsel of cheese, rather gritty, went beside them. The yeast crock was broken, but when he had picked out the specks and splinters, there was enough paste to set the day's loaves. The yammy flour was past collecting.

Only one pot was left whole. Kneeling in the rubble, Tacky lifted it—a stemmed cup—feeling how the smooth bowl fitted into the hollow of his palms. For as long as he could remember it had stood on the high shelf, but this was the first time he had seen it close. Rubbing away the thick dust and grime and yammy flour, he found that the bowl was sky blue and was cunningly encased in a copper sheath

25

turned green with age and neglect. The base and stem were lumpy, but as he turned the vessel in his hands, the lumps winked fire; they were bright-colored stones embedded in the copper. Tacky drew in his breath. This was never a cup shaped by Potter Ott's clumsy fingers.

Then where had it come from?

The answer stole as softly into his mind as the remembering had come last night: one moment he wasn't thinking it and the next he knew it was so. *The second jolt remembers the first.* The cup had been made by the people of his remembering: Starm and . . . the other one. Wonderingly, he rubbed his brow with his palm. They were of that lost time before he had become just Potter Ott's charge, a chidling with no dar, no domma, and not even a memory of either one. Starm and . . . ? Their very names had been buried with them under the rockfall that had taken them out of his life.

Getting to his feet, Tacky carried the suddenly precious cup over to the chest beside his pallet and knelt there, frowning. When Toothacher's Rock fell into the sea with Toothacher on it, the happening was immediately made into a story to be told around the firepit along with all the other Toothacher stories, but the rockfall that took Starm and . . . that took his dardomma . . . was never mentioned. Thoughtfully he rummaged out his soft red-dye festa gown, wrapped the cup inside it, and nested the bundle in the center of the chest for safety.

He remembered asking Potter Ott, a long time ago, if he had never had a dar and domma, and his uncle had said, "Some things are best left in the past, put out of mind." And so he had obediently left his dardomma in the past . . .

Without warning, the same unease, the foreboding that had come the night before, surged through him. Hurtling through the air . . . fright and loneliness . . .

He seized the broom and began to sweep. The choking dust he raised bothered Potter Ott not a whit except to

26

make him snore the louder, but the mouse revived and ran into her chink in the wall. Tacky left a few crumbs outside the hole and swept the rest out of the door and past the Belcher mound into a heap by the garden path. . . . There had been dust that other time too, the air choked with it, and a chidling's crying . . . *His* crying . . . ?

Abruptly, Tacky threw down the broom and went around the house to the oven-yard. Shattered pots littered the ground, but by groping about in the dust-hazed dawn, he found a jar with a broken lip that would do for holding water until his uncle got out the potting wheel. The days ahead would be full of the whir and shuttle of the wheel and the crackle of fire in the potting oven. These were the times Tacky liked best, for though his uncle made bad pots, he made them cheerfully, with many a song and a story to the creak of the wheel.

Slinging the water jar to his shoulder, Tacky set out for the spring.

The village lay eerily silent in the dawning, black stone in a gray landscape, and the air was heavy with burned dust, turned pink in the glow from Belcher's Rift. Not so much as a twig stirred; no gawk birds called to the coming sun. Even the storming of the sea far below was muted, and the only other sound was the soft rasp of his own sandals on Bump Lane. There were gaps in walls where Belcher had tumbled the stones, and a frayed look about the houses he passed. A corner of Mole Star's roof hung limp, bald of thatch; on Milk's house next door the rooftree was at a crazy angle; across the road, just beyond the nether spring, Trueline's small cottage wore an air of desolation.

Tacky found the dripping-pool scummed over with dirt and twigs, and the spillway choked by dislodged stones. Resigned, he unshouldered the water pot.

A sharp burst of sound shattered the unnatural quiet, and Tacky all but dropped the big jar. He stood stiff with fright for several moments before he realized that the sound was continuing and that it was only Trueline greeting the morning with her "Songchant of the Twelve Story Stones." Nothing ever stopped Trueline! If the roof of her house fell in, she would go on singing through a mouthful of thatch. As Tacky skimmed the pool with cupped hands and replaced the stones in the spillway, she worked her way through the first five Stones of the chant, pausing now and again to repeat a fractious line.

Tacky winced as she wobbled on a high note, but on she went, trilling and quavering her resolute way through the mournful tale of the Sixth Stone:

>"But the furls of Time uncurled
>Like leaves of cherrychoke,
>And hidden in the center,
>A Worm of Fear awoke . . ."

She took breath before the end line to deliver it in tones deep and dramatic and just a bit off pitch:

"And Belcher stirred and rumbled, but still he held his tongue."

Tacky filled his water jar and crept cautiously away, hoping she wouldn't look out of her window and summon him back, for Trueline craved listeners.

He escaped, but her voice followed him up Bump Lane.

>"They gouged his girdling flanks
>And ripped his vine-clad skin;
>In pain and rage the Belcher shook
>Till housewalls tumbled in."

Then, morosely:

"In spite, they sent no Morsel to still his hunger pangs."

Tacky got to his door in time to be spared the endless Eighth Stone. He knew every piercing note of it already—

how the ancient Firelings bundled their belongings on their backs to follow the Way of the Goat through fire and water and rock on the first day of the new season. As nobody knew which season that was supposed to have been, Trueline had made up twenty-four versions of the Bundle-back Stone. One of them *had* to be right, not that it mattered in the opinion of most Firelings.

"The Way of the Goat—*that's* what matters!" Potter Ott would expound whenever the subject arose. "Old Muddlehead needs to pull his nose out of the mudpots and go find it; otherwise, good folk, should Belcher sneeze himself inside out one fine night, we'll pull up the bed covers and find they're made of black corsa."

The bad feeling was with Tacky again as he recrossed his own doorsill. Potter Ott's snores had gone to a snuffling whistle, no more inviting of interruption than the awesome noises that had gone before. Tacky stood over him, willing him to wake up, but the loose lips went on puffing in and out, the loose cheeks flabbed away from the bones of his face, the loose body lapped over the sides of the bed. In a few hours, after the cherrychoke had worn off, his uncle would be his usual kindly, joking, lazy, happy self, ready to give ear to old memories and new forebodings. In a few hours . . . But *now* was the time he needed an ear.

He pressed an urgent hand against his uncle's shoulder.

"Rar-rr-gh!" With a massive shudder, Potter Ott heaved himself away from the hand and went back to his earlier garglings. Tacky prodded him again. Ott flailed the air with a warning arm.

Tacky stepped back, his courage leaking from him like air from a tree frog's chin. *But I'm grown,* he urged himself. *I'm no chidling to be bullied by a snore!* All the same, he didn't prod his uncle again. He picked up the bin basket and flour bag. If he whistled up Milk and Mole Star they could go to the binhouse together. Milk and Mole Star didn't talk much, but neither would they snore into his

29

face. And they didn't call MudLar names or seem to care whether his nose was muddy or not.

His spirits lifting, Tacky went out into the lightening day. Gawk birds were wheeling overhead now, drawing back the black sky curtain; the sun was edging out of the Swollen Sea; and the morning breeze had come to sweep the air clear. It was like any other morning. Even Belcher's smoke came out in gentle puffings as the daylight washed out the ill-boding pink glow.

But when he stopped at Mole Star's gate he was greeted by Mole Star's domma wagging a long spoon at him from the doorway as though he was a chidling in need of a scolding. "He's got no time for you today, Tacky-obbie, so just go along and don't be bothering us here." With a final waggle of the spoon she shut tight the door. Tacky stumbled away from the gate, his lifted spirits going the way of his short bout of courage.

Next door Milk's dar was on the roof whipping new tussock grass into the bare spots. "Save breath, Tacky-obbie," he called before Tacky could shape his lips into a whistle. "He's gone along."

What was wrong with everybody? Tacky caught up with two old gossips struggling along Bump Lane, but instead of giving over their bin baskets for him to carry, they barely mumbled in answer to his greeting and clutched the baskets against their thin chests, slowing their steps to a creep to let him pass. Then domma Floss, seeing him, turned quickly and went back inside her gate.

It must be last night's quaking that had jarred everyone, or maybe folk felt that there was too much to do and no time to talk. Grey Gammer would say the stew grows thin and weak when only words are stirred into the pot.

But as he came up to the binhouse, the air was alive with the buzz of voices recounting the night's terrors. There was no shortage of words here.

". . . the poor babling cried tears like rain. . . ."
". . . has a lump on his head like a gawk's egg. . . . !"
". . . flung pudding-flat on the slagstones, she was!"
". . . like Starm and Frail!"
Tacky stopped open-mouthed in the doorway.
"Hshhh-hh . . ."
". . . hshh-hh . . ."
The shushing sound swept along the crowded binhouse. Voices died; eyes turned towards him and as quickly turned aside. Stumbling, confused, Tacky threaded his way to the bins. A few dommas muttered "Mrnng" in the general direction of his head, but most silently gave way and looked everywhere but at him. Starm . . . and Frail . . . ? Frail! Starm and Frail . . . The names rolled easily together in his mind.

He bent over the first bin and scooped up a measure of yammy flour, feeling eyes watching every move he made. He took a second scoopful, wishing the buzz of talk would start up behind him, and a third . . .

"Morning, Tacky." The sudden voice in his ear was a startlement; flour went jetting out of the scoop. It was Grey Gammer come to his side, her face wrinkled into a twinkling smile. "And how did the windsong bird that swoops and soars pass the night?" she asked. "In its nest?"

Tacky laughed with sudden relief. It was just an ordinary day after all. "On the floor," he said, "trying to hold it still. But sometimes I didn't know whether it was Belcher or Uncle Ott's snoring that made the quaking. Are you all right?"

"Ah, it takes more than a bit of shaking to roust an older like me from bed the middle of the black hours." She took the scoop from him and emptied flour into his bag, then bent to fill it again. "But my granson's youngers went flying out of their roosts like gangling gawks." She sifted a fourth and a fifth scoop of flour into the bag and patted it shut.

"There, then, that should make five good loaves. Be sure to use all of it today. Loose flour scatters when Belcher trembles, but good loaves only bounce."

There was an oddness in her way of talking, as though she was saying something quite different from the words she used. Her eyes, always gleaming deep with thoughts beyond speaking, looked far into him now, telling him . . . what? The buzz of talk had resumed behind them and under cover of it Grey Gammer leaned closer.

"Be wary of MudLar's tongue today. There's a smell of fear." She said it so fast that he couldn't be sure he had truly heard her.

"You should tell Potter Ott," she went on in a louder tone, "that Venerable has already gone to get a Seth from MudLar, and to listen for the summoning bell to the Oathstone. And Tacky . . ." Her voice dropped again. "Mark me, Tacky . . ." but the words came in a whispered rush, and Tacky missed their meaning. *A time for . . . biding? . . . fighting?* It made no sense, but she had repeated it. *A time for fighting*—or was it *writing* she had said? And *remember,* she had said. The rest was garble.

He stared after her as she moved off nodding and smiling into all the somber guarded faces. Grey Gammer was old, old. But she was not so old that her wits had parted from her head. *Be wary of MudLar's tongue today?* What had MudLar's tongue to do with him? Potter Ott's tongue was more likely. *There's a smell of fear?* Of course there was. He had been smelling it from the moment he was thrown out of bed last night. But . . . *a time for writing . . . or riding? Hiding?*

With suddenly shaking hands he added strips of dried goat meat to his basket, then moved along to the dwindling supply of wrinkled yammies and running beans. Bits of talk drifted past, as though they had forgotten he was there . . .

" . . . and a burning coal jumped right out of the firepit . . ."

32

". . . but it's up to MudLar to say . . ."

". . . the day Belcher buried Starm and Frail!"

The runny beans spilled out of his hand, clattered back into the bin. They hadn't forgotten he was there—not at all! They wanted him to hear!

The buzz of their voices grew louder.

". . . what Belcher wants, Belcher takes . . ."

". . . a sly one Belcher is. Took Hulin down without a belch, when it wasn't the Crumplin he wanted at all. It was . . ."

"Hssh!"

"It's no time for hssh! It's time for truths!"

". . . no escaping it!"

Tacky grabbed up a fistful of the runny beans, rammed them into his basket, and got out of the suddenly stifling binhouse.

4

Tell a lie ten times by day and it will sound true before the sun sets.

—Very Old Toothacher, *Remembered Wisdom*

Outside the binhouse, Tacky drew a long breath and stopped his ears against the doom-laden voices behind him. Toothy Maw lay peacefully in the sunlight: saltlime trees sprouting green from the rocks along the cliff's edge; the candletrees in the center nubby with new buds, and the Belcher Mound a-sway with blowing grass. The constant wash-and-boom of the Swollen Sea made background music to the shrill cries of chidlings playing hopstone. Their chant drifted across the Maw:

> "Joke Eye made a honey tart;
> Then Joke Eye made a dumplin;
> But though I asked her pretty please,
> She gave it all to Crumplin.
>
> From webby toe to finger bone,
> Poor ole Crumplin turned to stone."

The village goats added a jingle of bells to the morning. Penned within their stone walls, they were clamoring to be milked and taken to morning pasture. Tacky had a sudden longing to be a goatherd again with the chidlings. Up on the Scars of Cherrychoke their concerns were small: finding the first corkleberries, or chasing the sharp-tusked piggers that worried the goats, or making their own dwarfed shadows on the mountain wall behind Skopple Guy . . .

Behind him, running steps pounded from the binhouse,

and Milk and Mole Star streaked past, their baskets held shoulder-high in one of their races. If they saw him, they gave no sign, no shout to join them. They ran whooping across the Maw, scuds of flour dust marking their passage, and Tacky thought meanly of the ear-bending they would get when they reached home with flour sifted over dried meat and yammy.

There was a sudden loud sniff just behind him. "Won't they have their big ears bent double when *they* get home!"

There was a smooth satisfaction in the voice—it was unmistakably Life's—that Tacky found irksome, no matter that he had just finished having the same thought. He was about to move off as though he hadn't heard when it occurred to him that, outside of Grey Gammer, she was the first person willingly to speak to him this morning. He turned around.

For once, Life's hair was shining smooth; her yellow pinover, though ill-patched, shone bright and clean. But she hadn't mislaid her high-handed manner. "Let's go talk to the goats," she said abruptly.

He had been thinking of doing that very thing, but, "No time," he mumbled. "Uncle . . . breakfast . . ."

She stared at him for a moment, opened her mouth, closed it—for a wonder. "All right, then I'll just walk along of you, as far as my house." She led off toward Puddingstone Lane without waiting for an answer.

Annoyed at her taking for granted that he would go the long way around just to walk with her, Tacky followed, bobbing his head at the grass-blown Belcher Mound. Life marched past it with her chin lifted. Behind them the hopstone chant had changed its tune.

> "Belcher's hungry,
> Can't you see?
> Give him a Morsel,
> But don't give *me!*"

"Likely you feel too old to be talking to goats," Life offered, "now that your hair is cut off? You're not going to make your first Oath, are you?"

"Nnn." He didn't feel old at all. The only difference he noticed since the cutting off of his hair to the ear was a chilly neck when the wind blew.

"No, of course not. You don't even know a trade yet. *No trade no wife . . . for Oath need both.*" She examined him with eyes narrowed critically. "Your ears look bigger," she said. "Otherwise no difference."

He scowled at her, but she rushed blithely on. "Do you know that my poor domma almost cut off *my* hair this morning?"

He tried to think of something scathing to say, but curiosity overcame him. It always did, with Life. "Why? Nobody ever cuts . . ."

"Why then, I'll tell you. You know how my poor domma sometimes gets confused, ever since they took Hulin, and how she . . ."

"I *know,*" he said hastily, before she could go through all the usual excuses. Confused was hardly the word for Joke Eye!

"We had no more got up this morning than Ven Ida came with her long nose all a-waggle to pay a visit." Life laid a knuckle to the end of her own nose and wiggled the end of her finger in the air.

Tacky started to laugh, then glanced warningly toward the Venerable house they were just passing. "Have a care. She might be watching."

"What a treat, seeing her own nose go past!" Life gave a bubbling of laughter. "So first thing, she complained about the jolting she got last night, and *then* . . ." Life stopped and gave a stomp of her foot . . . "and then she told my poor domma that Stone Hulin would have to be broken up! "That chunk of rock," she called him. She said if Hulin hadn't mercifully—*mercifully,* she said!—been taken by

36

Belcher in his third year, he would be full-grown by now, close to Oathing time, and certainly his hair would be short, so Stone Hulin is just a stone-shape with no meaning! Besides, she said, it's bad luck to remind Belcher that there had been a mistake all those years ago, that . . . that he wanted *somebody else* instead of Hulin . . ." Life said the last bit very fast, then added carefully, "Those were her exact words, Tacky."

He frowned. A mistake . . . He shied away from thinking what Ven Ida meant. Fear . . . "Ven Ida is shorter of heart than she is of nose," he said.

Life gave a brisk nod, but he could feel her eyes still judging him. "My poor domma just sat there, but the moment Ven Ida left she took hold of my arm and said, 'Come along inside, Hulin; it is time we cut your hair short—folk are beginning to remark it. Why,' says she, 'you'll be wanting to go before the Oathstone next thing!'"

"But . . ." Tacky looked at Life's shiny hair scrolling down her back . . . "But she didn't. How did you . . . ?"

Life waved an airy hand. "Oh, I just made whimpery Hulin sounds and said my stomach felt watery cold—and it did!—so she sent me to the bins for mustard plant. With any luck she'll dose Stone Hulin with it instead of me. Tacky . . ." She took two quick steps and planted herself in front of him. "Tacky, will you do a thing for me? Stop by my house for a moment, just a *whit?* When my domma sees your hair short, she'll think she has already cut Hulin's and . . . Please, Tacky?"

"I . . . but I. . . ." He didn't want to in the least, but Life was staring him into it. "But what if she thinks I *am* Hulin!"

"She won't. It's just to take her mind away from hair. She's not *daft,* you know. Just the littlest bit mixed up at times."

Chipstone's and Joke Eye's homing was the biggest on the Pillow. At the opposite end of Crossback Lane from

Potter Ott's, it too skirted the Stony Bib, though the house itself occupied but little of the space. In the field beyond the house gaunt shapes of rock reared into the air, a miniature version in gray of the goldenstone Scars above. The small court in front of the house was crammed with finished stone benches and stone tables, stone door lintels and stone mortars, stone rain-catchers and stone grills, and in the midst of these manifestations of Chipstone's artistry, forever immobile in a stone grotto, with a stone table at his stone right hand, stood Stone Hulin. Dark stone hair hung to his frail stone shoulders. The wind and rain of the chill seasons just past had wasted the painted blue of his tunic, but he smiled cheerfully with pale rosy lips and dark eyes, and stood staunch on his pedestal under a candletree, the unlucky webbed toes of either foot peeping out of cunningly carved stone sandals.

Beside him, on a low stone stool, sat Joke Eye, weaving bright threads on a small loom. A smile curved her lips, and when she looked up at Life and Tacky, her eyes danced over them like lights in the sky. She looked scarcely older than Life, though her hair was drawn up on her head like any busy domma's.

"Back so soon!" she called out gaily. "You *are* my quick child. And Tacky-obbie, our windsong bird! A bright morning to you."

"Bright morning, domma Joke Eye," said Tacky, surprised that she knew him at all, for he avoided her whenever possible. "Did . . . did you keep well during the trembling last night?"

"The trembling . . . ?" For an instant the lights in her eyes blurred, but she gave a quick shake of her head and they flickered back. "My dear Tacky-obbie, Belcher's greatest trembling is not to be feared as much as one bob of MudLar's head." She looked down at her weaving and jabbed the shuttle fiercely in and out, in and out.

"Yes, domma Joke Eye." Tacky felt awkward amongst

the stone clutter, not knowing whether to sit, stand, or leave quickly. Life had gone inside the house with her basket, and he was alone with this domma of the quirky tongue, who seemed to have forgotten him in her frantic weaving, but had not yet dismissed him.

Voices wafted from the Maw below; smoke wafted from Belcher above, high over Chipstone's untidy roof. Chipstone was a better stonecutter than he was thatcher: the tussock was loosely bound and dry, bunched in some places, too thin in others. Twiggy bits sprouted out of it like crazy straws stuck in a festive cake, giving the house an overall scared look . . . scared . . . Grey Gammer's words shunted across his mind, *the smell of fear* . . .

It was strange that both Grey Gammer and Joke Eye within the same hour spoke with the same tongue. *Beware of MudLar.* But nobody paid attention to MudLar any more, at least not much, the way folk did in older days. It was true that he sent Hulin down the Long Slip, but that was long ago, and it happened because everybody was frightened—Potter Ott said so many a time. They didn't know what else to do, so they listened to MudLar. It was different now. Folk were wiser. Such a thing could never happen again.

With a start he realized that Life had come out of the house and was talking to him—something about eating.

"No, I . . . thank you . . . I must go now. I wish you well, Life. I wish you well, domma Joke Eye."

"Wish-you-well," said Life.

"I wish you very well, young windsong bird," said Joke Eye. "And give my wish-well to dar Starm and domma Frail. I must send Life and Hulin over to get some more pots one of these days. They carelessly broke most of them last night."

A shiver started at the nape of Tacky's neck and traveled down his backbone. He stood stockstill and stared at Joke Eye.

"We'll do that," said Life quickly, and shook her head at Tacky.

He stumbled over a stone grill on his way out of the yard. As he closed the gate, he heard Joke Eye talking on in her bright voice.

"Do you know," she was saying, "Ven Ida grows weak in the headpiece. Just this morning she wanted me to cut Hulin's hair short—as though he wasn't the merest chidling."

Potter Ott was in his usual morning temper when Tacky roused him with a steaming cup of wickiup root passed under his nose. He made horrible growling sounds deep in his throat, followed by even more horrible lapping noises as he took the tea inside him. When Tacky gave him Grey Gammer's message, he squeezed his face up into an enormous grimace.

"Seths!" he mouthed with thick tongue. "Summoning bells! Oathstone meetings! What good are they! MudLar has had his head stuck in those mudpots for so long, his brain is mortified! And Venerable running up and down Belcher's pate like a silly gawk trying to get into the air! He can't even clear his nose without consulting MudLar which flap to blow first!"

It was not a good moment to ask questions about fears of the night. Tacky pulled his uncle free of the bed covers and onto his feet. Round as a potted cheese, Potter Ott filled a corner of the room even when standing upright. "And why not?" he liked to say. "I but fill the loneliness of my house since my finewife departed this life so many a season ago."

Potter Ott was likely as not to fasten his earlaps against any summoning bell, but this morning, instead of blowing endlessly and noisily on his second cup of wickiup, he sloshed it down and, pushing away his untouched bowl of stirabit, stomped out of the house long before the bell summoned him. He left a fat bundle of growled-out instructions behind him: gather firesticks; fetch blue clay; make bread; chock holes in firing oven; scrape potting wheel; work the clay . . .

Tacky, who had followed him to the gate, burst out desperately, "But there is something I would talk about . . ."

"*Talk!*" Ott stared at him and stalked out into the lane. "There's been altogether too much talk. The time has come to stuff the words back in." He gave a backward kick at the gate. "Oathstone meetings! Stick your finger in a stone to keep your tongue from wagging? Ridiculous!"

Tacky lingered inside the house only long enough to set the loaves. Then he was off to the Mudsock, hauling the two-wheeled cart behind him. Along the Stony Bib he rattled, past the firestick Thicket on the left and the steep Empty Forest on the right. It was lonely enough going along the path of bright loose stones where other Firelings seldom trod, but the Spewing, just ahead, sent tremors down his back.

It stretched, a great lumpy black tongue of corsa, all the way from Belcher's Rift, it was said, down his prone neck and shoulder and on down and down the side of his arm until its very tip lapped the Stony Bib. That's where the fiery melt of rock had stopped and cooled and turned to sullen black corsa. And under the jumble of burnt rocks there lay buried the Firelings who had looked for the Way of the Goat and never found it. Or, if they *had* found it, Belcher buried them for their pains before they could get out.

With a shiver of dread Tacky turned away from the ugly bare tongue and made his way down below the Stony Bib to the Mudsock, and taking the wooden clayfork and mallet from the cart, he began pounding out the first chunk. At first he kept his back to the Spewing, but it was worse to imagine a wraith's ghostly eyes boring into him than actually to catch one at it, and he turned halfway round to keep the Spewing in a corner of his own eye. Of course he was safe enough from the unquiet shades of those ancient Firelings, for everybody knew that they never left the Spewing. Not for the first time, however, Tacky wondered if the haunts knew the rules.

The midgins were circling his head in a solid mass before he had his cart loaded with all the clay it would carry. Tacky looked at the sky; the sun had passed the top. No need then to gather firesticks for firing the potting oven, not with his uncle's being at the Oathstone meeting all morning. Potter Ott was a man of habit, and he had a habit of not turning the potter's wheel once the sunball topped the sky.

But today went on being strange. When Tacky had finally pushed and hauled the cart over the last bit of Stony Bib and into the potting yard, he found his uncle growsing and growling and panting at the wheel. His face was measley with blue clay, his apron awash with the splash from the wheel.

"Work the clay," he grunted. "Then be off to get firesticks. After that, set up the pots. You can fire at sundown."

"Fire . . . those?" Tacky pointed at the row of lopsided, ill-shaped, sorry-looking pots collapsing in the sun.

His uncle glared at him from beneath blue-splatted eyebrows. "What else? Do you see any other pots hereabouts?"

Tacky held his tongue and began to knead the new clay. Whatever had been said through the secrecy of the Oathstone, it had brought no joy to Potter Ott. Gone was his usual careless talkative fashion of shaping pots. He worked furiously, as though a snake had climbed his leg. The wheel whirred and jerked, jerked and whirred; wet clay spattered everywhere; pot after misshapen pot was plunked down on the ground and another begun the next instant.

Tacky was glad finally to escape to the Thicket, but

outside the oven-yard he felt a weight of silence hanging over the Pillow. Nothing stirred, not so much as a wisp of smoke; no voices hung in the air; within the blackstone walls the houses crouched, waiting for . . . Nothing! He was imagining things.

When he got back from the Thicket with the second load of firesticks, the wheel had been cleaned—astonishing!—and put away, and the results of the afternoon's work sagged everywhere in the late sun. Tacky thought of the smooth, perfect cup wrapped in his red festa gown. His dardommma—if they *were* the makers of it—would never have bothered to bake such pots as these. Had Potter Ott's mind gone the way of Joke Eye's? Wearily, Tacky opened up the oven and began stacking the wretched pieces inside. Some of them fell apart as he picked them up; others collapsed as he tried to balance their rickety shapes in regular layers. It didn't matter. There wasn't a pot here that anybody would give houseroom to, even if, by chance, it survived the firing. All that digging and hauling and working of clay, the extra trips to gather firesticks, and now the setting of these sorry blobs in a leaky oven that might fall down at any minute: where was the sense? Tacky felt as caved-in as the pots. He had eaten one small hunk of goat-cheese since breakfast . . .

When the first faint aroma of baking bread reached his nose, he thought it must be borne on an errant wind from another homing, for another of Potter Ott's habits was never to take a hand at cooking. But then the savor of baking bread was mingled with that of hotchpot—rich, bubbling, gravied, thick hotchpot—and it came unmistakably on the down-draft from the three-cornered window far above him. So heady was the aroma that, looking up, Tacky half-expected to see the juices bubbling down the windstream.

He had just bricked up the oven opening when Potter Ott's voice drifted down to him. "Come and eat," was all he said. Tacky stumbled around the house and in through the open door.

The meal was as strange as the rest of the day had been. Potter Ott ladled bubbling hotchpot until Tacky could swallow no more. There was fresh-churned butter for the new-baked bread; there were succulent tips of speargrass; there were tiny sweet beancakes dripping with dark honey. Of all this feast, Potter Ott ate nothing. He talked. Rambling from subject to subject, he scarcely took time to draw breath and all the while he tore off small chunks of bread, which he shaped nervously between his fingers, then arranged in a border around his empty bowl.

"Your dar and I, we used to look for the Way of the Goat when we were chidlings," he said. "It was a thing all youngers dreamed of finding. And never did." He paused to count out twelve of the blobs of bread, which he then flattened with his thumb, *blunk, blunk, blunk* . . . "Nobody believes much in the Way of the Goat any more, but we did. It was in the old stories, and we believed." *Blunk, blunk.* "It's there somewhere, Tacky," he added softly. "Fireling found it once, and Fireling will find it again." He glanced up, and his eyes blazed deep with belief. Then he went back to his crumbs. *Blunk.*

"There wasn't fear in our young days. Fear had died out of Firelings. But then Belcher started up his shaking and quaking and fireshot. That was at the time the potting cave fell in."

"The potting cave," said Tacky quickly. "Tell about the potting cave."

"Used to walk the Spewing, we did," his uncle went right on, pushing the twelve flattened shapes into a straight line. "Never afraid of haunts, Starm and I. We didn't believe *all* the old stories, you see." His eyes flashed again, and again his voice dropped almost to a whisper. "Your dar and I decided that those Ancients followed the Way of the Goat and got out. Left Belcher's Body. Skaddled."

44

"But the haunts!" Tacky cried. "Folks have *seen* them!"

"We never saw any. Never went higher than the Aha, though. Some rules you shouldn't break without good reason. Good thing to remember. Be brave, you see, but not too brave. Where was I? Oh yes. Cave. We found a good hiding-cave. Under the Spewing. Still there, I shouldn't wonder. Took you there once, actually, to hide from . . . when . . . but you don't remember. In the Aha, behind the Sky Stone, through a crawl space? No, you don't remember, but you'll see." He tapped the blob of bread on the right end of the line and rapidly strewed a path of loose crumbs down from it, then looked sharply at Tacky. "Are you attending?"

Tacky roused himself from watching the pellets of bread. Twelve pellets, twelve Story Stones, and the one on the right end was the First, the Sky Stone, with the path running down the slope in front of it. "Behind the Sky Stone, you said. But the other cave—the potting cave that fell in?"

"It fell in," his uncle said shortly. "No secret about that. The earth shook and the cave collapsed. That's the all of it. There's nothing more."

"Uncle . . ." He finally got the question out in a whisper. "Where was *I?* Then. When it happened."

But Potter Ott had already got off on another tack: Mud-Lar. MudLar was nothing more than an ordinary Fireling with mud speckles. And Skarra? A poor weasling baby-thing with no more name than "The Dab," who became Skarra only because his dardomma had perished in a mining accident at the very time a new Skarra was needed.

"And that's the way it has always been up there on the Brow, all that fuddle-muddle and stir-with-a-stick! You mark well, Tacky-obbie, the day will come . . ." And Ott railed on, mixing past and present and future in such a confusing web that Tacky could take no meaning from his words at all.

"Do you mark this cracked stone?" Potter Ott suddenly

asked. Grunting, he leaned over to point with the ladle at the long diagonal split in the biggest slagstone.

"Of course," said Tacky. "It's always been there."

"Always . . ." mused Potter Ott. "And is your always the same as my always?"

"I . . . I don't understand."

"How do you think the slagstone came to be cracked?"

"Why . . . I suppose . . . I've always thought it cracked some time when Belcher trembled."

"And if someone were to ask you, like Venerable himself, let's say, how that crack came there, is that what you would tell him?"

Tacky hesitated, then nodded.

"And if Venerable were to stand up in Oathstone meeting and say that Belcher had cracked a slagstone in Ott's house, would others believe him?"

Tacky squirmed with discomfort, but Potter Ott waited for his answer. "Yes," he finally said. "Yes, they would."

"And if Venerable told MudLar and MudLar then carved what he said into a Story Stone, would everybody take it to be truth?"

"Of course."

"Ah," said Potter Ott with satisfaction. "Ah and hah!" He fell silent, a pleased smile wreathing the folds of his face.

"If you please," Tacky asked, "wasn't that the way of it?"

". . . the way of . . . ? Oh, the slagstone. No, that wasn't the way of it at all, not at all. *That* happened one day when my finewife dropped the flopcake skivver on it."

"Oh. Was it . . . was it because Belcher was shaking that she dropped it?"

"No." Potter Ott's smile grew even wider. "She dropped it because the handle was too hot."

Tacky's head spun with the effort to understand Potter Ott's quizzing, but the day had been too long and the meal too filling. His thoughts all fell together into one gigantic yawn.

"Sleep now," said Potter Ott. "I'll rouse you at sundrop to start the firing. I expect Flaw and Overshot for private talk and I would not have you hearing Oathstone secrets you *should* not hear."

And that's another odd thing, Tacky thought just before he sank into sleep. If his uncle wanted to have private talk, why put him in the oven yard where the strange up-down drafts through the three-cornered window would carry every sound to him as clearly as though he were in his own bed? More clearly! In his own bed he would at once sink into sleep, just as he was sinking now . . . He wished he didn't have that other sinking feeling in the middle of his middle.

5

The hungry stomach grumbles,
Cheated of its meal.
Choose the gaping passage,
The wrath no longer feel.

> —Seth given by MudLar to Venerable this
> Eleventh Year of the Gawk, in the Season
> of Singing Grass, on the Day of Salt, in
> the Hour of the Prancing Goat.

The great orange sunball had already fallen into the sea the other side of Belcher's Throat, where it would warm the Hollow One's useless legs during the black hours. On the Pillow, doors were closed against the chill night and lattices pulled tight over windows. It was a time for families to sit cosily round the firepit telling stories and toasting fat melon seeds, or painting masks against tomorrow's Festival of New Life, the day once known as the Giving of the Morsel. It was no time to be out of the house and alone.

But that's where Tacky was, and the strange day continued strangely into the night. Roused from his exhausted slumber at sundown, he had stumbled outside to light the potting oven and now, hunched against the rough wall of his uncle's house, he scrooched himself small inside his garben and kept watch on the firing. The kiln was a shambly cone of ill-fitted firerock, flung carelessly together when plain Ott perforce became Potter Ott. He had seemed a natural choice at the time . . . to everybody but Ott himself, who had no inclination to shape pots. But then he had little inclination for anything more than an evening's argument with cronies over their pipes.

The bitter smoke of cherrychoke leaked out of the three-cornered window above Tacky, and the whichway wind drafted it down the housewall along with his uncle's mutterings. Flaw and Overshot were long overdue. Tacky scrunched miserably closer to the wall, as though the descending curtain of warm smoke would hold off the glowering night and the deep forebodings that had taken up living-space inside him.

Halfway down Bump Lane, sitting on the big square memory stone under her greenthorn tree, Trueline hummed softly to herself as she too watched the night. Her dar had sat out his last years on a cliffside rock beyond the village in order to get away from folk, but she sat on her stone to be nearer them. "If you're always Inside," dar Toothacher used to say when she begged him to return home from his lonely lookout, "how can you know what is going on Outside?"

What was going on outside tonight was a heavy smell of burnt rock hanging in the air; an eerie pink haze enveloping the homings of the village; and a line of little smokes going straight up from each chimney hole, for the strong evening breeze had not yet come. Belcher's brummelling above the Pillow merged with the surge and swell of the Swollen Sea below it, but the village itself crouched in uneasy silence. Uncertainty leaked through the walls of the houses and clung to the black stones.

Whatever had been decided at the Oathstone meeting today, Firelings were keeping it locked inside their heads. Trueline hugged her dar's old fleece tighter around her. Never before had she failed to learn what went on at the Oathstone almost as soon as the dardommas, who were there, knew. Finding out, after all, was simply a matter of listening to what one saw, looking at what one heard, and telling naught to no one, for to gossip idly was to leak away

49

the certain knowledge of things. Toothacher had said it, and Trueline believed it.

The two shadows slipped so silently from the walkway between the houses across the lane that she didn't see them until they appeared at Mole Star's gate. Trueline abandoned her tune in the middle of a hum. Flaw and Overshot? Didn't they remember that only last season Mole Star's domma Willa had thrust them from her door with a long broom and sent their cherrychoke pipes clattering after them? Yet tonight when they tapped on that same door, it edged open and they slipped inside as quietly as the shadows they cast. Odd. Perplexing. Trueline picked up her hum where she had left off and waited to see what happened next.

When at last the door opened again, a third shadow had attached itself to the first ones. They turned right at the gate and went up Bump Lane: Flaw and Overshot—they walked with a swagger—and Witlatch draggling after. Their footfalls gritted away into the distance. Still Trueline waited.

Creak of a lattice. She smiled. Mole Star was leaving by his window to find out what his dar was up to. In a moment there was a scuffling—Mole Star going over his homing wall—and a low whistle. Trueline smiled again. A second faint scuffling: Milk joining Mole Star in the walkway between their homings. In another moment they appeared and went loping up the lane in the wake of the fast-disappearing shadows.

Trueline slid down from the memory stone, eased her gate open and, soft-footed, followed close after.

She came to the top of the lane quickly enough to see the first three shadows go through Potter Ott's gate, but when the housedoor swung open, only two of them went in. The third still lurked somewhere inside the homing wall. Milk and Mole Star separated and went opposite ways around the outside of the wall towards the back.

Trueline stood undecided between one step and the next:

"Elchery Belchery slippery toe,
Show me the way that I should go.
Thisser way, thatter way, I don't care,
But one thing I won't . . .
I - won't - go - *there!*"

There came out "thatter way," so she went "thisser way,"
left, round the homing wall to see what there was to hear
and hear what there was to see.

It was only by chance that Life joined the growing crowd
outside Potter Ott's house that night. Dar Chipstone had
arrived home from the morning's Oathstone meeting in a
bog of gloom, while Joke Eye was so distracted that she
spent the rest of the day in the stone grotto pouring a steady
murmur into Stone Hulin's ear. After supper Life tried to
interest her dar in a game of hole-stones, but he kept
miscounting the pebbles through inattention. Then she
traced the beginnings of a story game in the word-box:

"One cloudy morning three Firelings went walking in the
rain and when they looked at the sky . . ." But Chipstone
insisted that the story could just as well read: "At sundown
of a cloudy day MudLar went three times up the ancient
path to gather chortles, and then he flew into the sky," and
out of obstinacy would have it no other way. Nor would he
add a sentence to the story, in spite of her coaxings and
cajolings to play the game to the end. Vexed, Life tilted the
box of sand to erase the words.

"What does it matter anyway?" Chipstone muttered and
slumped deeper into his soggy state.

Life stomped out of the house into the chill twilight. She
walked past her domma, who never lifted her head from
Stone Hulin's ear, banged out of the gate, and stalked down

Puddingstone Lane. There was nobody else taking the night air except for the goats racketing in their pen on Toothy Maw. She spoke soothingly to them, but they only butted the gate harder and bleated louder.

Nothing stirred on Bump Lane as she rounded the curve of the road—but even as she looked, Life heard the muted clunk of a gate's closing, and a darker something moved into the roadway. And were those shadowy substances farther up the lane? Her head prickled with excitement. "Something," she announced to herself, "is afoot."

Slipping off her sandals in two quick sweeps, she half-ran after the shadow in the night until she was close enough to see that it was only Trueline who was afoot. Disappointed, she dropped back. So much for adventure. A moment later she saw light shine out from Potter Ott's door at the top of the lane and heard the murmur of voices in the air. Ott had callers, that was the all of it. Ott had callers; Trueline was taking a walk, and she, Life, never walked with Trueline by choice.

But suddenly the road ahead seemed full of skulkers, and Trueline had stopped short. In another moment she turned to the left and began circling the homing wall. Now that was a curious thing. Life hesitated and then, shrugging, went right, groping along the walkway between Ott's and Oldest Gar's homing walls. She stumbled over something and almost fell and felt her arm grabbed. A warning finger tapped her mouth.

"Hsssh." Mole Star removed his foot from her path and pulled her down to a crouch. "Life? Hsssh." Then he cautiously rose and, bent double, yanked her along by one hand towards the rear of the house.

Angrily, she tried to jerk away, but Mole Star only tightened his grip and towed her with him. Finally, with an additional "Hsssh!"—didn't he know any other words?—he turned her hand loose and made motions that seemed to say she could stand up, with caution.

She stood upright to look over the fence and, in fright, bobbed down again. Just inside the fence, no farther than the length of her arm, stood a figure. His back was to her, and he was peering around the corner of the house into Potter Ott's oven yard.

When her heart stopped throbbing up in her throat and retreated to its home, she dared to raise her head, slowly, above the wall once more.

The potting oven was roaring with flame through every crack and chink, throwing a fitful light on the yard walls and the back of Potter Ott's house—and the crouching figure of Tacky himself huddled close against the wall. There was a grumble of voices inside the house, but that wasn't the reason the quiet watcher—Witlatch?—was skulking inside Ott's homing. He was watching Tacky!

Inside the house, around the firepit, the three old companions had got the preliminary greetings out of the way and were down to the business of firing their pipes. Soon there was the familiar gurgle and gasp as they moodily sucked at the cherrychoke; the *hrumping* sound forced out of Ott when he bent his roundness to stir the coals; an occasional cough—Flaw; a hissing noise—Overshot spitting into the fire. It was Overshot who finally ended the silence with a great clearing of throat and the sizzle of spit.

" 'The hungry stomach grumbles,' " he began, but his voice suddenly stuck, so he went through the rites of *hmmm*-ing and expectoration again, and started over:

> " 'The hungry stomach grumbles,
>   Cheated of its meal.
>   Put him down the Long Slip,
>   My wrath no longer feel!'

There! What could be clearer than that! And tomorrow the very day of the Giving of the Morsel!"

53

Potter Ott took such a fierce pull on his pipe that it sparked up past his nose. "I'll tell you what's clearer than that! The Seth didn't say anything about the Long Slip. It said 'gaping passage.' 'Choose the gaping passage,' it said. I heard Venerable repeat it most clearly."

A fruity apologetic cough. "Well now," said Flaw, pulling nervously at the muffler wound around his throat, "it may be true it went something like that, but when Venerable gave the true meaning of the Seth, he said 'Long Slip'. Those were his very words. 'Put him down the Long Slip.' What else could it mean, tomorrow being the day of the Giving? *And on the first day of the Season of New Life in the New Year shall be the Giving of the Morsel.* You can't argue with *that,* Ott. It's all clear as the sun."

"Hoh!" said Potter Ott. He picked up the fire rod and rammed it at the coals in the pit. "Clear as the mud up MudLar's nose! How could anything be clear when a gap-headed, goat-witted old gawk like Venerable starts explaining what MudLar saw in his pink stew. And haven't we all sat round this very firepit agreeing that MudLar is fuzzled with age and fumes?"

There was a small weighted silence. Overshot nervously spat towards the firepit and missed it altogether. "Better not to speak of MudLar's fuzzledness in the old way, Ott," he said cautiously. "Times have changed now that Belcher . . . This is . . . ehh . . . just a friendly word to an old companion. Ehh. Why, there are many who wouldn't come near you after the things you said at the Oathstone this morning. There are *threats* against you, but Flaw and I . . . ehh . . ."

Potter Ott opened his eyes as wide as they would go in the fat folds of his cheeks. "Nonsense! Non- and *no*-sense! The truth about MudLar tonight is the same truth as last season, and as all those rounds of seasons ago, when he put that poor hapless Hulin down the Long Slip . . ."

"Everybody makes mistakes," Overshot said smoothly.

"But what folk are *saying* is that it wasn't *MudLar's* mistake that time. It was . . . *they* say, mind you . . . it was *yours* for hiding away Tacky-obbie. *He* was the one Belcher spoke for, they say. It was the chidling of Starm and Frail he wanted. But when he couldn't be found, well, it *was* the day of Giving the Morsel, and they thought the wrong chidling was better than none, and . . ." Overshot's voice faded away and he busied himself at his pipe to avoid Ott's terrible glare.

"And do you think I don't know?" Potter Ott thundered. "Do you think I would stuff my head with cherrychoke if I could keep the Crumplin out of my dreams any other way?"

"Now, now, old friend," said Flaw soothingly, "you couldn't know that Venerable would give another chidling into MudLar's hands. And Belcher seemed to be satisfied . . . for a time. But now . . ." Sorrowfully, he shook his head. "Belcher won't be put off again. Believe us, Ott, Belcher's rage will be with us until he has his full revenge against Starm and Frail. And—Ott, you heard yourself how Venerable said they were doomed from the moment they set the first pot in the Spewing cave, and the child doomed with them. If they hadn't thrown him clear when the quake came, he would have been buried with them, and Belcher would not now be demanding a Morsel."

Ott snorted with contempt. "It's easy putting words into the mouth of one who has no proper speaking tongue. Who is to say that Belcher didn't himself throw the child from the oven to save him?"

"Belcher has tongues enough." Overshot's voice was sharp. "He wouldn't now be licking the sky with them if it had happened as you tell it."

With an enormous effort, Potter Ott sat up as straight as his middle would allow, the better to shout. "They won't take him from me, I promise you! Even if I have to send him off to live with the wild goats, or on to the Spewing itself. Nor any other Fireling, half-grown or chidling, will they take. Ill-shaped my pots may be, but there is nothing crook in my heart. If Belcher's Belly is too hot, then I say slosh him down with cold water."

"Give over, Ott," Flaw pleaded, hunching himself farther away. "Belcher will have Tacky, no matter how you talk. Overshot and I will deliver him to the Long Slip, and we . . . Ott, Venerable has given the word, and everybody is agreed on it. Over the *Oathstone!* Give the younger to us peaceably for the sake of all Firelings. Venerable said we will honor him every Hollow Day."

"*I* didn't agree," Ott shouted, and whanged the fire rod onto the coals, sending up a fountain of sparks. "Venerable is a fool with a knot of grass for a head. If he is so eager to feed Belcher, then let us put *him* down the Long Slip. *That* would give Belcher something to hiccup."

The sudden silence was like a shock that ran through the room. The oil pot gave a small shuffling dance; a dish clattered to the floor; the very slagstones jerked and heaved. For a moment the three Firelings stared at the coals clattering in the firepit until it came home to them that the shock had come from Belcher himself.

Flaw and Overshot clutched and clawed at each other, their eyes swiveling with fear, but Ott gripped his pipestem in his teeth and puffed as though his cheeks were not all a-jiggle from the earth shivers.

"Belcher save me!" Flaw bawled. "Oh save me!"

The floor gave a long quake and then was still. Flaw and Overshot untangled themselves and lurched to their feet. Flaw, his muffler all unwound, reached the door first. Overshot turned to thrust a long, accusing finger at Potter Ott. "You have said too much at last," he got out in a strangled whisper. "Belcher heard your words and has warned you. I too warn you!"

"And . . . and I," Flaw echoed as he fumbled at the latch through his hampering muffler. "We all know your

56

tricks, Ott. That's why we came to get Tacky tonight, now and here . . ." The words dried in his throat.

The house had given a queer jiggle. Now it gave another. Stronger. Flaw's feet began a strange teetering dance as the slagstones shifted under them. With a roar Overshot yanked Flaw away and snatched the door open. "There'll be no hiding this time!" he bellowed. "We're taking Tacky with us . . . now!"

He didn't get across the sill. The house gave a heave that sent him sprawling along the floor. Flaw, vainly clutching at him, landed half in the firepit. Their howls were lost in the howling of earth and sky.

Potter Ott wasted no time on them. He had picked himself up and got through the door in one motion. The ground waved beneath his feet as he ran around the house to the oven yard. Lightning shot across the sky and voices shouted at him, but he lumbered on. A dislodged stone jumped at him from the wall and struck his knee. He stumbled and pitched forward, landing with a jarring thump. His head hung over . . . nothing.

Where the oven and Tacky had been, there was now a raw split in the earth, and Ott was staring into a chasm of such swirling dust he could not tell its depth.

"Tacky! Tacky-obbie!" His shouts were a whisper in the din. He wriggled forward, but unknown hands dragged him back from the edge of nothingness.

The rift in the earth was a monstrous slash that cut sharply across the back of Ott's cottage and ran on either side as far as he could see in the smoky glare. Stone fences, flax plots, trees—all had disappeared into the cut.

The unknown hands pulled at him again, but he flung them off. Somewhere in that trench, if he could only see him . . .

The earth moved again. Shuddering, grating, the two lips of the endless gaping mouth began to close. They came

57

together with a final crunch, throwing up earth and rocks and dust into a tumbled pucker that stretched all along the line where the ditch had been.

Potter Ott stood immobile under the shower of stones and dust, barely conscious of the arms holding him back and of Flaw's and Overshot's gibbering behind him. Belcher gave a monstrous sucking sound and shot out flames that licked the sky. Black ash rained down; smoke blanketed them.

"Fly!" Overshot shouted. "We'll be smothered! Witlatch, is that you? Let's get away from here! Flaw? Come away!"

Potter Ott stood on, oblivious to the rain of hot ash, the strange hands pulling at him, the beginning toll of the summoning bell from Toothy Maw. He stood and stared at the puckered barrier higher than any homing wall, as though he could will Tacky to rise up from it.

"The bell!" somebody shouted into his ear. "There's fire in the village. Come away now. There's nothing here for you to do."

Ott slowly nodded his head. A wave of pain and loss washed through him.

As they half-led, half-dragged Potter Ott around his house to the door, Life and Trueline, Milk and Mole Star were silent. Inside the cottage they lowered their burden onto his bed and then stared at each other over his recumbent form. There was no need for them to say what they were thinking. Just before they had been slammed down as though by a giant hand, they had all seen Tacky catapult through the air. The earth had surely swallowed him along with the rest of the oven yard.

6

"Tack . . . tack . . . tacky-obbie . . ."
The glad wild song still hangs on the wind . . .
O windsong bird, come swoop and soar—
From earth to sky and over the sea—
And sing your tackity song of yore!

—Very Old Song

Fire shot up from the binhouse roof, where a hissing hot cinder had lodged and smoldered and burst into flame. Summoned by the clanging bell, Firelings swarmed up the cornerstone steps to the roof and began tearing out the burning tussock.

In an excess of zeal, Venerable continued to pull the bell rope; its clamor mixed with the shouts and cries of the villagers, the explosions from Belcher, and the fainter hiss of falling cinders. At the bottom of all the sounds lay the beat and boom of the angry Swollen Sea. The ghastly red light cast weird shadows on familiar faces, hollowing eye sockets and blunting fine bones until neighbor scarcely recognized neighbor.

A long lightning flash stabbed down with a thunderous crack that set ears ringing. Life, on the ridgepole, looked anxiously toward her own house at the top of Puddingstone Lane. Domma Joke Eye would be crouched over Stone Hulin in the grotto, shielding him from the night's terrors. A small shower of cinders landed in the tussock at Life's feet; she stamped them out and looked again toward her house. Was that a lick of flame shooting from the roof?

"Pay attention!" yelled Big Spool next to her. She glared at him, but he was pointing sternly at a spark in the thatch. She stamped it out.

59

By the time domma Pooley came to spell her, Life was sure she could see flames at the top of the lane. She started to hurry past Big Spool, but he gave her another stern look. "Elders first," he growled.

A tremor shook the binhouse, and Life slammed down on the tussock, but Big Spool went sprawling past her down the roof. He went slipping and sliding over and dropped with a cry to the ground. Good enough, Life thought with relish. The next moment a great splodge of something stung her cheek, then another, and another. The night was suddenly filled with flying globs. Mud! Another splodge almost knocked her over. It was raining mud! Mud splattered and hissed and steamed on the smoldering thatch.

She didn't wait to use the cornerstone steps. Scooting to the edge of the roof, she dropped to the ground. Mudballs drummed everywhere. She ran into a mud-spattered somebody by the Belcher Mound, felt him—her?—go down.

"Ho, *you!*" the creature sputtered. Domma Crimmins. This was no time to wrangle with her. Life ran faster, terrified now that she would find her house burned out and her domma too stubborn to move from danger's way. The mud seemed to be thinning, turning into a thick rain, and the lane was slippery-slick underfoot. She kept on running.

Domma Joke Eye was exactly where Life expected to find her, in the grotto hovering over Stone Hulin. Dar Chipstone must still be at the Maw. There were no flames, and Joke Eye burst into words the moment Life flew through the gate.

"There you are!" her domma cried. "It's the oddest thing, Life. It appears to be raining mud! We were quite pelted with it. Not at all nice, but quite interesting for all that! Was it a big fire down on the Maw? I could see the glow of it from here, but of course with our own fire, which was *much* brighter being so close at hand, I forgot to watch!"

"There *was* a fire?" Life looked at the roof, but in the dim light and against Belcher's red glare, she could see nothing.

"Oh yes. On the back slant of the roof. A tidy blaze too, until he put it out. Well, he *was* just putting it out when this extraordinary mud came down and finished the job."

Life felt her heart jolt. "*He?* Who, Domma?"

"The one who came when he saw the fire."

"But who was it, Domma? Who was it?"

"Why then, it was the same one Hulin gave the food to. We just couldn't let him go off hungry like that, and not knowing where his next meal is to come from. Do you think your poor domma is so selfish-minded she never thinks of another? Really, Life, sometimes I worry about you. You must keep a firmer grasp on reality, really you must. There you are standing in all this . . . this mudpour. Come sit down here under the tree with your brother and me. It's not quite so bad here."

Life took tight hold of her temper. "Domma Joke Eye," she began.

". . . and Hulin," Joke Eye prompted.

". . . *and* Hulin, both of you listen to me. I want to know who he is and where he went. The one who put out the fire and the one you gave the food to."

"But there weren't *two* of them," said Joke Eye. "You're not attending, you see. There was just the one, and now you've driven his name straight out of my mind. But where he went? Why, he went out of the gate. The very same gate you came in by."

"*Domma,*" Life said warningly and took a step nearer. "Which way did he go?"

"Oh dear. I'm just not sure, but I don't think he went toward the Maw, or I would have seen, wouldn't I? Though it was raining hard by that time, or perhaps I should say it was mudding? And of course very dark in spite of that

61

annoying red glare. But why do you set such store by this
. . . this visitor?"

"Domma . . ." Life took another step toward her
mother. "I think I am going to slap Hulin, hard, if you don't
tell me which way he went, now."

"Oh very well, you graceless child. He went Stony Bib
way." Joke Eye sniffed disdainfully. "And hereafter, keep a
tighter hold on your tongue. It's in a wet place and easily
slips."

"All right, Domma," Life said. "I'm sorry, but this is
important, you see."

"I see a patch more than folk know," said Joke Eye tartly.
"Go then and give chase—all the way to the Aha if you
must!—but what is he to you or to Hulin?"

The thick rain had slowed to a thick drizzle and finally
stopped. A few stars had sneaked into the sky. Mud globbed
from the trees, thinning to long spidery strings that swung in
the air, and the ground was a thick syrup that sucked at her
feet. Life floundered along the footpath toward the Stony
Bib. It *couldn't* be Tacky. She had seen him flying through
the air. He had been thrown into the gash and the earth had
closed over him.

Suddenly she was at the new ridge of earth thrown up
when the big gash had closed. It was an ugly pucker that
ran along the back of the village as far as she could see. But
if it *was* Tacky who had put out the fire on their roof, where
would he have gone? The Aha? Or was domma Joke Eye's
hint only a part of her antic mood? Stooping, Life peered
at the bank of earth, but it was too dark to see if there were
footmarks.

She stood uncertainly under a dripping tree. Voices
drifted up from the Maw; folk would soon be going home.
Why should she stand here worrying about Tacky? If Flaw
and Overshot and Witlatch had gone to fetch him for whatever reason, it was none of her affair. He couldn't hide away

forever, so why not get it over with . . . and let the rest of the village go in peace. Hadn't she already warned him this morning?

Besides, she thought angrily, if Potter Ott hadn't hidden Tacky away all those years ago, Hulin wouldn't have been taken to the Long Slip in his place, and Joke Eye and Chipstone would have been like other dardommas instead of glomming about and sitting in a crazy grotto with a stone statue. So it was Tacky's turn come around, and it was nothing to do with her!

She stamped her foot and, turning to go, ran full into a wraithlike figure standing directly behind her. With a yell she backed off just as a sheet of lightning spanned the sky.

"There!" said the wraith in a matter-of-fact voice. "That's where he went over!" It was Trueline and she was pointing at the pucker of earth.

Life felt limp with rage and relief.

"What I have been thinking," said Trueline as though they weren't suddenly confronting each other under a mud-dripping tree in the middle of a night crowded with fear upon fear, "is that Tacky wasn't flung into the air by the quake. He flung HIMSELF! Otherwise we couldn't have seen him fly through the air, because we were all thrown, and that was *after* we saw Tacky go flying. So he isn't dead at all, and when he saw the fire in your roof, he came back to put it out."

Life managed a sort of croak in answer. She felt a new flare of resentment. Trueline must have listened to her talk with Joke Eye and then followed her here, too dense to know that she wasn't wanted.

"But," said Trueline, "if you and I have thought this tonight, by tomorrow Witlatch will have realized what happened too. He will tell Flaw and Overshot how he saw Tacky escape before the quaking started . . ."

"Ye-es." Reluctantly.

63

"And they will see . . . *those*." Trueline waved her hand toward the long ridge of earth. At that moment a lightning streak obliged and there, clearly revealed in the mud, was a set of telltale splodges marching up and over the top of the bank. Even Flaw would guess that Tacky was at the end of those tracks!

Life turned her back on the sight. "All right," she said belligerently, "what do you think we should do?"

Trueline made a thoughtful line of her lips. "Get rid of the foot tracks. Smudge them. Blot them out with other tracks."

"Hoh! Very clever!" Life cried. "They'll know. They'll never believe that the two of *us* would go for a night's walk in the mud unless we had to. *Nobody* in his right senses would. It sounds like something Milk and Mole Star might do . . ." She let her mouth hang open. "Milk and Mole Star!"

"Good idea," said Trueline calmly, and Life was infuriated to realize that Trueline had had Milk and Mole Star in mind all along.

"But they're . . . they're so unreliable! Always running about for no good reason—they don't have any sense! And how can you expect *them* to keep a secret? Nobody knows what they're really like. They're always together and they don't talk to anybody else . . ." She stopped short again.

Trueline nodded. "They hardly talk to each *other*. Why don't we just ask them?" She linked arms with Life, who unwillingly let herself be hauled along. "I almost forgot the reason I followed you! Domma Crimmins was complaining to Venerable that you knocked her down and left the Maw before the fire was out."

Indignantly, Life jerked her arm away. "I saw the fire on my own roof!"

"That's what I told Venerable," Trueline said equably. "So it's all right."

Wasn't there One Thing that Trueline didn't know!

Fuming, Life strode faster down the lane toward Toothy Maw. Trueline lengthened her own stride and kept up.

Of three things Milk and Mole Star were certain: running kept the head clear, talking muddied it, and working was for others. When Life and Trueline found them hauling food stores back into the binhouse, they whooped and would have set off at once for the Stony Bib had not Overshot borne down upon them, his scowl limned in soot.

"No more shirking here!" he shouted. "Flaw! Keep these two runabouts under your third eye!"

"In the morning, then," Trueline whispered. "Early."

Next morning Milk and Mole Star were out of their beds before the sun was out of the storming sea and, meeting in the walkway between their houses, set off up Bump Lane. The village looked as though a vast bowlful of flopcake batter had been emptied over it; trees leaned under pasty coatings; here and there walls had collapsed into lumpy heaps. Over all lay a silence that was delicious to their ears.

They ran to the top of Bump Lane and turned along the Crossback to Life's house at the end—she waved them on from her gate—turned again and loped along the footpath between her homing and domma Kirtle's until they came to the puckered ridge of earth and rock. Without breaking step they went up and over the pucker, and in the going they blotted out Tacky's footsteps that had gone before.

The Stony Bib was a long bumpy cake of mud, and down the center, heading for the tip of the Spewing, went the splodgy footprints. The mud was still soft enough for their own steps to squash out Tacky's. At least Trueline and Life said they must be Tacky's marks. Milk and Mole Star weren't much on opinions—everything was much simpler if you just *did* and let others argue the whys and wherefores of it.

They passed the rear of Potter Ott's house. Sounds of heavy snoring came down the wall from the three-cornered

window and they grinned at each other. Beyond Ott's homing the Thicket began. Mud webbed the firestick branches;
here and there the pucker had gulped down whole trees, and
their twisted roots dangled forlornly upside down over the
ridge of earth and rock.

The pucker ran on and on next to the Stony Bib, and
Milk and Mole Star faithfully ran along beside it, taking
turns at trampling out the telltale marks.

Milk punched Mole Star's shoulder. *Look.*

I'm looking.

The mud had gone. And just ahead, the pucker suddenly
ran out. With a whoop, they leaped over the last bit of
muck and landed on the familiar bright loosestones of the
Bib. The coming of the sun tinged the trees that marched
up the steep slope across from them, and beyond them the
Bib lay clean of mud as far as they could see—to the place
where it curled round the tip of the Spewing's black tongue.

Now what? They looked blankly at each other. They
were supposed to splunge out the footprints in the mud and
follow them until they found Tacky. But the footprints had
run out; there were no more to splunge and no more to
follow.

Mole Star frowned and bit his lip in terrible indecision.
Milk bit his own lip and waited.

At last, as though by signal, they moved. But Mole Star
went toward the Spewing's tip; Milk headed back toward
the village. They stopped in astonishment, questioning.

After a moment Milk had his way and they went loping
back through the mud, taking pleasure in making it splat
out from their feet. Laughing and puffing they followed
their backward trail until they came to the beginning of the
journey. They swerved with the trail and swarmed over the
pucker, half-sliding down the other side and landing with a
skid and two thumps at the bottom.

Angry hands seized them and hauled them to their feet;

scolding voices spat into their ears. Dazed, they looked into the glaring eyes of a circle of villagers.

Milk's mouth dropped open even farther than Mole Star's. *But . . .*

Mole Star pinched him. *Don't say anything.*

Milk indignantly pinched back. *I wasn't going to. I was just thinking . . .*

Then don't think so loud. They'll hear you!

7

Breathe the fume
Of Belcher's breath;
Taste the words
That Belcher seth.

The itching flesh,
The prickling hair,
The bite of Mud:
The Seth is there!

—*The Rule of Seths*

On Belcher's Brow the young Skarra woke with a cry and stared wildly about him. The dream again! Always the fear . . . the huddled shape . . . and then the long, lonely dark . . . and the smelly one coming back, bringing more fear . . . a sharp burning . . . and somewhere in the dark, a chanting . . .

Born of fire,
Born of ash. . . .

But even as he tried to bring them back, the words jumbled and ran together. They always did.

He struggled up from his bumpy pallet, sweat drops popping out on his forehead, his stomach still churning with fear. "MudLar! MudLar!"

Brightness lay along the beaten earth inside the small doorway, well past the etched line that marked the hour of Scurrying Insects. The other bed was empty. He was alone in the hut.

68

In a panic he flung himself through the doorway and stopped short, blinking in the sharp sunlight. Two wild black goats looked up from their grazing, shook their beards, and moved off a way. It was full morning! Where was MudLar? Why hadn't the gusher's spout wakened him?

Because . . . because . . . He rubbed his eyes and squinted across the grassy stretch to the smooth rock mound where early each morning Belcher spat the streaming night water high into the air, and where the blue basin lay into which the water fell and lay steaming for half the day until it had all seeped back into Belcher's Body.

But this morning there was no water—no water at all! A thin dust of ash and soot had sifted over the blue basin.

Ash. Slowly he crept out of the daze his dream had caused. Last night he'd thought at first the Brow was shaking loose and would be hurtled into the sea; then that Belcher was trying to suck the ledge back inside himself. He remembered a blast and the sky stained red, an ash cloud overhead, and rain rushing after it . . .

And MudLar? Skarra laughed aloud in his relief, and the two goats rolled wary eyes and moved farther off. Why, MudLar had yesterday taken the grit path up to Belcher's Throat, exactly as he had every last-day-of-the-season since Skarra could remember. And tonight, or more likely tomorrow, he would come limping down again in a flaring temper, and he would push Skarra out of the hut to sit over the Mud till called. He would then hunch over the writing scrolls that he kept hidden in the big chest forbidden to a Skarra. Afterwards he would demand a reckoning of every hour that he had been away.

Skarra came to himself with a guilty start. MudLar's parting instructions rushed into his mind: "Count the Blue Beads night and morning; taste the Mud thrice daily; bathe twice in the Blue Pool each morning; sweep the hut; bake the bread; prepare the day's scrattle; scrape the new goatskin. Other times, sit before the Mud and try to let Belcher's words enter your thick-boned head!"

Other times! There weren't enough hours between sun-bob and sun-drop to do the ordinary duties. But at least—Skarra eyed the empty pool—at least he was excused from boiling himself twice in the steaming waters. Even MudLar would have to admit there was no water there. Could it be that Belcher had taken pity on him for once? He looked up at Belcher's peaceful breathing-in-and-out for a sign, but Belcher just went on emitting litle puffs of smoke, with an occasional pale lick of his tongue, like one who has eaten well.

Back in the hut, he seized the besom and scrabbled it over the earthen floor. A wide crack had opened up overnight; he pushed the sweepings into it. He shook out his skimpy pallet and straightened the scratchy coverlid. From the foodshelf he took down the flour crock and the yam yeast pot. There was enough flour for one loaf, but the yam yeast had turned a poisonous green. Five good loaves there had been yesterday, and MudLar had taken them all with him. There was nothing in the hut but orts and oddments until next food-bringing from the Pillow.

He finally made a meal of scrapings of black honey, clabbered goat's milk, and one wrinkled parsnap. By that time the sun had stretched into the hour of Limp Grass. With a hungry sigh, Skarra folded himself crosslegged on his pallet and pulled the string of bulky blue beads from under his plaingown. One day he would be MudLar himself, and some poor jar-headed Skarra would sit miserably here and tell the days and seasons for him. Once he had asked what use there was in telling over the days, for they came and went in any case, with no help from a poor Skarra. Mud-Lar's answer had been a double-dose of bitter tea for the clearing of his head, and no food—not even scrattle—for three days. After that Skarra emptied his mind twice a day and told the endless circlet of beads without question.

He gathered the Belcher cone and the five Hollow beads into one hand, and with thumb and forefinger picked out the swaddled Morsel stone for the season of New Life, just beginning; with the other hand he named off the fifteen days as their shapes passed through his fingers: the jagged arc of the Sky, round Sunball, crescent Moon, pointed Star, and Lightning Flash . . . he gave a sigh . . . then Cloud and Sea, Wind and Thunder, and . . . *yawn* . . . Rain; and last came hewn Rock, Metal, Soil, grain of Seed, and the gritty Salt. His hands were clumsy, the beads skipping out of his sweaty fingers like tiny leafhoppers.

He exchanged the New Life bead for the next, Pure Brightness, and told over the days, starting from the beginning again: Sky, Sunball, Moon, Star . . . Through the seasons of Shimmery Rain and Oozing Rocks and First Shoots he groped and bungled his way. His back began to itch. He couldn't scratch, for if he dropped the beads, he would have to begin afresh. His fingers grew more slippery as the itch of his back grew worse. The beaded days of Shining Meadows shook and jounced on the endless hide string. His stomach growled; a trickle of sweat crawled down his back, and he hunched his shoulders to blot it with his plaingown; but always he clung to the beads.

The sudden jangle of the bell made him jump, and the beads, only half-told, clattered against his chest. He stared down at them in despair.

The bell jangled again, louder.

"I'm *coming*," Skarra said through his teeth. Tearing his plaingown off over his head, he scrambled into the second-best Sethgown. It dribbled on the floor around his feet, though on MudLar it scarcely covered the knee. He pulled the hood over his head. It dropped down to his nose, and the point fell over on one side. There was no help for it. Leaving the hut, he tried to walk with MudLar's dignity to the mudpots, but the Sethgown kept tripping him and he could see that Venerable, waiting at the bellrock, was nowise impressed. He stumbled to the Sethseat and a moment later Venerable came and squatted beside him.

"Speak," said Skarra, trying for MudLar's deep tones, but producing something nearer to "squeak." He tried again. *"Speak."*

Venerable spoke—a long discourse of fires and ash and mud and a tacky bird and a big pucker (had he heard aright?)—and Skarra kept nodding as wisely as possible with the hood tickling his nose at each bob of his head. The Pillow sounded a terrible place, full of bickering and hates and names like Flaw and Overshot. A long time ago, when any place at all seemed better than the Brow, he had tried to run away to the village, and each time MudLar had tied him up for his pains. Wise MudLar. But *he* shouldn't have run off with all the loaves.

Finally Venerable stopped talking and Skarra fastened his eyes on the slow roil of pink mud. There were five mud-pots plus one small splutter, but Belcher spoke only through the largest one directly below the Sethseat. The thick mud bubbled and plopped and Skarra breathed deeply of the fume, trying to put out of his mind the stonetruth: Belcher had never yet spoken to him. Belcher's breath smelled worse than usual, and Skarra's back still itched horribly.

Itched! But that was the first omen! Never before had he got as far as the itching. Bending lower over the large roiling circle, he took in a great searing breath. Now, now would surely come the second omen! But there was only a fiercer bubbling, and a blob of flying pink mud bit his chin.

"Belcher speaks!" cried Venerable, scooting his thin haunches closer.

Skarra nodded. But he hadn't had the second omen! The scratchy Sethgown prickled, and a rivulet of sweat ran suddenly cool down his chest where the blue beads dug secretly into his flesh. He wanted most desperately to scratch, both front and back.

"Belcher speaks!" said Venerable more sharply. "What

says the Hollow One? What is the Seth? Hurry on, then!" His scolding voice nagged at Skarra. "In times like these, we need MudLar, not a . . ."

Skarra held up his hand. Just so he had seen MudLar silence questions while Belcher spoke to him. But if Belcher was speaking this day, Skarra couldn't understand him. *Plup-plup . . . plu-plup* was all that came to him from the mudpot. *Plup-plup . . . plu-plup.* Another blob bit him, this time full in the mouth. He dared not spit it out in front of Venerable, and it gritted hot on his tongue. He swallowed painfully and the mud went rasping and burning down his throat.

Swiveling his eyes under the hood, he looked despairingly up the grim rampart of Belcher's Throat for some sign. If only he could see MudLar returning down the grit path! But that couldn't be. There hadn't been time for him to go to Belcher's Rift and return . . . not enough time even if Belcher had lain motionless through the night. Skarra suddenly clutched at the beads through his gown. What if MudLar had been caught in Belcher's fire last night! What if . . . Skarra's scalp prickled. What if Belcher spoke now through the mud and told him to go after MudLar . . . to go up the Throat! But he didn't know the way, not beyond the Long Slip! The prickling spread over his head, and new rivers of sweat crawled down his back and front.

Prickling? The second omen! *The itching flesh, the prickling hair, the bite of Mud . . .* But the bite had come too soon, before the prickling. And the pink mud still said only *Plup-plup . . . plu-plup.*

Venerable shifted restlessly. "The Seth," he urged. "What is the Seth? Hurry then! The sun grows hot on my old bones."

Venerable would never have dared to hurry MudLar, not if he had to sit there on his bony bottom the livelong day. Skarra stared more fixedly at the seething mud, blanking

73

from his mind the picture of MudLar's bones blackening in Belcher's fires somewhere above the Brow. The hair-prickling had disappeared now, but the itching was worse than ever.

"Perhaps," Venerable goaded him, "Belcher does not speak to Skarra because you have neglected your duties. Did you bathe properly in the steaming pool? Have you eaten of the pink mud thrice daily? Do you . . . ?"

Eaten of the pink mud! Venerable had just seen him swallow a dollop that would choke a goat. His mouth was still raw from it, his eyes still watering. Venerable nagged on at him, worse than MudLar. MudLar would have snapped his feet, or deprived him of bread, and let it go at that. The itching had drawn together into one unbearable twitch—just *there,* between his shoulder wings. He had to scratch, he had to!

Throwing his head back, he brought words out of his torment. "Strike dumb the tongue," he moaned, and Venerable's voice chopped off in mid-sentence.

"Strike dumb the tongue . . ." Skarra repeated, desperately searching in his mind for more words to go on with. Words to rid himself of Venerable, whose mouth had already started to open again.

". . . that Skarra mocks!" cried Skarra. He couldn't stand the agony another moment . . . "For Skarra seeks . . . the sea-splashed rocks!" He held his head back for another moment and then collapsed into a miserable huddle. "Go now," he groaned. "That is the Seth."

Venerable creaked to his feet, muttering over the words of the Seth.

> "Strike dumb the tongue
> That Skarra mocks!
> For Skarra seeks
> The sea-splashed rocks!

74

"And what does Belcher mean by that?" he demanded,
". . . erh . . . good Skarra?"

"What he says!" Skarra cried out. "Yesterday he sent
MudLar up the Throat to the Rift. Today he bids those who
mock Skarra to hold their tongues." Skarra pointed to the
mudpot that had now subsided into a slow swirl. "He has
finished speaking. Come back tomorrow."

Skarra forced himself to wait until Venerable had
disappeared beyond the bell-rock that marked MudLar's
domain, and then he tore the Sethgown off over his head.
And scratched.

Skarra raked at his flesh with a deep shiver of ecstasy, but
his fingers couldn't reach the worst itch of all, and he fell
backward to squirm with exquisite pain in the grainy dust.
Beside him the mudpots burpled on, and in the distance the
water jet gave a gurgle and a half-hearted spout. Skarra
jerked upright. There was a sudden scuttering and a frightened *baa-aa-aa,* and the two small black goats ran stiff-
legged past him, as if Belcher himself was after them. Skarra
laughed, and scrambled to his feet to watch the gusher.

But the water jet, having cleared its throat, fell silent
again. The pool had collected only a few drops of water in
its layer of ash. If MudLar were here, he might tell Skarra
to sweep out the ash, but MudLar was far away. Skarra's
heart felt suddenly light. MudLar was on Belcher's Throat
—and Belcher had spoken to *him,* the Skarra!

Back in the hut, Skarra folded the white Sethgown away
and pulled his own faded blue plaingown over his head.
The frayed edge tickled his knees, and that reminded him
of the itch between his shoulder wings. But he had no more
time for scratching. He must put down his first Seth on the
goatskin and think of what it meant.

From the niche above his sleeping mat he took the top
goatskin roll and the sharpened gawk quill and knelt over
his work. Some of the previous Seths were blotted and

75

spotted from the splutter of the quill, and the lines ran uphill. But this, his own first Seth, must be perfect. He dipped the quill in the pot of inkberry and held it poised over the soft creamy skin while he tried to call up the moment of the Seth. First the itching, then the prickling . . . No. There had been the terrible itching, and then the bite! Two bites! The prickling had come after. But then . . . ?

Then the itching kept getting worse, but Venerable nagged on and on, and finally there was no bearing it and he had thrown his head back and words had popped out. He hadn't thought about them. They just came out of his mouth. *Strike dumb the tongue.* Yes, that was how it went:

> Strike dumb the tongue
> That Skarra mocks,
> For Skarra seeks
> The sea-splashed rocks.

Sea-splashed rocks . . . ? For Skarra seeks the sea-splashed rocks . . . ?

The rock pool!

His jaw dropped. Belcher wanted him to go back there. Belcher knew! Belcher had known all the time! It was Belcher who had sent the small black goat to show him the way that first time; it was Belcher who had sent the two black goats today as a sign to go back a second time. Belcher had caused the terrible itching—and stopped the gusher—to prepare him for the delicious salt chill of the secret pool!

With sudden urgency, he plunged the quill into the inkpot and began writing the Seth. Purple spluttered and splotched on the goatskin, and the lines ran uphill like the others, and he wasn't sure what sign was proper to write for "dumb" or "mock," but no matter. It was his first Seth, and Belcher had commanded him to find the rock pool again!

He left the goatskin open to dry, changed his soft sandals for heavier ones with ankle thongs, and went out into the sunlight again. The black goats had gone, but that was no matter either . . . he didn't need to be led this time. Even though two rounds of seasons must have passed since the small black goat had shown him how to go, he remembered the way. High overhead a gawk bird flaunted against the sky, sending down its jeering, *Yih-yih, yih-yih.*

"Yih-yih," Skarra hollered back. "Drop me a fish!" He watched the gawk soar down to its run on the distant Scars, and laughed when it dipped down, failed to make a landing and flapped off again, looking foolish. It came circling around for another try, but Skarra didn't wait to see if it got down this time. He set off for the rock pool.

The steep hollow between Belcher's Head and left Shoulder was filled with lofty trees. Farther up the Neckline the trunks wore thick skirts of brambles and stickery bushes, but hard by the Brow the forest was almost empty of undergrowth. Just behind the MudLar hut the ledge offered a steep shelving descent to the forest floor.

Clutching two clumps of tightgrass, Skarra gingerly waggled his legs over the lip of the Brow until he found a foothold. Some worrisome moments later he had half-slid, half-skidded down the side of Belcher's Head and was on his way across the slope of the Empty Forest toward the Spewing. When he came to a wide gap in the trees, he paused long enough to make sure no Firelings were on the Stony Bib just visible far below, though there was little danger of that. Villagers seldom walked this way.

His thoughts trudged along with his feet. When he got to the Spewing, dared he walk across it? Or must he make his way, a long way, on down to the tongue tip and up again the other side? Once he had thought the spew of rough black chunks was Belcher's real tongue, but MudLar had dismissed his fears as idle superstition. "Belcher sent forth the Spewing and destroyed those Firelings who tried to leave

77

him. As for his Tongue . . . it is flame, and may we never see it, for it forks forth from his great Throat and is shown only in anger. The Eye is the gusher," MudLar went on, for he never stopped with a simple answer to a question, "and each morning he sheds his bitter night tears into the pool. The mudpots are his Mouth through which he speaks to us . . ."

"But how is it," Skarra had asked, "that his tongue is so far away? Why doesn't it come out of his Mouth?"

"It is not for us to find fault with Belcher's way of life," said MudLar. "Contemplate your beads."

And Skarra had contemplated, but strange fancies about the shape of Belcher came into his head. These fancies he kept to himself, and never so much as whispered them, for fear of Belcher's anger—or of MudLar's, which was even more to be dreaded, being closer at hand and usually followed by a good leg-snapping.

But MudLar wasn't here, and Belcher had sent him the Seth. Clutching the blue beads through his plaingown, Skarra felt an unaccustomed surge of will. He was tired and hot, and the way to the pool was long. Marching past the last tree, he set foot on the rearing black corsa of the Spewing.

8

"Who goes there?"   "Who goes there?"
"Sneakity-sneap."   *"Snippity-thread."*
"Hold one toe   "Go and find
  And go to sleep!"   A crust of bread!"

"Who goes there?"   "Who goes there?"
"Snackity-tack."   *"Snobbity-stone."*
"Give your hand   "Go up the Spew
  A mighty whack!"   Bring back a bone!"

—An Ancient Rhyme Game called "Threat"

Life had intended to wait by her gate until Milk and Mole Star came back from their search for Tacky, but Joke Eye was full of mewling plaints this morning, and there was no end to the house chores she insisted on before breakfast.

At the loud outcry, however, Life ran outside. She was in time to see Milk and Mole Star come floundering over the pucker directly into the triumphant arms of Flaw and Overshot, who bore them off by the scruff of their necks, like chidlings taken to be punished.

"What happened?" she demanded of the few villagers who were nattering to each other at the scene, but they shrank away from her. Only Yoe the Beekeep spoke up.

"No passage!" he declared officiously, throwing out his skinny arms. "By order of Overshot. Things here are not exactly what they seem. Best go back to your own house, Life. Not a day to draw attention to yourself—any of you that's not yet stood up to the Oathstone, that is."

She retreated under the unfriendly scrutiny of the gossipers.

When the summoning bell rang soon after, she went to the Maw. There was no sign of Milk and Mole Star; Trueline skulked near Flaw and Overshot, her ears alert. Venererable told everybody to get busy and clean up the Pillow and stay this side of the pucker until Belcher's purpose in creating it had been determined. Meeting dismissed.

Disquieted, Life collected provisions at the bins and went back home. Joke Eye had not gone to the Summoning, nor had she cleared any more of the mud and burnt thatch from the house, nor had she made breakfast. She was sitting in the grotto with Stone Hulin, threading her loom with blue. "For a cloak and hood against the next mudstorm," she explained brightly. "I've scrubbed him twice from top to toe . . . he does get so grubby! But do you know, Life, he's got his old appetite back. He ate every scrap of food last night!"

"I'm glad, Domma," Life said with stiff lips, and went inside to make the breakfast stirabit, clean and sweep, bake the overnight bread, and fill the soup pot for the noon meal. Before she had finished, Chipstone came back from his inspection of homing walls in the village and moodily climbed up on the roof to ruminate over the fire damage. Even moodier, he climbed down again and set to scraping mud from the outside of the house and from his stoneworks.

Ven Ida came to pay a consoling call and to snoop at the damage done to the roof; she had no more than gone when Grey Gammer came to the door with a basket of spottybuns.

"I'll just pass the time of day with your good domma and be off again," she said. On the threshold she hesitated and gave Life a long look. "Might there be too many spottybuns for your family," she said thoughtfully, "might you find somebody hungry to give them to."

Life stood staring at the doorway long after Grey Gammer had left it. Then, her mind made up, she sorted through the house chest and hauled out a raggety old shoulder wallet almost thrown out a dozen times and began stuffing it with half the provisions she had brought from the bins: runny beans, salt nuts, chortles. She thrust in a loaf of new bread and filled up the empty spaces with Grey Gammer's spotty-buns. Rummaging in a cupboard, she came across the foolish wadding coverlid she had long ago made for Stone Hulin —to please her domma. It hadn't pleased her domma overmuch, so now she thrust it into a basket as rickety as the wallet was raggety, and put another loaf and more spotty-buns on top.

The wallet she slung over her shoulder, and picking up the basket, she went outside. "I am going to talk with Potter Ott," she told domma Joke Eye.

"Do that." Joke Eye nodded without looking up. "Give him my good-day and to the windsong bird a greeting as well. Ven Ida would have it that Tacky has been, that is, has disappeared, but we know that is untrue, don't we?" She sighed heavily. "Ven Ida should not mock me, but there, each must have his fault. And even if there were one without a single fault, that itself would be a fault, would it not?"

"Yes, Domma," said Life, shifting from one leg to the other.

"My thoughts run back and forth with the thread, and that is better than the swirling thoughts that come with stirring a pudding. Pudding thoughts are deep down and dark, but thread thoughts weave bright in and out and are never broken. Though the shuttle dips under and out of sight, it must come to light again. Do you see that, Life?"

"Yes, Domma." Life took a deep patient breath and let it out slowly.

"You don't, of course, for making a pudding and weaving cloth are one and the same for you—a something that needs must be done to avoid a scolding. But one day you will know the difference of thought that goes into every movement of your hand."

"Yes, Domma." Life changed the wallet to her other shoulder.

"But I can feel that just now your feet are having escaping thoughts, so wish your brother well and run off to wherever you are going."

"To Potter Ott's . . . first," said Life. "And then . . ." she watched her domma's face ". . . to the Aha to find Tacky . . ."

Joke Eye bent closer to her loom. "Give him my good wishes," she murmured, "and Life . . . have a care."

"Yes, Domma. Wish-you-well, Hulin." She patted her stone brother on the head. "Tweak-your-ear," she said under her breath. "Wish-you-well, Domma."

She started along the Crossback, going with a sort of skip that would discourage anybody's wanting to talk and pry.

Potter Ott didn't answer her knock, but when she leaned hard against the door, it popped open and she half-fell inside, into darkness and a reek of cherrychoke that stung her eyes and nose.

"Phoo!" She swung the door wide to let the sunlight and air stream in. The window lattices were all closed tight. "Potter Ott?"

There was a sudden great commotion to her right, a hrumphing about that froze her to the slagstone, and a growling groan that stiffened her hair.

"P-P-Potter Ott?"

A groaning snore.

She pushed her way through the wall of stale smoke to the bulge on the bed and stood long moments looking down at the lips blubbering in and out. If Potter Ott knew where Tacky might have gone, he wasn't going to be telling anybody for a good long time. She stalked away from the lumpish bed, her eyes darting everywhere about the dim room. There . . . against the opposite wall. A clothes chest.

The chest was almost empty: a wadded-up something-heavy on top; nothing but flimsy thin garments beneath. Where were Tacky's warm clothes, then? Surely he had more than the garben on his back! Irritably, she picked up

82

the wadded-up something-heavy to throw back into the chest. Wait. Scrambling to her feet, she carried the bundle toward the light streaming through the doorway. It was Tacky's red festival garben, a good thick one. It was wrapped around . . . She stepped closer to the doorway, and froze.

"Who's in there?"

For a moment Life stood transfixed, staring out at the gate. It was Pickler and Anner from next door! Silently, carefully, she began to back off from the doorway, trying to hush the small gritting of her sandals.

Perversely, Potter Ott ceased his snoring. Life froze again.

"He's stopped breathing!" Anner cried. "We'd best go in!"

"Oh, leave off," groaned Pickler. "Can't a one change his tune when he sleeps, without neighbors rushing in to sound his chest?"

"But his door stands open!"

Life drew in her breath. *Why had she been so stupid!*

"To let the smoke out, I shouldn't wonder. Can smell it from here."

Life let out her breath. *She hadn't been so stupid.*

"But what was it Oldest Gar saw, then! Hurrying past, was what he said."

She had been stupid.

Pickler's voice was running out of patience. "His wits departing his head, most likely."

"We're going in there, Pickler." The gate creaked. "Something's amiss."

Potter Ott, as though in protest, half-raised up and then fell back with a crash that sent clattering echoes round the four walls.

The footfalls on the path sounded nearer.

In a silent frenzy of movement Life flew to the clothes chest, lifted the lid back on, thrust the wad of vermilion garben into her wallet, and crossed to the deep shadow behind the open door. Why hadn't she answered them when they first called out! Made some excuse for being there—bringing food—something! And why, oh why didn't Potter Ott go back to his snoring again!

And then he did. Just as Pickler and Anner stood on the threshold, blocking out the sunlight, Potter Ott blasted forth.

"There!" Pickler announced. "You wanted breathing; you now have breathing. It's back home for us. We've got enough to do without chasing Oldest Gar's wits around the Pillow."

Anner still stood resolute. "Oldest Gar said somebody came in here, and I . . ."

"Or some*thing!*" Pickler suddenly roared. "To my mind, we'll be seeing that younger's shadow in all the time to come!"

Behind the door, Life caught her breath again.

Anner's voice was scornful. "Shadow! A haunt? *Here?* On the *Pillow?*"

"*Think!* Use reason! There are shadows dwelling on the Spewing because Firelings were swallered there. Why should there not be a shadow here where the lad was swallered last night!"

"*If* he was swallowed . . ." But Anner sounded suddenly doubtful of her own doubt. "Flaw and Overshot . . ."

"He was *swallered,*" said Pickler.

Life held her breath so long she felt dizzy, but nothing else happened. When at last she dared peek around the door, there was nothing but sunlight on the dried mud of the path. She slid through the doorway.

At the back corner of the house, stones angled out of the pucker like crazy steps—flatstones from the oven yard wall, firebrick that had been the potting oven, shards of baked clay that had been pots. Life gingerly planted her foot on the lowest tilted stone and started up. Near the top she abandoned all caution and scrambled over and down, the wallet bump-bumping after her. If Oldest Gar could see her from his house, let him think she was Tacky's shadow go-ing back to earth!

Suddenly her feet felt light and she did a little jiggling dance in Milk's and Mole Star's dried tracks. She had got away from the place where everybody was talking doom, and that was enough for now! Here there was space to breathe and the sun was shining. She flew down the Stony Bib, the wallet banging against one side, the basket against the other.

"*Plock-plock* goes the bag," she chanted in time to her steps. "*Squiff-squiff* go my feet," but then the mud ran out on the Bib and the sound her feet made in the loosestones was "*skronch-skronch*." "*Skronch-skronch* go my feet," she tried, and laughed aloud. Trueline wasn't the only one who could make songs.

She reached the Spewing and, still laughing, leaped high across the tip that lapped over the Bib. Leaped and, in the middle of the leap, she saw him.

He lay sprawled out face down just the other side of the Spewing tip. Frantically she twisted, kicked out her legs to turn herself, and came clumsily down beside him. The bas-ket flew out of her hand. The wallet was squashed under her shoulder.

"Tacky!" she cied. Alarmed, she sat up and yanked at his arm.

It was very limp.

9

The long wind blows down the empty black tongue;
The Long Slip waits for the old and the young.
Then keep to your cotts;
Walk not in the wind,
Lest you give up your song before it is sung.

—An Ancient Keening Song

Tacky had not been named after the song of the bird-that-swoops-and-soars for naught. Cowering against the wall of his uncle's house, he had been frozen with fear, but when he heard Flaw and Overshot threatening to take him away, he had swooped out from the safety of his nest and soared over the oven yard wall like any bird whose song was "Tack . . . tack . . . tacky-obbie." He heard the oven yard collapse behind him as he went sprawling onto the Stony Bib; and the loosestones jiggled and scuffled him about like a chortle in a sizzling frypan until his teeth rattled in his head. Lightning ripped and tore at the sky; thunder slammed against his ears; Belcher spat out a blast of flame that reached the stars and then a blot of black smoke that erased them from the sky. Ash fell like hot rain. Tacky buried his face in his arms and waited for Belcher to finish him.

What happened next and then next and next, he couldn't quite string together. There was a long groping-about and a stumbling and a climbing over some sort of rubbly stuff and a thinking that everybody else must be dead. There was a fire, too, and he was on a roof tearing out the thatch, but something . . . a hard ball . . . hit him and knocked him off the roof . . . and there was a lot of mud. And a domma! . . . a satchel of food. And the Aha. The scary, moaning hide-hole in the Aha.

But between the domma and the hiding place there was the walking. Walking in mud and on loosestone, walking in moonlight and starlight and black night and walking up the slanty path in the shadow of the Spewing to find the deep cavelike place behind the First Story Stone that his uncle had described. And in all the long walking, somewhere along the way, he had found a few tag ends of courage and knotted them together. He had defied Belcher; he had escaped the Long Slip; he had got through the ghost-ridden night.

He wasn't so sure of the new day. In the grim morning light of the Aha, he huddled dejectedly against the First Story Stone. His teeth chuddered with cold, and hunger gnawed at him; but the satchel of food was still inside the hide-hole, and he was not. Nor could he find a spare slip of courage to send him back inside.

When his uncle Ott told of the hide-hole, he had not spoken of haunts. He had said nothing of the tormented spirit that dwelt in that upside-down bowl the size of a potting oven and made itself known with the coming of day.

The moaning had started as a sigh, almost imagined. Grieving.

Ahhhhh-hh.

And then it grew louder. Hollow. Despairing.

Ahhhhh-hh. It came from the floor, from the walls; it was in the thin air, pressing all around him. *Ahhhhhhhhh-hh. Ahhhhhhhhhhhh-hh.*

Fear jabbed at Tacky's back. Terror thrust him through the narrow entrance tunnel into the early sunlight. If the groans pursued him, he couldn't hear them for the wind that *shrrrrd* down the looming bulk of the Spewing.

Even in the morning light the Aha was dim and chill. The dismal Story Stone tablets stood along the cliffside, dark gray and forbidding; only a narrow path lay between them and the crumbly outer wall of stone. The far end of the gallery of stones was a wall face that, when one said "Ah," called back "Ha!," but the sound was not the haunted *Ahhhh-hh* of the hide-hole. The gallery smelled of goat and must and decaying rock.

Tacky's stomach grumbled with hunger. If he were to crawl just partway into the burrow, he could reach in and grab up the satchel and be outside again quicker than thought . . .

He must stop thinking about food! Jumping up, he began walking up and down the gallery. Only the first six Stones, running left from the Spewing wall, were standing free; the rest were part of a greater rock in the cliff wall, each with a border etched round it. All the space on the cliff side had been used, and Tacky wondered idly if the Thirteenth Stone would be on the end wall or carved on the crumbling rampart walls, and whether he would ever see it. Or would he become the main figure *on* it? Gloomily, he turned for another look at the Twelfth Stone. It showed a small figure, Hulin, sliding down the Long Slip above the Brow. Tacky decided it would be better to think about food after all.

He went back to leaning against the First, the Sky Stone, and stared down the path to the Stony Bib far below. After a while, he knew that he would have to brave the cave and the moaning once more. A vision had been growing in his mind—a vision of a succulent red chortle spurting juice down his parched throat . . .

He was in and out of the hide-hole before he had time to think a second thought—before the haunt could so much as fetch up a sigh—dragging the satchel after him.

Unfortunately, the satchel had come out upside down. It was empty.

That's when he had decided to go down the slanty path to wait.

* * *

"Tacky!" The voice kept nagging at him. "Tacky! Tack-ieeeeeee . . . !" It raised to a shriek.

He rolled slowly over, blinking in the sunlight. "Wha-at?"

"Are you hurt? What's happened?"

Dazed, he sat up, looking round him. "It's you," he mumbled. "Life. I must have fallen asleep."

"Asleep! Here? Anybody might have found you! Did *they* find you? Milk and Mole Star?"

He couldn't think what she was talking about. "There were moans, Life! Terrible moans! In the Aha, the cave behind . . . My uncle didn't tell me about the moans!" The story of the night tumbled out of him all of a-scramble, with the tag ends of courage coming untied as he talked.

She was picking up scattered spotty-buns and putting them back in her basket. "Wind," she said absently. "Probably just the wind you heard."

"No. It wasn't. The wind made a different sound. This was like groans."

"Sun-splinters, then." Briskly, she stood up and pulled at his arm. "The sun splintering on cold rock, just the way it does on housewalls in the morning. You shouldn't have left the Aha!"

"It was *moaning*, Life."

"Sun-splinters." She handed him the wallet she had fallen on. "Food." Doling out a spotty-bun to him from her basket, she started up the slanty path beside the lowering Spewing.

"Moaning," he repeated stubbornly, but only to himself. He fell into step.

The new voice came from behind them. "Dar Toothacher used to say that only the listener knows the true tune."

Life whirled round so fast she knocked Tacky against the Spewing. "Trueline! Where did you come from!"

Gravely, Trueline held out a hand to him as Tacky picked himself off the side of the corsa. "Domma Joke Eye said you were at Potter Ott's, but you weren't. Then I found your

89

foot scuffs all over the pucker behind the house, and after I rubbed those out as best I could, I found *these* along the way." She flipped open the lid of the basket on her arm and took out two spotty-buns well-dotted with mud from the Bib. She dropped them into Life's basket.

" 'nks," said Life ungraciously. "Tacky, are you coming?" She started up the path again.

He hesitated, looking from Life's disapproving back to the aloofness of Trueline's face, finally gave a helpless wave of his hand and followed after Life. Trueline promptly fell in behind, and they started the long climb to the Aha.

Next to the path, on the right, the Spewing brooded like some gigantic worm crouching above them. Along its lumpy back, well over their heads, the wind swept with an eerie *shoooooo* and *shrrrrrr,* but no breath of it stirred on the slanty path. Lizards, disturbed in their sun-basking, skittered away or turned to unblinking stone. Farther off, grazing on the scrubby slope, a family of three goats watched nervously through barred eyes and finally went stilting off with an urgent *baaaaaing.*

The three Firelings moved closer together and before very long, Life's back lost its starch. She began to spill out the happenings of the night and morning; Trueline added a good share; Tacky told his part; and soon they were chattering and laughing together against the rest of the world—until suddenly they were at the Aha.

It reared broodingly above them, a blank-faced rampart wall against the greater wall of Belcher's Arm. The slanty path led to the narrow entrance next the Spewing, and they stepped into the chill gallery of stone that knew the sun only when it was directly overhead.

Life gave a shudder of distaste. "I came here with my dardomma once. Hulin too. That was before he . . . well of course it was *before!* He didn't like it and he cried, and I gave him a good shaking." She glared at Tacky and Trueline. "He deserved it, being so mealy . . ." She dropped her basket abruptly. "Let's eat. Then we'll listen to your sun-splinters. Or whatever they are." She gave Trueline a grudging glance.

They hunched down in front of the First Story Stone where they could keep an eye on the slanty path. Trueline opened her small, neat basket, took a bright cloth from it, spread it tidily on the ground, and began to set out food in a pretty pattern. Each dish was handily wrapped in big cumber leaves.

Shrugging, Life took the wallet from Tacky and pulled out, first, a big wad of red cloth, which she shoved at him. "Only warm thing I could find in your chest. There's something wrapped in it, but I didn't have time to . . ." She dug farther and brought out a loaf and some spotty-buns. "Squashed," she announced cheerfully. Then she found a leaf-wrapped bundle of chortles, dripping with juice. "Also squashed." She held out a handful of the mangled fruit and motioned with it. "Just what *is* that thing?"

He had unrolled the red garben and sat looking at the green-stained vessel. "It's a cup," he said slowly.

"Of course it's a cup. But *what* cup? Why was it all wrapped up?"

"I'm not sure." He sat up straighter and started to rub at one of the knobs on the stem.

"Not *sure!* Didn't you wrap it?" Life began licking at the mashed chortles in her hand. "I hate folk who don't answer when you ask them something."

"Perhaps you oughtn't to ask," Trueline murmured, as though to herself. "Have some pickled cumber, Life? Tacky?"

"N' thanks." Life swiped at her dripping chin with the back of her hand.

"No, thanks," Tacky said absently. "Here. Look at this." He thrust the cup between them.

"All I see is scratches," Life said, and added grudgingly, "Oh, all right, it's a bird, a flying bird. So?" She pushed the cup away and thrust her hand into the wallet to bring up the other loaf . . . flattened. "Your cup squashed everything. I can't think why I brought the silly thing along." She tore the loaf apart and offered hunks to him and Trueline. "Here. Eat."

He put his bread down and went on smoothing the etched place on the cup. "It's a windsong bird," he said softly. "My dardomma must have made it. Starm and Frail, before they . . . you know. And I'll tell you something else." He kept his head down and began talking very fast. "I've thought it all out. I was in that potting cave when it started to fall—it was on the other side of the Spewing, I think, and down closer to the Stony Bib. And my dar—Starm—threw me out of it. Way out on the grass. By a tree. I remember going through the air!"

Life cleared her throat and Trueline made murmuring sounds, but he plunged on. "Then they took Hulin. And that was because Potter Ott hid me from them. I think it must have been in this same place here, the hide-hole, and that was the second time I got away, so it's no wonder the Seth said that I cheated Belcher!"

"Oh, *Seths!*" Life bit off a big corner of bread and chewed angrily.

"But don't you see? The moans last night . . . Belcher won't ever let me sleep again until . . . until . . ."

Trueline suddenly put a warning hand on his.

"Something's down there," she whispered, and pointed.

A tiny figure, a dot of blue against the dun ground and the black Spewing, was toiling up the slanty path.

"It wasn't there a moment ago—I've been watching. And then suddenly it *was*."

Life was the first to move. "The hide-hole. Quick!" She stuffed food back into the wallet in a scramble. "Get the

92

rest, hurry! The cloth, everything! Go on, Tacky, show the way!"

The First Story Stone stood crookedly from the cliff wall, as though long ago it had been shoved out of place by the Spewing. Behind it, in what looked like solid corsa, there was a crawl space that quickly dropped away into the heart of the Spewing itself. One by one they wriggled with their bags and baskets through the narrow opening and crammed themselves into the inverted bowl. A little light leaked in through crevices in the corsa over their heads, and rather a lot of the wind's *shrrrrring* sounds.

And now another sound was joined to the wind's song . . . the excited piping of birds.

Life broke their own startled silence with an urgent whisper. "Did we bring everything? Tacky, did you get the cup? And your festa-thing? And the bread? Did you get the bread?"

Cup . . . yes. Garben . . . yes. Bread . . . He fumbled through his armload.

"Did you pick up your *bread?*"

"I . . . that is . . . No," he said.

He could feel the glare from her that he couldn't see. "I'll get it," he said hastily.

"You can't," said Trueline. "Let it go."

"Get it," said Life.

Tacky pulled himself up to the crawl space and wriggled through into a noise of alarmed chirpings and flutterings of wing. Standing carefully upright, he squeezed along the back of the Story Stone and peeped round it. Yellow windsong birds were whirlwinging overhead; a few of them, braver than the rest, were already sailing down again to their interrupted dinner.

Beyond them, down the slope, the blue dot had turned into a figure—an undersized younger from the farmings, by his smock. Alarm sounded in Tacky's head like clicking stones.

There was no chance of retrieving the bread, for Blue Smock was looking directly at him. No, not at him. He couldn't possibly see half a head poking round the Story Stone. He must be watching the windsong birds.

Eat, Tacky commanded the birds. *Eat it all up!*

When the figure turned into a raggedy-haired, sharp-faced scrawny thing—a chidling!—Tacky pulled back his head and edged into the deeper shadow of the Stone. And waited. He felt someone pulling at his foot, and gave it a wiggle to show he knew what he was doing, even though he didn't.

The windsong birds gave the signal of Blue Smock's arrival with a whir of wings and scolding tongues. Tacky held his breath.

There was a long pause. He could feel the scrawny one looking at the bread and wondering how it had come there. If he started searching . . . if he stuck his head behind the Story Stone . . .

There was a small scraping sound, and a crunchy sound like the breaking apart of a crusty loaf, and a little thunking sound as of bread being thrown down, and then Blue Smock spoke, in a voice that had an odd unused croak about it.

"You can come back, Tacky!" he called out. "I'm only taking half the bread."

Tacky's mouth fell open—how did Blue Smock know his name, or that he was there? He already had a foot lifted to step forward when the voice turned into a coaxing whistle. Blue Smock was talking to the windsong birds!

Footsteps grated close to the Sky Stone, and Tacky got ready to catch hold of the stranger should he poke his sharp face round the corner of the Stone.

Blue Smock didn't stop. In a moment Tacky could see

him walking along the gallery past the other Stones. When he came to the rearing slab of endwall, he went right on walking.

And then he vanished.

10

Follow the goat
To the end of ever;
Come back home
Never, never.

—A Hopstone Game

When Skarra almost stepped on the big chunk of bread at the Aha, he backed down a few steps and stood staring at it. Overhead the yellow windsong birds cried their tackity disappointment and anger and went darting off in a flight of whirring wings.

Bread—here? Uneasily Skarra turned to look down the way he had come, first bent-backed in the wind across the Spewing, then up the sun-beaten path. A small family of goats browsing nearby kept a watchful eye on him. Goats were a good omen. But—bread? Windsong birds could not have carried it here.

He picked it up. It was fresh. He stepped cautiously into the Aha and looked down its length, and then up the sheer face of the cliff behind the Story Stones. Overhead a gawk scolded, *"Yih-yih."* Skarra suddenly smiled. Somebody on the Pillow was missing a loaf today. The gawk had helped itself and then awkwardly dropped half its looting.

He tore off a good-sized piece to leave for the windsong birds, called out to them to come back, lifted the rest of the loaf in salute to Belcher, and bit gratefully into the crust.

The sunball was so high now that its beams spilled over the Story Stones and crept along the musty ground. Skarra walked slowly between the Stones to the rocky wall at the end of the gallery, chewing on the good bread. He wished

96

the two black goats at the Brow had come with him, but they were likely too fat to go through the slot. It had been a very small goat that showed him the way that other time.

He had been dutifully tracing the picture-markings on the Eighth Stone with his finger when the black goat had appeared. "They put bundles on their backs and made ready to follow the Way of the Goat," the story went, and suddenly the little goat had appeared in the Aha, startling both of them. And then it had run back and vanished through the slab of rock, he following, sure that he had found the Way of the Goat. But of course he hadn't. He had found the way to the rock pool instead.

The sunlight showed no break in the rock mass at the far end of the Aha. Only if you had seen a very small black goat walk through solid rock could you know that the great slab had cunningly parted from the cliff and that the prickle grass filling the crack was actually a dangling thorn hanging from above, easily brushed aside.

Still chewing, Skarra wriggled through the crevice. His feet remembered the step off to the left, then right again through the split-apart rock. He felt the old panic as the rock clasped him front and back . . . what if Belcher chose *now* to put back together this rock he had opened! For *Belcher never opens a door that he does not close again, though it be countless ages that pass.* Skarra shuddered, but the next moment his hand closed on the far edge of the rock and he slipped on through.

The cliff wall of Belchers' arm curved away on the right; on the left a jut of rocks thrust skyward; between the two faces the ledge descended swiftly, opening into a broad grassy valley that continued in a gentler slope down to sun-glinted rocks. Beyond them rolled the sea, but still far below the meadow. If it weren't for the downslide he had found in the rock barrier, he would never have discovered the rock pool.

97

He followed the cliff face until he could see the two great slabs leaning against each other just as he remembered, then struck across the meadow toward them. The grass rattled at his ankles but deep down it was spongy cool on his feet. Yellow flowerlets laced the green, their petals folded prim against the heat of sunhigh, and a drift of blossoms fluttered pink and white from a score of trees. The bright air was astir with the flash and dart of chatbirds; in the distance a few fat goats browsed; and over all hung the lazy thrum of bees.

I'm the only one who knows this place, Skarra thought, and suddenly the qualmishness was back with him. But he was here at Belcher's will! He had the Seth. A true Seth. *He* would never have dared say those words to Venerable had Belcher not put them in his mouth. He walked faster. Sweat poured out of him like water from the Oozing Rocks, and the itching started up again. He was thirsty, and his middlings had already forgotten the bread he had sent down. When he got back to the Brow, he promised his rumbling stomach, he would dig down into the coddle bird's oven mound—that biggest one near the hot spring—and bring up a feast of eggs. And mayhap tomorrow Belcher would speak through the mudpots, telling Venerable to bring food before the usual bringing-day. The more he thought of it, the more it seemed certain that Belcher would do just that. The words were already forming in Skarra's mind, the way Belcher might say them:

> Five fat loaves,
> Wrapped in vine . . .

Or Belcher might even put in something about the loaves being crusty:

> Crusty loaves,
> Honeyed through,
> Cool froth of milk . . .

With the furious pounding of the sea beginning to throb through his feet, he broke into a run down the last tilt of land to the jumbled golden rocks that marked the cliff's edge. Just beneath those rocks lay, unseen and unimagined from above, the big sandy open cave beside the Swollen Sea itself. It was a downward scoop in the lower cliffside, as though some great hand had lifted out of the sea just high enough to gouge a living space from the rock.

Skarra licked his dry lips. Only moments separated him now from the sheltered pool at the outer edge of the sandy cave.

The two tilted slabs—like a Belcher cone—were just as he had last seen them. Eagerly Skarra seized hold of the flat stone he himself had placed over the downslide and hauled it away. Earth and pebbles rattled down the funnel, a tiny sound in the thunder of sound from below. He hadn't remembered how loud was the sea . . . Carefully he let himself into the opening of the funnel and went slithering and sliding feet first to the bottom.

For one long scaring moment, he thought he had come down at the wrong place. Where was the roomy sunlit cave of that other time? The floor of softest sand? The gentle pool girt with rocks to keep the sea out?

The cave was a rile of slapping, foaming, angry water. Gone was the girdle of protecting rocks, hidden beneath the foam. Only tips of them showed; from these wicked teeth great showers of spray shot into the open cave, wetting him through, runnelling down his legs and feet.

He felt bitterly disappointed. All day, ever since the Seth, he had looked forward to bathing in the rock pool—Belcher had promised! But how could he step into that swirling churning mass of water? He would be dashed against the outer rocks—he would eat water and breathe water and die. Was *that* what Belcher meant for him to do? No. No, Belcher had taken pity on him—he had *felt* Belcher's pity wash over him. Hadn't he? Had he? Skarra felt a great uncertainty weigh on him. He shivered in the cold spray, and his lips tasted of salt. He had been so sure, back at the mud . . .

The whumping sound behind him gave warning—too late. Something struck the back of his legs, knocking him off balance. For a moment he teetered desperately, arms flailing the air, and then he went plunging forward into an ice cold ferment. The water sucked him in and down, scraped him along the bottom, and finally lifted and hurled him against the far wall of rocks. He clawed at the stones, but a new surge of water swept in to drag him back, and the sucking and the scraping and the battering happened all over again.

Belcher, save me, he cried, but the words were drowned in brine and bitter despair. Belcher had tricked him. Belcher had sent him here to die, after all. Rotten, rotten . . . Belcher . . . He could feel himself smashing against the rocks one last time.

11

The tastiest dish when seasoned with tears gives
the tongue no more pleasure than Bleak Soup and lies
heavier inside than Stickytoe Pudding; while a single limp
parsnap chewed in happy company is a feast.

—Grey Gammer

Life hadn't meant to push Tacky quite so hard, but his
fidgets and twidgets finally outwore her patience. If she
hadn't tugged him through the danglethorn slot he would
still be dithering in the Aha; he would have stood on the
ledge all day if she hadn't pulled him down to the meadow
beyond; she had hauled on his arm all the way across the
flower-dotted grass; he had hung back so cravenly that, when
Blue Smock disappeared again, she couldn't be sure just
where the vanishment point was. Trueline hadn't been help-
ful.

"Perhaps he likes to make up his own mind," she had
protested in the middle of a fiercely whispered argument in
the meadow.

"*What* mind?" said Life, and yanked at Tacky's arm.

Even after they found the opening between the tilted
rocks and heard the enticing slap and surge of water come
funneling up to them, Tacky must stand urging caution until in exasperation Life gave him a sharp shove, and
phlumpf! Down he went, disappearing as thoroughly as
Blue Smock.

Still fuming at Tacky's obstinacy, and now a bit anxious,
Life slung the wallet of food over her shoulder and pushed
off after him. The slide was steep and long and curving;
once started down it, there was no stopping. She went

shooting out of the narrow darkness into an ear-shocking din. Her feet struck a something that gave way before her—Tacky!—and the rest of her bounced down on cold wet sand. The wallet dumped itself on her head.

In a flurry of runny beans and mashed chortles and spotty-buns and salt spray, she scrambled to her feet. "Tacky!" The boom of waves swallowed the voice out of her mouth. She felt the first sharp squeeze of panic. He was gone! They were both gone! She stood alone on a narrow strip of sand, with water lashing at her in front, rock wall thrusting against her back.

Of a sudden Trueline was standing beside her. Pointing. But Life could see only waves of water shattering against a rim of rocks that stood out from shore. No . . . There! She saw them. In the foaming water just inside the rim of rocks—a bobbing head and a sodden sack of blue. Tacky's one arm was wrapped round a tip of rock; with the other he was dragging Blue Smock's head up. Wild water boiled furiously round them.

"Coming!" she cried. "Hold on!" Something to throw to them . . . The wallet? Not long enough. Beside her, Trueline was . . . was . . . Distracted, Life watched her pull her pinover off over her head. Of course! She jerked at her own pinover, lost precious time disentangling it from the wallet still on her shoulder, and willingly let Trueline help knot the wallet to both overgowns while she kept shouting, "Hold on, Tacky! Hold on!" as though he could hear.

The lifeline looked too short. Snatching it from Trueline, Life pushed off her sandals and waded into the foam. Icy water dragged at her ankles; sand treacherously sank away under her heels. She was glad to feel Trueline's grip on the hem of her undergown. She groped forward until, suddenly, between one step and the next, the slope shelved off into nothing. Floundering back, she dug her toes and heels into the oozing sand and flung the end of the line, the wallet, with all her might towards Tacky's head.

A sudden jerk snatched the other end out of her frozen fingers. She clutched after it, overbalanced, and plunged into the seething water . . . but she had got hold of an end of the cloth, and she clung desperately to it. Then she felt Trueline's arms around her waist, lifting her; and floundering, choking, coughing, she got her feet on the treacherous sand and stood up. Tacky still clung to the rock tip holding Blue Smock's lolling head above water, but now he also held a strap of the wallet in his fist. A wave slapped into his open mouth, and his head disappeared, reappeared, went under, emerged . . .

Trueline's hands fastened around the line next to her own fingers. Life set her teeth and pulled, stepping backward against the dragging water, digging her heels in with each step, feeling Trueline's exact movements beside her. At last they were clear of the water and, bracing their feet in the wet sand, hauled Tacky and Blue Smock the rest of the way in.

Tacky flopped on the sand, his sides heaving; Blue Smock showed no signs of breath at all. There was a purpling lump over one eye, but the rest of his face was death white. His scrawny body stretched limp under the skimpy blue garben, the skinny legs dangling pitifully below the frayed edge. His sandals were gone, his knees and feet scraped and scarred. Life put her hand over his heart and was startled to feel clumps of something under the cloth. He made a small gurgling sound, like water bubbling in a clay pot.

Trueline made motions, and they took hold of his legs, dragged him round until his head was lower than the rest of him, rolled him over to let the water leak out. A small dribble ran from his mouth and nose.

Tacky groaned and tried to lift himself, but slumped down again. Telltale water seeped from his mouth. Alarmed, Life abandoned Blue Smock to Trueline and yanked Tacky round to face downslope. A little more water drained out of him. She tried lifting him by his legs to make the water run out faster, but they only bent at the knees. Exasperated, she tugged at his waist until she'd got his middle lifted off the ground. Water gushed out of his mouth and nose. It was like tilting a pitcher to pour the last of the milk! She lifted him again, higher . . . and again and again, until no more water came. When she rolled him on his side, his eyelids were flickering and there was a small purply smile on his lips.

She went back to help Trueline. Together they managed to lift Blue Smock partway up by his middle, but they were too tired to hold him. Life took a quick look round. Nothing to prop him over. Nothing. Just scattered food and the sodden lifeline. And the sodden Tacky . . . ?

Trueline touched her hand and nodded. Gripping one of the sticklike arms each, they dragged Blue Smock bumping across the sand and tugged him up and over Tacky's shoulder until he folded at the middle. His head waggled alarmingly, but more water spurted out of his mouth and nose.

It was the best they could do. Life sank, exhausted, to the cold wet sand. In a moment she would think about getting them back up to the meadow . . . If the water came higher . . . In a moment she would . . .

She awoke to a flood of sunlight, a sharp pain in her cheek, the sound of Tacky's voice blending with a long, slow wash of water, and a grouchiness of spirit that started at her hairstems and lasted through to her toes. Raising her head, she stared around her with a disfavoring squint. Astonished, she hitched up on one elbow, rubbing her cheek and blinking in the glare of sun on sand. A *lot* of sand!

The sea had retreated beyond a great tumble of rocks, leaving behind a gentle sparkling pool and beside it, like tipstools drawn up to a firepit—waterpit?—four broad flat rocks. Tacky and Blue Smock and Trueline were sitting on three of them.

"But Belcher had nothing to do with it," Tacky was saying. He was working at one end of the knotted lifeline, Trueline at the other. Blue Smock was sitting with his legs drawn up to his chin, the blue garben pulled taut round them—as though he would like to wrap himself completely out of sight.

"So you don't have Belcher to thank. You can thank me for pushing you in—that was by accident—and you can thank Life and Trueline for pulling us both out and pouring the salt water out of us. That was good sense."

"But the sea!" Blue Smock had a voice like fingernails scritching along stone. "It was Belcher pushed back the sea to save us!"

"Dar Toothacher called it Drag-outs," said Trueline. "That's when I was a child and he told me stories."

"Tooth . . . ? Drag-what?"

"Drag-outs. Toothacher—my dar—said there were Drag-ins and Drag-outs, and they pull the sea back and forth and eat the moon between times. Don't you know about Very Old Toothacher? And The-Place-Where-Toothacher-Fell-off-the-Cliff? The far side of the yammy patch?"

"No-o."

"I thought everybody . . . Well, from there you can look down and watch the sea rise and cover Hungerbite Rock, and then after a while it goes the other way, and you can see all of Hungerbite again. That's what dar Toothacher was doing when the cliff broke off under him—watching. He could tell you just when it was going to happen, too . . . the coming and the going, that is, not when the cliff would fall. Of course, folk said he wasn't good at much else, but he was no harm, either." Trueline's last words came muffled through the knot she had put her teeth to.

"How is it," Life broke in crossly, "how is it you know about this place, and don't know about the sea's coming and going? Where did you spring from? And did MudLar give you permission to go to the Aha?"

Blue Smock cast a quick look over his shoulder at her and ducked his head lower into his knees.

Trueline delivered a disapproving look over the knot. "You're awake," she said. "Have something to eat. The spotty-buns are soggy and more than a bit salty, but I've brushed most of the sand off; and there are some salt nuts."

Life rubbed her aching face and looked down at the imprint of her head in the sand. A lumpish stone bulged just where her cheek had been. She pushed herself up. Her undergown was clammy and salt-stiff, and her hair felt lank and cold on her shoulders. Then something about the stone stopped her. She stared at it.

"Need help?" Tacky asked.

"No-o-o . . ." She scraped the wet sand away from the stone. The two holes in it were chocked up, and now she could see a third hole. She went on scraping.

"What are you digging at?"

"It's a . . . I think it's a . . . it *might* be . . ." The roundish lump came sucking out of the sand. She turned it over in her fingers, scraping at the clogging sand. "I'm sure it is! As soon as I get the sand dug out, I just know it will be!" It was only a crumb beside the one that stood on Toothy Maw, and it was smoother, and whiter, but . . .

"Will be what?" Tacky demanded.

"What?" . . . but if it was a true one, and found here, then it must mean something . . .

"Will be *what?*" Tacky repeated.

"Don't go on asking 'Will be what?'! It's tiresome." The three holes had to connect with each other through the middle of the stone, else it wasn't a true one. "Do you have a bodkin?"

"Why would I have a bodkin?"

"I didn't ask *why*," said Life. "I asked if you *did*. Why don't you help instead of chewing on my pinover. You, Blue Smock, find me a twig!"

"A . . . *twig?*" Blue Smock croaked.

"Here's a bodkin," said Trueline. Amazingly, she held out a long pin.

" 'nks." Life began prying with it into the secret recesses of the stone. "I don't understand you," she scolded at them, "I find a true Oathstone and all you do is sit there eating cloth and not even trying to help!"

"Oathstone!" Tacky dropped the knot and came scrambling over, Blue Smock after him. "Why didn't you say so!"

"Did. I kept on telling you!"

"You kept on saying 'It's a, it's a . . .' But are you sure?"

"Almost." Two of the holes were cleared into the center of the stone, where they met. If the third one . . . "Blue Smock," she said sharply, "I can't see through your thick head."

He hunched back from her a trifle and looked fearfully up into her face. "You shouldn't . . ." he said in his scritchy little voice ". . . if it is an Oathstone, you shouldn't be . . . doing that. Not unless you're making an oath."

His face was pinched-looking, as though it had been caught in a slammed door, and the scare in his eyes made Life uncomfortable. She didn't like cringy, scrawny things. And now this cringy, scrawny thing was putting out a cringy, scrawny hand to take the stone from her. She slapped the hand away, and he shrank even further into himself.

"He's right," said Tacky. "And you don't have to slap at him."

"Then he should learn to keep his hands off." Life went on with her probing. She would *not* be made to feel sorry for this scared thing. "Besides, it's not an Oathstone until it has three holes meeting in the center, and this one so far has just two holes, so it's just a stone." She took time out to glare at Tacky and then at Blue Smock. "Do I hear any objection to picking sand out of a stone with two holes?"

"But . . ." said Tacky.

"But . . ." said Blue Smock.

They looked at each other, shrugging. Trueline stayed aloof.

"Well, *then*," said Life, feeling that the three of them were turning against her. She jabbed the bodkin defiantly into the third hole again and again. "There! That's it!" She gave one last dig with the bodkin and blew into the opened hole. "Look, it's a true Oathstone!" Triumphantly, she passed it to Tacky. "Be careful not to stick your finger in it," she cautioned, "now that it *is* an Oathstone."

Tacky squinted into each of the three holes against the sun. "It is. It really is," he said wonderingly. "What ought we do with it?" He passed it to Blue Smock, who took it gingerly between finger and thumb and brought his eye to it.

"Make an oath. What else?" Life got briskly to her feet and shook out her clammy undergown. "As it's not safe for Tacky on the Pillow, he'll have to stay in the Aha, until . . . well, until it's safe again. Of course I know *I'll* never tell anybody where he is, but what about . . . *others?*" She darted a brief glance at Blue Smock, raking Trueline in passing. "So we'll take a binding oath to keep Tacky's secret. We'll do it properly just as soon as we've eaten. Blue Smock, give the stone to Tacky to keep. Tacky, put it in your belt pocket and don't lose it."

Tacky accepted the Oathstone back from Blue Smock. "And now," he said mildly, "if you've finished telling everybody what to do, let's eat."

They sat on the four rocks and gulped down spotty-buns crunchy with sand and soggy from salt spray, chewed on salt nuts turned slippery from the sea water, and grew thirstier by the moment. Life tried not to watch Blue Smock's irritating way with food. Before every bite, he lifted the morsel in both hands above his mouth and then tilted his head back to eat it in small nibbles, like a mouse. It was no wonder he was so scrawny—everybody else would have cleared the table while he was working up to his third bite!

He troubled her, this spindly creature from nowhere. He

108

had a bumpy something on his chest hidden by his smock, he had never even heard of Very Old Toothacher, and he had a way of looking apprehensively over his shoulder. His garben might have come from a ragbag, and his sandals—somebody must have found them in the pool—were very strange, with thongs that wrapped right round his legs. He was very strange altogether, this . . . this . . . She wasn't even sure if he was chidling or younger. His hair was so thin and scribbly there was no telling if it had ever been cut short to mark the difference.

When, finally, the last crumb had gone down, Life smoothed a circle in the sand; Tacky took the Oathstone from his belt and placed it in the center; and they all scrooched closer with their heads over it.

"You start, Tacky," said Life. "It's your secret we have to oath on."

Obligingly, Tacky put the tip of his finger in one of the holes, and then looked up with surprise. "But I don't know how to do it!" he exclaimed. "None of us knows! We've never been allowed at an Oathing!"

"Why you just . . ." Life looked at him in exasperation. "All you do is . . ."

"Tell who you are," said Trueline, "and what it is that needs oathing. Then you end with binding words and clasp the hand of the one next to you. Usually the oath is done in threes, with two people oathing and the third as a witness, but this way is just as binding."

"How do *you* know all that?" Life demanded.

Trueline shrugged. "I listen a lot," she said, "while others are talking."

Before Life could retort, Tacky started. "I am called Tacky-obbie, named for the call of the Windsong-Bird-that-Swoops-and-Soars, and I live with my uncle Ott . . ."

Life watched Blue Smock while Tacky told about his dardomma's death and the Seth and how he was hiding away to avoid being sent down the Long Slip. He ended with the binding oath: "We have eaten together and therefore you are bound to me as your other self, and I to you, whatever befalls us." He reached out and clasped one of Blue Smock's hands in his.

Blue Smock looked bewildered, and scared too, Life thought. She motioned to Trueline to go next and kept her eyes fastened on Blue Smock's downcast face while they heard the whole story of Toothacher and the memory stone for Trueline's domma and the songchant Trueline was composing. She started to sing a sample of it, but Tacky cleared his throat loudly, and she went back to the binding oath, clasping Tacky's and Blue Smock's hands when she had finished.

Life got through her part quickly, but when she got to the binding oath, she added "Breaking this oath will burn out your tongue. So *beware.*" She joined her hand with the others', and Tacky guided Blue Smock's limp finger to the Oathstone.

Blue Smock licked his lips, swallowed several times, opened his mouth, shut it.

"Go *on,*" Life prodded.

"I . . . I am . . . I am . . ." His scritchy little voice kept sticking to words. "I . . . that is . . . I don't really have a name of my own. I don't have a dar or domma, and I . . . I live mostly by myself. Sometimes I'm called names like Ten Thumbs or Gawk Awkward or . . . Stumble Foot, but I should like to be called . . . be called . . . that is, if I'm to be something like your brother, why you could give me a real name, couldn't you?" He cast a hopeful look around at them and dropped his eyes again. His lower lip began to tremble.

Trueline broke the short silence. "Why not? You're welcome to use my dar's name if you like. Though," she added in apology, "Toothacher doesn't seem to fit you very well, even without the 'Very Old.' *Quale* might do better. There hasn't been a Quale for a long time . . ."

"Or Starm," Tacky offered. "That was my dar. We could call you Starm."

Life felt them all looking at her, waiting. "There's Hulin," she said grudgingly. "Nobody is going to use that name for a long, long time. Hulin Blue, maybe. It has a good sound, and we could call you just Blue for short to keep from getting mixed up with . . . with . . ."

"It has a very brothery sound, Hulin Blue does," said Trueline.

When everybody nodded in quick agreement, Blue Smock's mouth formed into a tremulous smile, or at least his teeth almost showed and his lips almost went up at the corners. He bent to the Oathstone once more.

"Then I am Hulin Blue," he said, as though tasting the name and finding it sweet on his tongue. "I live on . . . ng . . . in the uplands. The way I found this place was . . . one time there was a goat went through that slot in the Aha, and I followed, and I found this rock pool, but I never told . . . anyone."

"Did you get a permission to come to the Aha today?" Life demanded.

"A . . . a permission?" He looked uncertain.

"Did *we?*" asked Tacky quickly. "Finish your oath, Hulin Blue. I'm getting a crick in my shoulder."

They had to help him with the words—he might know the rules about fingers in oathstones, but he didn't know a scoop's worth about oaths—and, that done, Tacky knotted the stone carefully inside a bit of cloth Life tore from her undergown so that nothing could rub against their oaths. He stowed it in his belt.

"These four rocks," said Hulin Blue suddenly, motioning toward the stones they were sitting on, "and four of us. It's like a sign, isn't it?" When he puckered up his face like that, Life thought, he looked like a withered turnip. "Belcher really meant us to . . . to meet here, didn't he?"

"Why not?" said Trueline.

"Witless as Murkle himself," Life muttered to no one in particular.

"Who is Murkle?"

Life gave a *hff!* of exasperation. "Really, Blue, you must live in a deep hole! And why does everything have to be a sign! Belcher has nothing to do with us . . . we met here because we followed you. That's *all*. And Tacky was in the Aha to begin with because he thought nobody would be coming there. And you thought the same thing, didn't you!"

"N-no, I felt a feeling, that is, it was like being *told* to come . . ."

"You mean you came because you were hot and wanted to bathe in the pool!"

"Did I?" Blue whispered. "No, I don't think so. Because I'd forgot about this place until . . . until . . ."

"Until you 'felt a feeling,' " Life said scornfully.

He gave her a stricken look and turned beseechingly toward Trueline, who had gone rummaging at the bottom of the slide.

"I've found eight runny beans from the spill," she announced in her determinedly cheerful voice. "Now *there's* a sign—two beans each! I think I see another, but I'll leave it there and not spoil the count. Life, are you going to wear your pinover or is it still wet?"

"Both," said Life shortly. She yanked and jerked her way into the damp, salt-stiff gown. "Let's get out of here, if we can, and find some water to drink." She gave Blue a little push towards the funnel. "Murkle," she explained to Blue, to make up for her shouting at him, "isn't anybody real. We just tell stories about him; you know, like Windlestraw."

"Who is Windlestraw?"

Life stared at him. "Just start climbing," she said.

It was Blue who pointed out a line of darker green in the meadow and led them to a place where water ran in a clear sparkling channel. They drank from their hands, sloshed their heads, and finally rolled in the stream until all the stiff salt of the sea was washed out of them. Then they spread themselves out to dry near a nest of white boulders, chewed on the eight runny beans and talked, and when the beans were gone, they chewed on juicy grass stems and talked. The birds went on singing, the bees went on thrumming, and the fat goats never stopped wagging their lower jaws.

Blue didn't know about firepit stories or flying straw kites or chase-games; he had never been to the Pillow or the yammy patch or the Scars of Cherrychoke; he had never even been to a festival!

"You are bone-ignorant, do you know that?" Life demanded. "Where do you live? Under a stupid-stone?"

"I . . ." He turned in confusion to Trueline. "You said about dancing the Scorched Rock dance. How do you do that?"

"Oh, you just pretend you're barefoot on scorching hot rocks, and the dance comes naturally. Here, we'll show you."

They had to haul him forward and back on his awkward feet and hoist him into the air for leaps and keep from stumbling over him when they came to the *stamp, stamp, stamp.* He did better when they slowed down to the yammy dance and went winding in and out around the boulders as though they were mounds of newly planted yammies.

They finally threw themselves on the ground to rest.

"That's supposed to make the yammies grow better," Tacky said. "But Potter Ott thinks it's just a good excuse for a frolic. One planting time it was too wet for the yammy dance, and the yammies were twice as big that year. Potter Ott said they were probably grateful for not being jumped on."

Unexpectedly, Blue laughed, but immediately became sober again. "This Potter Ott you live with . . . does he keep food from you when you do something wrong?"

Tacky stared. "Now why should he do that?"

"To . . . to teach you."

"Hoh!" Life scoffed. "Who ever heard of learning anything on an empty stomach!"

"Oh," said Blue. "Oh."

"Speaking of yammies and empty stomachs," Trueline said reflectively, "do you remember the year when lots of the yammies didn't sprout? And when the mounds were dug up, they had stones in them? And MudLar read the mudpots for Venerable and said Belcher turned the seed yams to stone because chidlings had been digging on the big Belcher Mound and made him angry? Do you remember that?"

"Of course," said Life, and Tacky nodded, but Blue looked blank.

Trueline bent her brows into a serious frown. "It wasn't Belcher did that to the seed yams." Her voice got very small. "It was me."

"That's *ridiculous*," said Life. "How could *you* turn seed yams to stone?"

The eyebrows turned even more serious. "Because I planted them in the first place."

"Planted! Stones? You must be daft!"

"That is very interesting," said Trueline in maddening earnestness. "You believe Belcher can turn seed yams into stones, but if I plant stones and they go on being stones, you say I'm daft, without even knowing the wherefore!"

"What is the wherefore, then?"

Trueline looked pleased with herself. "It's that dar Toothacher was in charge of the seed yams that year and he didn't save enough out of the last crop. When it was time to plant, there weren't nearly enough. I didn't want my dar scorned at a Summoning, so I filled two of the planting bags with stones and put them in the ground myself when the day came. Of course I couldn't ever tell, but *I* knew why they didn't grow. And that's more than Venerable or MudLar, or even Belcher, knew!"

Life stared at Trueline in astonishment and admitted a

tiny sliver of admiration to her thinking. Then she saw Blue's face. He looked . . . stunned? Horrified? Or just witless?

For a while, then, they lazed, listening to the burbling stream, the soft sing of insects, and the distant low wash of the sea, while the shadow of Belcher's enormous arm crept steadily across the meadow.

Suddenly Blue raised his head, like a warning. While the others froze, he skulked low across the grass to one of the boulders, where he knelt briefly, watching and waiting. Then, swift as a lizard's tongue, his hands shot out. There was a sudden shrilling, and he held up a struggling little brown furry thing. In the next moment it fell limp in his grasp, its little head hanging over his wrist.

"You killed it!" Life gasped.

Blue shook his head, stroked the little thing's pinkish ears with his thumbs. Its eyes flicked open, squinted shut again, and it bunched up its orange rump till it was a small round furball.

"But what is it?" Trueline asked.

Blue shook his head again and went on stroking the furball. "I just call it a Friendly One. Once I had . . . but I wasn't allowed to keep it. This one's very young. I wonder . . ." Carefully he turned it over in his hands to look at its legs. "Yes, you see, its toes are too soft for burrowing. That's why his family left him. He'll die."

"Oh, but . . ." Tacky put out a finger and stroked the little head. The eyes squinched open and shut, and happy rumbling sounds came from Friendly One's interior. "If he's going to die here, maybe I could . . . What do you think?" he appealed to Hulin Blue. "Couldn't I keep him with me? In the Aha?"

Blue looked dubious. "You'd need lots of grass. They eat all the time, these creatures. I suppose, though . . ." He thought further, then, "Here," and gave Friendly One over. But the little beast eluded Tacky's hands, went clawing up his chest, ducked under the neckline of his garben and skittered out of sight—down to the last sprawling leg.

"Ah-ooo," Tacky yelped, clutching at the front of his tunic.

Blue laughed and yanked Tacky's belt tighter. "There. He can't fall out."

Life stared at Blue as he and Trueline fell to digging roots for Friendly One. In those few moments while he was holding the creature, Blue had stopped blundering through his words and had talked—even laughed—like any ordinary younger.

Not that she trusted him any the more for it, she hastily told herself.

They were on the ledge leading back up to the Aha when Life felt, suddenly, an overwhelming . . . loss? She looked down at the others somberly toiling up the shadowed slope, and beyond them to the tranquil meadow, still sunlit at the far reaches. A wisp of longing curled through her mind. If they could stay here . . .

They could build a shelter—a house—with tree branches . . . eat wild yammies and chortles and bitter root . . . milk the fat goats . . . fetch clothing and coverlets in plenty from the Pillow, and seeds to plant in gardens . . . and nobody would ever find them. And then, one day . . .

Absently she edged through the split rock . . . *and then, one day, when she went off to follow the sun, why then . . .* and turned to go through the slot . . . *why then, they might go with her and they would all follow the sun together . . .*

She eased herself back through the danglethorn into the Aha, and her dream shattered.

There was a flurry of movement at the other side, a hissing intake of breath, like a rearing nest of snakes.

Life fell back against Blue, fright shivering all the way down to her toes.

There were two flurries, two voices, wildly waving arms, staring crazy eyes . . .

She had already shoved Blue back through the slot against Trueline and Tacky when the echoing shouts from the Aha sorted themselves into intelligible words.

"Life! Come back! It's *us!*"

Milk and Mole Star!

12

Long ago, when Firelings had nothing better to do they went Hunting the Balefire, that Chopper of Piercing Virtue so long lost to them.

Windlestraw, however, being as wise as he is foolish, grew tired of scratching about in the spidery crevasses, nasty ditches, and fusty caves that were deemed possible finding places for a longknife as tall as the candletree on Toothy Maw. He went off alone to spy out ant dens, poke into pesker burrows, examine bee hollows, and generally enjoy himself in a small way. Soon the villagers were twitting him about looking for the chopper in the feelers of a scurrying insect.

"Even Murkle," they scoffed, "has enough sense to look in places *big* enough to hold the Balefire!"

"Ah yes," said Windlestraw agreeably. "But then even Murkle has never found it there!"

—Legends of Windlestraw

Trueline felt a small quaver of dread as she eased back through the split rock into the meadow, calling after Milk and Mole Star to follow. With each passage it seemed to her that the crack grew narrower, as though the rock was trying to rejoin itself. But Milk and Mole Star were as full of *Hoi* and *Halloo* as ever, and once through the split, flung themselves down the slope to the meadow with their usual joy and abandon. Blue, walking beside Trueline, watched them with big eyes.

It was only after the six of them had settled against a stone outcropping at the foot of the ledge that they began to piece together the garbled tale brought by Milk and Mole Star—neither seemed able to finish a sentence without the other.

Ever since they had been caught spludging out Tacky's footsteps on Stony Bib, Milk and Mole Star had floundered deeper and deeper into the bog of Flaw's and Overshot's suspicions.

After sun-high they had been hauled along to the Aha with a special search party, there having been introduced grave doubts that Tacky was at the bottom of the pucker after all; and just as unceremoniously they were then hauled back down to the Pillow. But while they were in the Aha, Milk had almost backed into a narrow opening behind the First Story Stone, and Mole Star had stepped on a red chortle still so fresh that it squished under his heel. By dint of standing firm in the shadow of the Sky Stone, they kept their discoveries from the searchers until Flaw and Overshot decided that Tacky, if he still lived, must have gone to hide in the Mudsock or the Thicket and moved the hunt down the slanty path. It was much later before Milk and Mole Star could break free from their grasp and only then because Flaw had lost his muffler in the Aha. He had stuffed it into his sleeve when his neck got too hot.

"And then," said Mole Star, "happened it fell out . . ."

". . . quite by accident," said Milk.

". . . and nobody else wanted to come all the way back to look for it . . ."

". . . except us." Milk pulled the wadded muffler out of his own sleeve and swung it around in the air with a triumphant flourish.

"But it's all right then!" Life cried. "They won't come back here to look. So Tacky only has to stay in the hide-hole another night, and then the Day of the Morsel will be past and it will be safe to go back home!"

But Trueline had listened to Milk's and Mole Star's patchy tale with growing uneasiness, and what she heard in the pauses and hesitations was more than they spoke with their mouths. In the minds of Flaw and Overshot, she knew as clearly as though they had told her, one day had become as good as another for the Giving of a Morsel . . . if it would save their own skins.

The shadows lengthened; flowerlets closed. The bees, out of work for the day, went home and were replaced by midgins. It was time to leave the meadow.

Back in the Aha once more, Trueline insisted they all crawl into the hide-hole to listen for the sounds Tacky had heard last night. Almost no light now filtered through the chinks into the cave, nor was there any sound beyond that of the wind's *shrrrr* as it swept down the Spewing overhead. She helped Tacky spread out the wadding that Life had brought, while Milk and Mole Star sorted the remaining food into Tacky's satchel and Hulin Blue fed roots to Friendly One. Life, meanwhile, rattled off a series of advices to Tacky; wear the red festival gown for warmth; stow the windsong cup in the satchel; don't mind sounds in the night because it was only sun-splinters no matter what anybody said; stay hidden until they came back in the morning and then they would all go to the meadow . . .

Even when they crawled outside, and Milk and Mole Star were dancing to be off, Life wouldn't let them go until Tacky had produced the Oathstone for them to swear through. They obligingly poked their fingers into the holes and said the proper things, and then went racing down the path. Flaw's muffler streamed in their wake. Life and Blue and Trueline set off together.

Halfway down the slope Trueline turned to look back at Tacky. He stood tiny in front of the great tablet of the First Story Stone; it, in turn, was dwarfed by the shaft of Belcher's outstretched arm, a towering cliff face behind the Aha. A small feeling of fear stirred inside her. It was easy to make light of night-moanings and to talk against Belcher when the sun was shining on green grass and yellow flowerlets and the world was still and you had found a way to the Swollen Sea; but when the sun had gone and the chill mist rose up about you, and you were on the slope with a strange younger from the uplands you knew nothing about, and . . . *and only the Shadows of the Doomed roam the Spewing, their anguished cries shivering down the long black tongue* . . . She hurried to catch up with the others.

At the tip of the Spewing, Life stopped. "How do you go from here?" she asked Blue.

He hesitated and then waved one scraggy arm vaguely toward the trees of the Empty Forest on the other side of the Spewing.

"But what if MudLar sees you?"

"I have my way to go."

"Or the other one . . . the Skarra?"

Blue shrugged.

"What is it like, where you live?" Trueline suddenly asked. There was a strange wildness about Blue, as though he only existed through others, as though, when they walked away from him, he would stop *being*.

"It's . . ." For the first time, Blue's eyes met hers and then Life's without wavering. "It's very lonely," he blurted, and turned and ran stumbling up the other side of the Spewing, up through the steep Empty Forest.

As they stood watching him disappear among the trees, a shiver started low in Trueline's back, like a thumbworm arching its furriness before creeping forward: *hummmp* . . . *crawwwl* . . . *hummp* . . . *crawwl* . . . Like a warning. A premonition of a thing she knew deep inside herself. . . .

Something had started that would not be stopped until—until it was finished. One way or another.

The tremors that began that night were of only bed-quivering strength on the Pillow, but Firelings were overstrung. Gone were the times when they would have smiled at the prospect of poor old clumsy Belcher trying to get to his feet, and now they lay a-tremble under their coverlids.

Flaw, even though he had properly denounced Ott's friendship, packed up his family and took the Pubbly Way for the uplands just in case Belcher confused him with his former friend. But when they reached the upper yammy patch, they met farmers who came jolting down the Pubbly Way to seek safety on the Pillow. They all huddled together inside the tumbled stone walls of the yammy patch, and the more Belcher sprinkled them with ash, the louder they talked of his goodness.

Venerable got up a dozen times, thinking he should calm the villagers, but he went back to bed as many times, for he could think of no words. Belcher had truly put a stop on his tongue in the morning's Seth. He tried not to think of the young and untried Skarra seeking "sea-splashed rocks." He tried not to think of MudLar on Belcher's Throat, for he could remember a MudLar of long ago who had gone to speak to Belcher's inner fires and never come back. In fact, he tried not to think at all and pulled his fleece up over his head.

Life heard her domma get up at first tremor and go outside to comfort Stone Hulin, but when she in turn went out to comfort her domma, she was sent back to bed. The wallet, swollen with the loaves she had baked that evening, lay under her bed where she could stretch out a hand to feel it from time to time.

Many a pipe of cherrychoke was smoked through that night to fuzzle the head against danger, but only Potter Ott, who had got an early start on fuzzlement, slept soundly in his jolting bed. Having lost everything, he had no reason to lose sleep as well.

Milk and Mole Star never went to sleep at all—for fear of being awakened and seized by Flaw and Overshot. When the tremors began they were out of their windows like two shadows, and like two shadows they melted into the red darkness of Bump Lane. There was no one to see them go, except for Trueline, of course, from her memory-stone across the lane.

High up in the Aha, Friendly One gave shrill warning of the first tremor moments before it came, bit Tacky's ear, and went scrambling wildly into his hair.

"Wait! Wait!" Tacky cried. "Hold still!" He pried the quivering ball of fur loose from his hair and held it close in his hands until the small shrieking gave way to despairing little bleats and whimpers and an occasional hiccup.

Tacky raised his head to listen. A pale pink glow filtered through the crannies in the Spewing, outlining the opening into the Aha, but there was only silence outside.

And then there was something. A whisper? It grew into a faint moaning, like the moaning he had heard the night before. But then it changed. It sounded almost like . . . like words. His scalp shrivelled.

Ar-rahr, it said, and the voice, if voice it was, sounded as close to him as the ball of fur mewing against his chest.

Ar-rahr, ar-rahr, it repeated.

Clasping Friendly One tighter to him, Tacky groped round the walls of his small cave, but he felt only the rough rock on all sides. A trick of the wind over the Spewing? The wind had stopped. There was no sound of any kind anywhere except for the moaning and the clappering of Friendly One's heart against his own.

And then, faintly shivering at first, growing to a grinding rumble, the hide-hole shook around him. Shook again. And again . . .

123

A rock chunked at his feet; another hit the side of his head and made his ears sing. Under him the ground suddenly sagged and at the same time jutted up under his left knee, dragging his leg upward against the rocks overhead. Friendly One shrilled into his ear.

"All right," Tacky said shakily, trying to get his leg back from where it was pinned, and right himself at the same time. "We'll get out of here."

He worked his leg free at last, but before he could squeeze through the narrow passage into the Aha, there was a booming crash over his head. A shock ran through him. Friendly One dived down the neck of his gown and scrabbled at his chest. Everything was suddenly deathly still.

The pale pink light had been completely blotted out. Dust choked the air.

Far on the other side of the Spewing, Skarra had been dreaming a new dream of shadowy figures dancing . . . of laughter and voices, when suddenly it was bent into the old terror. A swirling mist curled round the figures, blotting out the bright meadow, and in the center of the mist was the bundled figure, the steam, and the terror that were always a part of his dreams.

At the second tremor he sprang up, calling out to his shadowy friends to be careful, but they had disappeared into the mist. The third brought him fully awake. He was standing alone in the dark hut clutching the blue beads so hard that his hand ached.

The beads! He had fallen asleep in the midst of telling over the beads! MudLar would never have let him do that. MudLar would have prodded him awake until he finished. MudLar would have called him a thousand names and kicked his feet to bruises, but he would somehow have seen that the beads were read twice each day—he would have kept the wrath of Belcher from touching Skarra! MudLar . . . MudLar . . .

Belcher made a terrible rumbling sound directly below his feet that drove Skarra, terrified, into the open. The Rift glowed a red warning above him.

"I will! I will!" Skarra shouted over the noise of the jarring earth. "I'll do it now! Only let MudLar come back!" He stumbled to the ledge above the mudpots and sank to his knees. "I'm here, I'm here," he sobbed.

A sudden roar drowned his voice. The gusher! Pent up for two days, the steaming water jet shot boiling and hissing into the sky. Skarra covered his head. Scalding spray needled his back. The roaring went on and on as though all the water in the world was spouting from Belcher's Body.

Frenziedly Skarra fumbled out the cone of Belcher and the five Hollow stones with his left hand, and with his right the Season of New Life. His mind wiped clean of all thought by his fear, he began telling over the days . . . Sky, Sunball, Moon, Star. . . .

The jet at last dropped off with a gurgling and a gargling, shot one final spurt into the air, and fell silent.

But Skarra remained crouched over the mudpots, his fingers picking up beads and dropping them for the next in turn. Through the long night, from the hours of Stealthy Rat through Creeping Footfalls to Deepest Dark, he told the endless cycle of days and seasons.

Sometimes he fell into a half-sleep, but each time a new tremor awakened him, and his fingers staggered on at their work.

At last Belcher was mollified. He gave a final shake; his flames paled in the coming dawn. The rough beads fell out of Skarra's raw hands and he slept where he lay.

13

When the mouse jumps up
And his whiskers fall,
It's quick past the net
And up to the wall!

—"Mouseway," an ancient tag
and chase game

The Pillow was chill and mist-wrapped the next morning when Life set out for the binhouse. Goat carts, ghostly in the early light, went thumping across the bottom of Puddingstone Lane to Toothy Maw and more came rumbling down Pubbly Way from the uplands. Fog-shrouded figures plodded alongside, their muffled shouts mingling with the creak of harness and wheels.

The village was in disarray. Trees leaned; the roadway bulged here and sank there; new holes yawned in stone fences. Two goats browsed on Flaw's roof, while below, bounding round and round with threatening lunges of a rake, Flaw charged in pursuit of four more strays. A long shred of cloth hung from the mouth of one of them and waved in the breeze of its passing for all the world like Flaw's muffler.

Grey Gammer, encircled by the usual ramble-scramble of children, joined Life to watch the spectacle from the lane. "Flaw forgot to shut his doors when he ran off to the uplands in the night," she said with relish. "There is a narrow line between honest fear and witless fright, marked by the time it takes to close the gate." She turned an intent look on Life and added slowly, "On the other hand, those who

126

linger too long sometimes risk worse than goats eating holes in their shirt tails." She shook a chidling off her skirt and shooed the rest away, and they went off tootling through their fingers and chanting:

> "Strike dumb the tongue
> That Skarra mocks,
> For Skarra seeks
> The sea-splashed rocks!"

"Their new game song," Grey Gammer said. "Venerable was so flustered that he forgot to give yesterday's Seth over the Oathstone, and of course the chidlings picked it up. Poor Venerable. Not even MudLar has ever stoppered his tongue so neatly." She frowned then. "You know of course that MudLar still hasn't come back? Venerable went for a Seth at first light, but there was nothing in the mudpots but a lengthy request for crusty loaves, well buttered, to be delivered this afternoon." Her eyes went back to their twinkling. "When MudLar is away, the Skarra has an appetite."

From Flaw's gatepost to the binhouse Grey Gammer rambled on. She speculated on the possibility that Belcher's rage came not from anger at Firelings but from a giant seaworm that was biting his toe way the other side of him where Fireling couldn't see. She reported that Ven Ida wanted to have Stone Hulin put down the Long Slip because, she said, Belcher was jealous of images other than his own. She remarked that whereas Milk and Mole Star had been much in evidence yesterday, today they were not to be seen—and she gave Life a searching look. She spoke darkly of the suspicions and dark broodings that lay over the Pillow, of the skittishness of people's minds when they were in the grasp of fright.

They rounded Venerable's homing into full sight of Toothy Maw. Carts stood in haphazard array; goats *baa*-ed and reared in their traces; children scuttled underfoot; dardommas scolded; and above the clangor, Overshot's hoarse voice bawled instructions from the speaking bench.

Grey Gammer put a restraining hand on Life's arm and faced her, eyes deep-down serious. "Listen to me, Life, and listen well. I have heard Belcher's belly-rumblings all my days. I know them better than the belly-rumblings of my granson's chidlings. And I tell you now that they are not the simple gripe that comes of eating green chortles, or the pain of having a toe bitten by a sea-worm. Belcher is sick! Life, I fear for all of us. With MudLar away, and only a dab of a Skarra . . . Life, Skarra needs to be warned of the danger! By someone he will listen to. I've been thinking . . . He might listen to someone close to his age, Life!"

Grey Gammer held Life's startled gaze a moment longer, then suddenly wheeled and went off into the jam of scatterlings and carts, leaving Life to stare after her. Gammer's ramble-scramble of children went straggling past, their high spirits draining out of their feet, their chant only half-hearted now, and already altered to roll easier off their tongues. "Skarra seeks the sea-splashed rocks" had become "Skarra sees the bee-bash-bocks!"

Out of the jumble of Life's mind, a memory of yesterday jumped clear: Blue Smock crossing the flowery meadow on hurrying feet towards the rock pool. The sea-splashed rocks? Blue . . . ?

Even as the thought wandered into her head, she laughed. Poor scrawny, cringing, anxious, scared Hulin Blue! Whoever or whatever he was, he could not, ever, not possibly, not in the giddiest imagining or in the most outlandish dream, be Skarra!

"Oh there you are!" said Joke Eye when Life walked through the door. "I've been wondering what had become of you."

"I've brought the flour for your baking."

"So you have!" Joke Eye left the pile of goat's hair she was carding to take the basket. "What a thoughtful chidling you are."

"You asked me to fetch it," Life reminded her.

"Did I! I must have forgotten. Why don't you go out and speak to Hulin? He gets lonely, not being able to run and play like the others. Still, it's better now that he always stays in our own courtyard, don't you think? The others used to tease him until he cried, do you remember?"

"Yes, I remember." Life knelt by her bed and carefully pulled out the wallet she had filled the night before. The milk hadn't leaked, and it was still sweet.

"Are you taking that to your dar? I believe he is at the upper yammy patch. Mending wall. Or perhaps it's Bump Lane. It's very thoughtful of you, Life."

"He's cutting thatch down by the thicket, Domma, and he took food with him." She turned away and said softly, "I'm going to the Aha, Domma."

Joke Eye paused in the act of shaking the flour into a bowl. "Yes, to be sure." She suddenly shook a great deal of flour, and white powder dusted over her hands. "Life, Kirtle has been telling me strange tales. She says Flaw and . . . but, there, I've decided not to believe such gossip. Flaw and Overshot, indeed! As soon speak of Murkle. Still, you will be careful going out and about, won't you? These are odd times. Folk empty their heads of sense, come troubles like these."

"I'll be careful, Domma."

"Just speak a word to Hulin as you go out. He does get lonely, you know."

"I will."

"And tell your dar I'll bring some new-baked bread to him for his meal . . . Oh there, I am forgetting again— you're taking his meal to him now, aren't you? It's very thoughtful of you, Life."

Life paused in the courtyard to pat Stone Hulin's head.

Though the rest of the garden was still spattered and smeared with mud, Stone Hulin had been polished clean and his table washed down. The mud drips had been broken off the candletree that shaded him, and even the tumbled homing wall had been rebuilt—to keep Stone Hulin safe in his own yard.

Yoe the Beekeep, unrelieved of guard's duty from the day before, was flat out asleep with his mouth ajar when Life skinned over the pucker onto the Stony Bib. There she paused, looking at the welter of footprints scuffing the dried mud. Grey Gammer's words slid into her mind. Most of the tracks went along the Stony Bib toward the Spewing, but there were others that made a neat little track between the pucker and the steep path opposite. Venerable's tracks. To and from the Brow. To the Skarra. *Someone should talk to the Skarra,* Gammer had said, *somebody close to his own age, somebody he would listen to . . .*

How would you go about meeting the Skarra? Go up the steep path and knock on the Brow and say, "Excuse me, Skarra, but do you know about Belcher's bad bellyache?" Ridiculous. Skarra wouldn't listen to her. And even the *thought* of going up the Venerable Path brought a bad memory that wouldn't be crammed away again once it had come to her head . . .

It was after Venerable took Hulin to MudLar that long ago day, and Joke Eye had followed them in her despair. Afterwards she talked of nothing else until Chipstone finally carved the Stone Hulin to comfort her. ". . . All wrapped in a shroud so snug he was already limp as any dead one, and MudLar himself carried him from the Brow, slung over his shoulder like a long bag of wool, up that sorry path to the awful place, and then *Whuuuuuushsh* down he went into a big hole there in the clearing, high above the Brow, it was . . ."

Whuuuuuushsh, Life reminded herself with a shudder, and hoisting her own heavy bag to her shoulder, she turned towards the Spewing.

A hand fell on her arm, and she swallowed a shriek.

"Shhh-hh, don't wake Yoe," Trueline hushed her. "And you can't go along the Bib—old Larking is watching by Ott's house. And Zook is guarding the thicket."

Life shrugged Trueline's hand off her arm and said the first angry thing that came to mind. "Who says I was going along the Bib?"

"Oh. But. Where *were* you going then?"

Life gave her head an upward bob. "Brow."

"The Brow?" Trueline, annoyingly, looked only faintly surprised. "Then we'd better go before Yoe wakes up," she said briskly. She peered along the Bib. "Can you see old Larking? There, I see him. He's looking the other way. Run!"

She snatched at Life's hand and suddenly they were across the Bib and on their way up the Venerable Path. Fuming, Life pulled away from Trueline's grasp and at the same time she was sudenly glad of her company—as long as she didn't start to *hum*.

She didn't. Instead, "Milk and Mole Star went to the Aha last night," she said.

Life stopped in surprise, and Trueline stumbled into her. "Have a care!" Life said sharply. Then, "How do you know? About Milk and Mole Star?"

"Saw them," said Trueline. "I knew they would go, didn't you?"

"Nnh." How would she know a thing like that!

Surprisingly, considering Venerable's perpetual grumblings over his trips to the Brow, the path wound pleasantly back and forth up the steep way; birds sang in the laced trees overhead; a few wild flowerlets pushed up here and there . . . and suddenly they had arrived. Or at least they had reached some great rocks and hanging beside one was a bell with a rope that hung down in front of Life's nose. She peered round the rock.

So this was the Brow! It looked rather scruffy. Shaped

like half a mooncake, it nestled into the hill that rose directly behind it, and Life felt a pang of disappointment. There was no nose, no chin to Belcher's Head! The Brow, Belcher's Brow, was nothing more than a ledge, and not a very big one at that. On the left, where the rim of the half mooncake ended, there crouched a low stone hut with rotted thatch. Stubbly grass lay between it and a stony mound that was well to the right of the bell rock. Past this stony place, before the mooncake curved around again to the mountain wall, a line of trees marked a small burble of a stream. Greening branches flickered a pattern against the gaunt Scars of Cherrychoke looming beyond the Brow.

Tentatively Life pulled the bell rope. The bell had a rusty, clanky clatter, not sweet-toned like the summoning bell on Toothy Maw. Nothing happened. Nobody came.

Trueline leaned over and gave the rope a harder yank. This time the bell gave an angry clang, and Life jumped in fright. Frowning at Trueline, she stepped up beyond the bell rock. High overhead Belcher just went on with his peaceful daytime smoking.

There was a strong smell on the Brow. Trueline pointed to the right, where a blue pool steamed in the middle of the stony mound. Together they crossed the grass. There, to the left of the pool, were the famed mudpots. There were five of them and a little ploppy bubble that hardly counted, and they curled and swirled and sometimes they blubbered into a *pop!*, and when they popped they gave off a stinging acrid smell that made the eyes smart. Life backed off, choking, but Trueline stood watching the slow, slow, slow swirl and bubble as though a spell had been cast on her. But then she began to hum, and Life knew that another chant was about to be born. Hastily, she crossed the grass to the crazy stone hut.

"Hallo?" she called softly, and then louder. "Hallo!"

There was nobody at home. She edged her way to the door and peeped in.

The hut was a dark hovel, reeky with stale air. Life's nose wrinkled, but she took a good look, now that she was here. Dirt floor. Two pallets, one soft and fleecy, the other flimsy, with bumps. Niches in the walls. Pieces of hide rolled up. A few crocks and jars. A pile of clothes. That was everything. Whatever else MudLar and Skarra might be, they were not rich in possessions.

She backed away from the door and turned toward the hill that rose steeply from the Brow. There looked to be a path through the thick growth of grass and scrubby trees—would that be domma Joke Eye's "sorry path" where she had followed MudLar as he carried Hulin to the Long Slip?

It appeared to be the only other way off the Brow. Did that mean, then, that to find Skarra she would have to go up the sorry path?

Not she! She had had enough of prying. If Grey Gammer thought it would do any good to talk to Skarra, she was wrong for once. How could you talk to anybody who lived in this place? It wuld be like living under a stone. A big fat stupid-stone . . . Under a stupid-stone . . . The words rang inside her head like an echo.

She gave a shout at Trueline and started running. Half-way to the bell rock she remembered Yoe and old Larking on guard below and ran distractedly back to the crazy hut and around it, searching out another path to the Spewing. ". . . I have my way to go . . ." The mooncake of a ledge sloped down sharply behind the hut, but there were flattened bushes and grasses . . . it was a path of sorts. With another shout at Trueline, Life went skidding down the side of Belcher's Brow, regained her feet and ran off along the slant of the Empty Forest. When she saw the Spewing looming ahead like a vast snake worming down the edge of the Empty Forest, she went leaping down to the Stony Bib to round the tip of the black tongue and so up the slanty path to the Aha.

The slope was eerily silent. There were no browsing goats,

no lizards flicking across the path, no windsong birds sounding their tackity song. Even the soft chirpings of tiny things in the grass were missing. There was only the scrape of her own slippers—and Trueline's close behind—and the *shrrrr-ing* of the wind down the Spewing.

When she stopped for breath, she stood, arms akimbo, frowning up at the ramparts of the Aha. Something was different. Wrong. Distracted, Life squeezed her eyes shut . . . Yesterday, when she came up the path she could see the First Story Stone framed in the entrance to the gallery. She blinked her eyes open. The Sky Stone was, simply, no longer there.

"Tacky!" she yelled. The Spewing gobbled up her voice.

She felt Trueline's hand on her arm, fiercely shook it off, and went flying up the rest of the slope.

The Sky Stone was still there, after all. It lay on its side, crushed into the Spewing. It was Tacky's hide-hole that had disappeared.

"Tackieeeeee . . . !" Her cry bounced between ramparts and Story Stones and came back to her. ". . . eeeeee . . ."

The meadow! He had gone through the slot to the meadow!

But Trueline was before her. She stood motionless at the end of the Aha, the danglethorn held aside in one hand.

"Go *on*," Life yelled at her. "He's got to be there!"

Trueline turned stricken eyes on her. "It's . . . it's Milk. Something happened to the stones. They've shifted."

Standing sideways in the narrowed slot, his head turned to face them, eyes pleading, stood Milk. He was clasped firmly, front and back, in the vice of rock.

". . . help," he whispered, ". . . I'm stuck."

No matter how they yanked and pried at him and bade him pull in his chest or his stomach or his ears, there was no removing Milk from the jaws of the slot. The two rock faces had closed on him like a mold and until the earth moved again, he was stuck fast. His eyes stood wide in his poor tortured head as he answered their questions. When he and Mole Star got to the Aha in the night, they had found the Sky Stone over the hide-hole and so had gone through the slot into the meadow in the hope that Tacky was there. He wasn't. Coming out, Milk was edging through the slot when the ground moved and shifted the stones, trapping him. Mole Star was still in the meadow, unless—Milk shuddered —unless the split rock had closed and caught him too.

"Dar Chipstone!" Life exclaimed.

Trueline jumped and looked with startlement back into the Aha.

"Chipstone!" Life gave her an impatient shove. "Go get him! Tell him to bring chisels, hammers . . ."

"But . . . the guards . . . unless Yoe is still asleep . . . ?"

"Oh don't be so *witless,* Trueline. Dar Chipstone is cutting thatch down by the Thicket. If you're not a complete bungler, nobody will see you. Now *run,* and I'll go try to dig Tacky out of the Spewing."

Infuriatingly, Trueline only nodded briefly and set off at an obedient run. Life scowled. Trueline should have yelled back that she couldn't have known where Chipstone was. That she wasn't a bungler either. A hummer, yes, but not a bungler. People should stand up for themselves.

Life spared a few minutes feeding chortles from her wallet into Milk's grateful mouth—his arm was pinioned at his side—and doling out words of cheer. "You'll see. Mole Star's safe in the meadow. You're the unlucky one, getting caught. And poor Tacky." She beat down the rising panic. "We'll all laugh about getting caught by rocks before the day is over. I promise."

Still calling words of encouragement over her shoulder, she hurried back to the fallen Sky Stone. How much time had passed since Milk and Mole Star got to the Aha and found the Sky Stone smashed over the hide-hole? How long since the quake had closed the slot on Milk? And—there

135

was no use dodging the thought—the split rock on Mole Star . . . ? No. Mole Star was safe in the meadow. Her dar would chisel Milk out of the rock and then chisel through the split rock if he had to, to reach Mole Star. That left Tacky . . .

Where the passageway to the hide-hole had been there was now only rubble, but she yelled Tacky's name over and over and listened between calls for an answer from the corsa. There was none.

She climbed up the fallen Sky Stone, looking for some sign that Tacky had got out. There was nothing. Leaning perilously from her perch, she began picking at the broken chunks of black corsa in the hope, not of finding Tacky underneath the debris, but of not finding him.

At first she was mindful of keeping her feet off the Spewing itself. There had been enough bad fortune! Then her foot slipped, and when she finally uprooted the huge rock she was tugging at, she found she had all unwittingly stepped on the place where nothing could ever grow.

I am on the Spewing, she told herself, looking down at the foot planted squarely on a big chunk of corsa. *I am standing on the Spewing and it's really just burnt rocks. I stood on the Brow and I saw the mudpots and the blue pool and the house of MudLar and now I am on the Spewing and I am all right.* Gingerly she slid her other foot off the Stone to join the first, still half-expecting a blast from Belcher. Nothing happened at all, except that some of the rubble slipped underfoot, and she had to clutch at the Story Stone for balance. She stepped carefully onto a broad slab and stood up straight into a buffet of wind. It dragged her hair into streamers, as abruptly let it go limp; but she was too full of amazement to turn her head away.

An immensity of Spewing still lay above the Aha, a sweep unsuspected from the Stony Bib. It lay like a vast double waterfall the length of Belcher's high shoulder.

Slowly she scanned the upper part of the Spewing for a sign of Tacky . . .

When she saw the figure above climbing slantwise down across the Spewing toward her, her instant thought was of Tacky. But even as she opened her mouth to call, she recognized the blue smock. *Blue!* On the Spewing?

No, not *Blue!* . . . Sea-splashed rocks . . . stupid-stone . . . A terrible anger welled up inside her. Anger at smashed hide-holes and shifting stones, at Flaw and Overshot, at . . . Recklessly she started toward him, leaping over the crazy jumble of corsa with no care for the jagged edges tip-tilted to catch her. She was almost upon him before he looked up.

"Life," he whispered, shrinking into himself.

With another bound she was in front of him, not knowing what she would say or do to him. But when she saw his hand fly protectively to his chest, she thrust at his neck, felt the thick strand round it, and yanked it out of his smock.

Beads went flying in all directions. Bright bits of blue danced and bounced and clattered on the cinder rocks—into crevices and crannies and down holes—until they had all disappeared.

Life looked into his horror-stricken face, and the rage all drained out of her.

"I'm sorry," she said. "Truly sorry . . . Skarra."

14

To be a Skarra is to be
  Fearless as the dawn,
  Enduring as the Scars,
  Strong as thunder,
  Trusty as the coming of night,
and above all,
  As inquiring as the sun shining in the morning.

—Very First MudLar

When Life called him by name, Skarra cringed as though she had struck him.

"But I'm *sorry*," she said over and over. "Deep-inside sorry. Watch, I'll find every bead, every single one, even if it takes forever!" She saw a blue bit shining near her foot, and pounced on it. "See, I've found one already!"

"Don't touch that!"

Startled, she dropped the bead, and it went skittering off to a new cranny. She looked up at Skarra's stricken face. Two big tears rolled down the hollow of his cheeks. "Why? Why can't I touch it?" She put out a hand toward him.

He shrank back from her. "Because . . . because nobody is supposed to! Nobody is supposed to touch a Skarra or . . . or the beads."

Life examined the pitiful figure he cut, the scrawn and skin of him, the shag of ragged hair that almost hid his eyes. "Too bad we didn't know yesterday," she said flatly. "Next time you fall into a rock pool, you can pull yourself *and* your beads out and drool your own water without *me* to pour!"

"Oh." He stood looking at her uncertainly. "I didn't think of that."

"Of course," Life said, frowning with thought, "you weren't Skarra yesterday. You were Blue. *Hulin* Blue. Like my brother. It makes a difference." She fetched up a coaxing smile. "And if I hadn't broken your beads just now, I would still think you were Hulin Blue, wouldn't I?"

"Ye-es," He looked only half-convinced.

"That's decided, then," she said. "Today you are Hulin Blue, and you are looking for Skarra's beads for him! And I'm helping. And Tacky . . ." Life's hand flew to her mouth, and she gave a sudden wail.

"How could I forget! Blue, you've got to help me find Tacky. The hide-hole caved in . . . and Milk is wedged in the slot, and Mole Star . . ." Words tumbled out but the wind swept most of them up and away, and Blue went on looking stubborn. Life felt pulled from all sides . . . and she'd forgotten Gammer's stricture to see the Skarra . . . though if Skarra was Blue, and Blue was Skarra . . . There just wasn't time to sort everything out, and Blue was stammering again.

"But my beads! And . . ." Blue waved his hand toward Belcher's smoke drifting skyward . . . "and I have to look for . . . for him!"

"That's what I just said, but he certainly isn't up there!"

"Not *him*. *Him*." Blue gave her a pleading look. "Mud-Lar. He went up Belcher's Throat and hasn't come back, and I have to go look for him. That's why I came . . . I started up the grit path from the Brow, you see—to find him, that is—but then I remembered the oath we made yesterday—and thought I should tell you why I couldn't come to the Aha . . . and I came straight across the Empty Forest and the Spewing, the quickest way . . . and . . . well, now I've told you, so . . ."

"So we're wasting time talking, aren't we? You come help me dig out the hide-hole and *I'll* . . ." she heard herself saying recklessly ". . . I'll go with you to find Mud-Lar!"

"But . . ." New tears welled in his eyes. "I can't go *any-where* without the beads. I can't, Life. You don't understand. I've never *not* had them. A Skarra . . . they're the most important thing about a Skarra, the beads . . . And Mud-Lar on the Throat . . . it's dangerous up there. I *need* the beads."

She wanted to shake him, shake him until his hair spun in circles. Crying over spilled beads while Tacky moldered in the Spewing! Cramming back her impatience, she brought out the voice she used for domma Joke Eye's bad moods. "It will be all right, Blue. I'll look for the beads and *you* can pick them up. *Though,*" she put in cunningly, "as I've al-ready touched them, I don't suppose it would matter too much . . . No, no, don't blubber again! I won't touch them. Look, there are at least three right there at your feet!"

Faster than winking he whisked them out of sight into the deep pocket of his smock.

"How many are there of these beads?" Life asked after a time.

Skarra glanced around guiltily before answering. "One for every season . . . that's twice-ten and four more . . . and one for every day of the season . . . that's ten and five . . . and five more for the Hollow Days."

"That's . . ." Life quickly gave up the sum ". . . good and many. What are they *for?*"

He eyed her nervously. "To count. Tell over. Twice a day."

"Why?" She saw another speck of gleaming blue and pointed it out. "Why do you count them if you already know how many there are?"

Skarra's voice was muffled as he bent to scrape the bead up into his pocket. "Because . . . because . . . MudLar says so. All Skarras count the days."

"Sometimes *I* count the days. To the next festival, I mean.

It would be like a game if I had beads to count instead of fingers and toes."

"You wouldn't like it, not if you had to count out the whole year twice every day."

"I should skip," she said firmly. "Here you got all the beads now?"

He turned his back on her while he counted them out of his pocket. "Two Hollow Days missing," he said, facing her again.

"We'll have to find *those*. Extra Days are the best days of all. Better than festivals even!"

But search as they would, they found only one of the missing beads. Life kept looking back to the Aha. "What does a Skarra *do?*" she asked after a while to distract Blue from noticing that she was moving the search down toward the fallen Story Stone. "Besides counting beads?"

"Lots of different things," he said cautiously. "Like charts. I'm learning to make charts now."

"What are charts?"

"They're like . . . pictures. Of where you've been or where you're going."

Life stared at him in perfect astonishment. "That," she pronounced, "is the most ridiculous thing I have ever heard. What's the use of them?"

"I haven't learned that yet," he said humbly, and bent closer to the search.

"Charts," Life muttered. Her face burned, her knees were crimped and scored from the sharp corsa, and her mind bulged with worry . . . There was so much gnawing and nagging of fear in her head that she stood for long moments staring down at the shreds of red-dye cloth before she realized what she was looking at.

"Blue! Come quick!"

"Did you find it?" He came hobbling eagerly across the corsa to her. His face fell when he saw what she was pointing at. "Oh. Just old threads."

Life faced him, exasperated beyond endurance. "Old threads! On the *Spewing?* How do you think they got there! It's Tacky's festa gown they came from! The one I brought to him yesterday. He got out, Blue! He got *out!*" Tears sprang to her eyes. Angrily she swiped them away and went down on her knees on the corsa slab, *willing* the threads of cloth to produce the rest of Tacky. The slab bordered a deep hole half-full of rubble . . . and one great chunk of corsa that lay ominously across the downward side of the hole.

"How do you know," Blue suggested darkly, "Belcher didn't push him *in,* and that chunk on top of him!"

"Why don't you put a pin in your tongue?" Angrily, she stuck her head over the end of the slab and called into the rubble. "Tacky . . . ? Are you there?" The fallen chunk of corsa gave a dull echo of her voice.

"If he *was* here," said Blue, making peace, "why? What was he doing?"

"Maybe he . . . maybe he . . ." but she couldn't think of any reason. "Why don't you go back and look for your selfish old bead!" she said meanly.

After a moment she heard the scrape of Blue's sandals on the rough corsa going away from her, and she was alone with two shreds of red cloth and her head hanging down a hole trying to read its mystery. She began pulling little chunks of rubble out from under the slab, watching them bounce on the bigger chunk below. *Chink. Chink. Chonk.* What if Blue was right and . . . ? *Whumpf . . . Splut!* The last one was a bigger piece that flew into bits. She dug about in the bank of rubble on a knobbly piece, and she gave it a good jerk. Cinders *plop-plopped* from all round it, and then the big piece ripped loose, and she almost went down with it.

A sudden rush of cool air fanned her hot face as she hung half over the slab, staring back into the small opening she had made in the rubble slide. Cool air . . . and something else? With a strangled shout at Blue to "Come quick!" she scrambled down into the hole and began raking at the scree, careless of raw-scraped fingers and torn nails and the rain of stones on her feet.

Blue's taut face appeared above her. "What happened?"

"Stick your head over and listen. Do you hear it?" She stopped pulling out stones long enough for him to put his ear to the hole.

Blue's face pinched up with fear. "There's something *in* there! It's . . . it's grunting . . . and, and scuffling."

"Of course there's something in there! It's Tacky! Don't you see? He's stuck in there! It's some sort of tunnel . . . maybe even a brill!" Her mouth fell open. "Blue! The moans he heard in the hide-hole! That's why he went in . . . to find . . . to find . . ." Suddenly she felt as scared as Blue looked.

"Well, *I* don't want to find whatever he found," Blue said hastily, and withdrew his head from the hole.

Neither do I, Life thought. *Neither do I. But if Tacky is in there . . .*

"You, Blue! Come back here!"

She could sense his hesitation.

"At once!"

She heard the rasp of his sandals, and his head slowly edged out over the rock slab above her.

"Wh . . . what now?"

"Be of some use." She got her hands around a sizable chunk of corsa and began wiggling it out of the bank. "Stick your head over and keep calling while I dig."

Blue started to back off.

"Do it!"

His face reappeared once more, white as clabber. "But what if s-something answers?"

"Oh . . . !" She glared fiercely at him. "You put your finger in the Oathstone and took a binding oath. Now put your headpiece down here and shout!"

Fearfully Blue slid forward until his head hung over the

opening into the brill. "Tacky?" he whispered. "Tacky? Are you there?"

"Louder!" Life yanked the big chunk out of the bank. A hail of smaller rocks bit at her legs and feet. "Don't you know how to *yell?*"

"I don't think I can," Blue said. "I just never have." He swallowed, and two big tears dripped from his upside-down eyes to splash on Life's forehead. He put his mouth close to the opening and waveringly cried. "Tacky? Are you there?"

"Yell!"

Another tear splashed down on her. Past endurance, she stretched on tiptoe and gave Blue's nose a fierce wrench.

"Owwwwwww!" he howled.

"Much better!" Triumphantly she raked a pile of scree from the brill. "Just keep that up!"

15

"Once," said Very Old Toothacher, "I was a Fireling of many parts. To my finewife I was the Toothacher who didn't mend the gate; to Flaw and Overshot I was the Toothacher who botched the thatching of a roof worse than Chipstone; to Chipstone I was the Toothacher who couldn't lay a proper wall; to Venerable I was the Toothacher who dozed off at Summonings. To everybody on Belcher's Body I was somebody who didn't do something.

"But now, to one and all, I am the Toothacher who sits at the cliff's edge and thinks about the water that comes and goes on Hungerbite Rock. I am a simple Fireling doing a simple act, but one that I do well, and it pleases me to know at last just who Toothacher is."

—Very Old Toothacher, *Remembered Wisdom*

When Tacky's hide-hole collapsed on top of him in choking dust, he knew his end had come. Belcher had claimed him after all.

"I'm sorry, Friendly One," he said. "I should have left you in the meadow."

The hide-hole shook again, like an afterthought, and the bottom fell out from under them. Tacky braced himself to keep from going down, for this was surely the end of the end . . . a long slip opened up especially for him. A slip that would take him down and down into the very center of Belcher. To his gizzard, he thought wryly.

Unexpectedly, the moaning came again . . . last night's moaning, but louder, clearer. Tacky's back crawled. The moaning came from below—from Belcher himself!

"All *right*," he said. His arms and legs trembled from the strain of pushing against the shattered remains of his hide-hole. "All *right,* I'll have to come, but just remember that you cheated when you said it was *you* who turned the seed yams to stone, when it was really Trueline. And just remember . . ."

His strength gave out.

Pictures of his coming end shuttled through his mind before he had even begun to fall: he could see himself sliding fast, faster, down into the middlings of Belcher; faster still, until he turned into a blur, the blur of wings of a windsong bird flying, dying. Down, down, down . . .

Whumpf!

He landed abruptly on his back with a jar that rattled his teeth.

The pictures evaporated. He had fallen no more than twice his length. Friendly One bit him.

"Yow!" Tacky's voice boomed back at him. Before the echo had quite died away, a long low moan surrounded him, ending with a distinct "Help . . . me . . ."

Tacky's eyes flew open. Blackness. And a weak shaft of light, pink light that pulsed brighter and then faded. At the end of this . . . this . . .

"Help . . . me . . ." The voice came from the direction of the pink light.

Tacky sat up, groping about in the darkness. Wherever he had come to, the satchel, the wadding, everything, had journeyed with him. Still shaken, he ferreted out a juice root for Friendly One, and then bundled the wadding into the satchel while he tried to think where he was. The pink light pulsed again, and a word crept into his head. Brill. He was in a brill.

There were dread tales of these mysterious tunnels—these

brills—that went on for ever, burrowing below the surface of the Spewing; dire stories of hermits who had wandered into them never to reappear, of strong bodies reduced to a miserable pile of bones moldering somewhere inside, of piteous calls for help never answered.

"Hold close," he whispered to Friendly One. With one arm outstretched he started toward the pink light, sliding his feet with care to avoid stepping on the hermit he expected to find. For of one thing he was quite certain. Belcher might speak through the earth and sky with his shakings and fires, his thunders and ploppings of mud, and just possibly he could make moaning sounds, but never, never, had he been known to beg for help. Whatever was calling him now was of flesh and blood. A wandering hermit. A solitary not yet reduced to a heap of bones.

New tremors shook the brill and there were sounds of falling rock ahead, but when the shaking was over, the window of pink light was larger, coaxing him onward. He moved faster up the tunnel, and then, abruptly, he was there, with only a sloping bank of rubble to climb. Tacky licked his dry lips. This wasn't the real end of the brill. It was only a place where the top of the tunnel had fallen in. His hermit must be on the other side of the cave-in. Dimly remembered learning stories told by Arkive began to come back: *brills are long galleries of sound . . . whispers travel farther than shouts without getting lost . . .*

When he heard the *cr-i-i-ck* he looked up sharply. An overhanging block of corsa teetered just above his head. Tacky didn't stop to consider. He took three running steps up the bank . . . and as promptly skidded down the treacherous cinders. Friendly One gave a shriek and dug into his shoulder.

"No!" Tacky yelled. Jagged pains shot through his hands and knees. Dizzy, he leaned his head against the rubble slope.

"Help . . . me . . ." It was the merest whisper, and it

147

came fluttering through the cinders. His hermit. The solitary.

"Yes!" Tacky shouted in answer. "I hear you! I'm coming!" Slowly and laboriously this time, he dug his toes into the shifting scree. The overhang gave another ominous *cr-i-i-ck* just as he lapped his hands over a firm slab of rock at the top of the hole. The wind licked his knuckles with encouragement, and at last he wriggled free of cinders and crawled out into its full sweep down the Spewing. Belcher had not swallowed him after all!

Friendly One gave him a warning nip, and Tacky scrambled farther along the corsa to safety. In the tremor that came moments later the overhanging rock gave a sudden *cr-r-rack!* and toppled into the hole Tacky had just crawled out of. Dust whuffed up in a cloud-shower. With an exhausted shrug of wonder he put his head down. He was on the dread Spewing . . . and glad to be there!

When Friendly One next nipped him, he jerked awake with a thought that had idled, all unbidden, into his mind. Supposing, back in the time of the Eighth Story Stone, that some of the Firelings *had* escaped the Spewing? Had found the Way of the Goat and got out of this perilous shaking land? Supposing *he,* Tacky . . . Ruefully he shook the impossible dream from his head before it could take shape, but his heart beat a little faster.

Gawk birds were batting away the last of the Deepest Dark to prepare for the bobbing of the sun. The Rift showed a pale point of flame and smoke rolled down Belcher's Throat, but on the Spewing itself the powerful wind swept the air clean and clear. Tacky turned his back to it and looked down the steep slope to where the Spewing bulged beside the Aha and the Sky Stone lay tilted into the smashed hide-hole where he had sheltered the night before. Friendly One sauntered across his shoulders and stopped by his ear to make mubbling sounds into it.

With a start Tacky remembered the last whispered cry for help . . . He had answered, had said he was coming! How long ago? He leaned over the edge of the hole into the brill and called into the rubble.

"Hallo . . . ? Hallo in there!" There was no answer. Had so much rock fallen that it cut off the voice? Or had the rock fallen on the voice and finally silenced it? He almost *hoped* . . . Flushing with shame, he pushed himself to his feet.

The call for help bound him to answer it—there was no other choice for a Fireling. But if the voice came from far up the brill and there were other cave-ins along the run of it . . . Consideringly, he looked up the Spewing.

At the top of Belcher's arm, where the corsa swept down, a faraway thumb of rock stood against the sky like a remote misplaced Scar. It seemed to Tacky that a hump ran from where he stood above the cave-in straight up the Spewing to the thumb. The brill? If he climbed the corsa . . . Torn, he looked down the Spewing again. Life and the others would be coming . . .

One foot willed him to go up; the other wanted only to go down. Neither foot would follow the other. He stood there in the buffeting wind, unable to make up his mind. And then, as though Potter Ott was standing in front of him with the familiar horrible grimace that went with his tempers, there fell into Tacky's mind the words: "Move! The worst is to do nothing at all, so *move!* Make up your mind for better or worse, and *move!* And after that, *never . . . look . . . back.*"

Tacky shrugged Friendly One onto the saddle of his shoulder, poked a long juice root at him until he felt the small teeth take hold of it, and began picking his way up the corsa against the sloping wind. For better or for worse, he was moving.

When the sun bobbed, he was already high on the Spew-

149

ing, but the thumb of rock he had marked out seemed no nearer and the hump, real or imagined, showed no more cave-ins. The gawk birds had gone off to do whatever gawk birds did after sweeping away the dark, leaving only the *shrrrrr* of the wind to keep him company. It burned his eyes when he tried to watch the yellow windsong birds flitting up and down the side of Belcher's arm, but it blew their heartening tackity song to his ears.

He climbed on. Still the Thumb beckoned golden above him, looming larger now. He could see how the melted rock had flowed round each side of the shaft to join again lower down, forming a shiny black cupped palm at the base of the Thumb. Tacky skirted the palm and climbed on to the top.

The savage blast, when it came, almost turned him over. Wind screamed and tore at him; his festa gown flapped behind him like a weather-banner from a pole. He had reached the top of Belcher's arm!

He crawled the last of the way to the Thumb with eyes squinted against the wind and pulled himself up against the sentinel rock's towering safety.

Belcher's arm flung out towards the glinting sea in a great barren ridge, but Tacky gave it only a scant glance. Across from him was another ridge bulking out of Belcher's Body in a gigantic barrier against the sky. Belcher's leg!

But what lay between arm and leg took his breath away. Corsa. A sea of corsa. It swept down from Belcher's Throat in so vast a spread that the familiar Spewing looked no more than a small spillover. The corsa ran to the very edge of the lapping sea far below, but all along the bottom, trees and grass grew thick around the black humps.

Trees grew far up the steep mountain of the leg, too, giving way near the top to stone outcroppings in fantastic shapes. A glittering sheet of water cascaded from the highest jumble of rocks.

Suddenly the wind shifted to a breeze that came gentling

across the barren arm. There was another sound. Friendly One stopped his restless journeyings around the inside of Tacky's gown and froze on Tacky's stomach.

Tacky moved away from the Thumb along the ridge of the arm. He lost the sound and turned back, but the wind made another sudden shift and filled his ears with its roar. He cast down the corsa to the smooth dip of land that was palm to the golden Thumb and ducked his head below the wind.

There! He stepped to the left and back onto the corsa. A jutting piece sheered off under one foot, scoring his heel as he went down.

"Help . . . me." The voice came from beneath his foot!

Tacky eased himself away from the treacherous rock. It was an overhang masking a hole in the corsa, for all the world like the overhanging block that had given way just after he had crawled from the brill far down the Spewing. The same brill! He had found it!

"Hallo . . . ?" he called cautiously down the black hole.

"Arrahr . . ."

"Who . . . what are you? A . . . A . . . A hermit?"

"Ar-rahr . . . help . . ." The voice sounded feebler.

"All right, then," Tacky said in a loud voice. Gingerly he stretched his arm into the blackness, half-expecting to have it grabbed and himself dragged after it. "Take hold of my hand."

"Ah . . ."

"Come on!" said Tacky. "Take my hand before I change my mind. Stop *mumbling!*" he shouted as still another *"Ar-rahr"* floated up from the black hole.

Friendly One, roused by his shout, bit his ear.

Tacky gave a yelp of pain. He was suddenly frightened through and through. Frightened of who or what was down the hole; frightened that the shelving rock above him might give way at any moment; frightened, suddenly, at being so far and away from all he had ever known, fishing for this . . . this bodiless voice lurking beneath the corsa. Even his fingertips, stretching into the blackness, were frightened.

Now the fingertips touched a hand, a bony, feebly grasping claw of a hand—a hand so trembly weak it could never do him harm. Unless it belonged to a haunt . . .

"Ar-rarh . . ."

"Stop your foolish mutter and *help!*" Tacky grasped the hand so tightly he could feel the bones of it grind together and yanked, but he was dragging a dead weight. "Listen to me, you down there! There's nobody but me to pull you out, and if you've got half the wit of a goat, which I doubt, you'll help!"

There were little scrabbling sounds, and the drag against Tacky's hand lightened. Tacky almost smiled. *An insulted goat clops faster.*

He pulled steadily, wriggling backward to haul out whatever manner of thing was at the end of his arm. If it attacked him, he was ready to drop it back into the hole.

What it was, was not a pretty sight. White hair, half-matted, half-sticking straight out, like the feathers of a blow-weed after the rain. A face of sharp bones with a thin stretch of not very clean wrinkled skin. A long stringy neck ending in a dirty garben that concealed the rest of him. A feeble thing it was that Tacky had claimed from the brill; the only strength in him was an ancient frowsty smell that rose up like a solid wall. He was a thing of the corsa, but never a haunt. A haunt smelled of sunburnt dust.

Tacky dragged the wretched old bone-bag clear of the overhang and, pulling Life's wadding out of his satchel, tucked it under the old one's head. He licked a wet spot on to a corner of his festa gown and wiped the ancient face with it. Then he rummaged in the depths of the satchel for the last few strands of rootbite, which he pressed into a soft moist ball. When he squeezed the juice over the old one's lips, the sunken mouth opened. He eased the ball inside.

The hermit slowly blinked open his eyes. They were almost colorless, so faded they were, and they had a wild look. A shrunken tongue crept out, licked around the sunken mouth, and then the creature spoke.

"Get . . . out . . ."

"That's right, Old Gawk," said Tacky. "I got you out, for what that's worth. What are you doing here? How did you get into the brill? Where do you live?"

The mad eyes stared at him, and the tongue came out for another slow journey around the lips. "No . . . ar-rahr . . . goat . . ."

"But I don't have a goat. Listen to me, Old Gawk. I'll have to do something about you. Water. Food." His nose twitched. "And a bath. If you don't mind my saying it. Now where do you come from? Where's your homing? Your *home?*"

But the old one's eyes flickered shut and he gave himself up to a shuddering sort of breathing that was terrifying to hear.

Tacky looked down at his prize in despair. The sun was burning hot in this cupped palm of corsa that the wind skipped; his tongue felt thick and swollen; his bruises throbbed and his scratches stung and this thing of the corsa had become his to look after. *It is not enough to find a lost one; you must see him all the way home . . .*

Suddenly the ancient legs flailed; the body shook all over. Tacky grabbed at him to keep him from knocking against the jagged rocks near his head, but with unexpected strength the creature shook him off and struggled to sit up. His mouth worked agonizingly to shape itself around words.

"Away," he finally croaked. "Fine go." He tore at the neck of his garben as though to rip it off, and then before Tacky could catch him he keeled forward, his head banging on the rough corsa at the edge of the hole.

"No!" Tacky shouted. "Don't do that!" But the harm was

already done. As gently as he could Tacky raised the matted head to rest against his knee. The hermit didn't even twitch.

Tacky bent his ear to the bony chest. Life still flickered inside. It almost seemed that deep within the bones and soiled flesh something was calling his name. "Tacky, are you there? Tacky, are you there?"

He jerked his head up. The voice went on calling. "Tacky, are you there?"

It came scritching up through the corsa itself.

Up through the corsa . . . ? The brill!

"Your pardon, Old Gawk," Tacky said for form's sake, though Old Gawk looked past hearing him. He shuffled the matted head off his knee onto the wadding and flung himself flat alongside the brill's opening.

"Tacky, are you there?" The faint voice was in his ear now.

"Yes!" he shouted into the hole. "Blue! Is it you?"

There was the sound of indrawn breath, then a shoveling and a crunching, and suddenly the brill was a gabble of cries and shouts pounding against his ears.

"Listen to me!" he shouted. "I need help. I . . . I've found something!"

Another gabble greeted him, and then thinned into Life's voice. "We can't get through! We're trying to dig you out. Blue and I . . ."

"But I'm not in the brill. Come over the top. Straight up the Spewing. To the big rock like a thumb. You can see it from there. But hurry!"

Blue's voice wailed up the long tunnel. "But I can't find the last bead! I can't go anywhere till I have the bead!"

Bead! What was Hulin Blue talking about? Tacky suddenly laughed. He felt lightheaded. A bead!

"It's all right, Blue," he called. "Come without the bead. It's not a festival. But hurry! I need you!"

"Coming!" Life sang out.

There were further scramblings and muffled talkings, one thin and wailing, the other sharp and scornful, and then the brill fell silent.

Tacky went back to the creature he had saved and knelt beside him. Though the old solitary was dirty and matted and probably completely out of his senses, Tacky felt oddly close to him. "It's all right now," he said comfortingly. "Somebody's coming to help. We'll take you home . . . or . . . well, we'll take you somewhere. Life will know. Life always knows."

The wrinkly mouth stirred into speech, but all that came out was another *Ar-rahr.*

"Yes . . . well . . . Blue is with her, so that makes three of us to carry you. We'll get you off the Spewing soon. And Life will have something for you to eat . . . I told them to come to the big thumb rock at the top. You don't have to worry."

The old one was trying to say something again. "Thuuummm . . . thuuummm . . ."

"That's right. Thumb. The rock that's like a thumb. You can't see it unless you're partway up the Spewing, you know. I never knew it was there. Not until I came up the Spewing to find you." Tacky couldn't seem to stop talking. "I was in the brill, you see, and I heard you moaning . . ."

The old one lifted a trembling hand and sought Tacky's clasp as though he was giving his thanks.

"That's all right," said Tacky, not liking the feel of the dry old bones. But the bones hung on to him. "If . . . if you would just try to tell me . . ."

The eyelids fluttered, the mouth worked, and finally words rasped out.

"Thumb . . . shadow cross . . . cross . . . listen!" The grip on Tacky's hand grew tighter. "Must follow . . . must . . . everyone . . . follow way. Go . . . *goat!*"

Tacky felt the skin crawl on his neck "The . . . goat? The *Way* of the Goat?"

"Listen!" The creature's body strained and jerked. "Doom! Get . . . OUT!"

"All right." Tacky wished that Life would hurry. It wasn't good for the old gawk to be so stirred up. "Yes, I understand," he said soothingly. "Doom . . . and the Way of the Goat? Don't get excited. I'm listening."

The ancient body began to shudder violently. The eyes opened wide, but there seemed to be no sight in them. "Thumb!" The voice was a gasp. "Shadow . . . look for . . . shadow . . . *goat.*" The clawed hand bit into Tacky's palm.

"Yes, yes," Tacky said, wincing. "I'll look for the shadow . . . on the Thumb."

A cry of utter despair burst from the wrinkly lips. "No . . . *no!*" Feebly the hermit beat the ground with his other hand. *"Cross . . . a . . . crooooooooossss . . ."* His voice ended in a wail that left the poor old thing limp. Somewhere deep inside him a new shuddering started and grew until his whole body was wracked.

He made one more effort. "Look . . . chest!"

Then his body sprawled out as though the strings holding it together had twanged apart.

16

Striding tall
He spans the Scars
And walks the wind
To the shining stars.

—An Old Riddle

The Pillow bulged with scatterlings like a bolster stuffed with gawk feathers, and still the carts rattled down from the farmings and minings, disgorging whole households onto Toothy Maw. Horrid tales came with the scatterlings and went flooding through the village. ". . . and just on a sudden the ground blew open, right there at my feet. A nasty great belch, it was!"

". . . Blasts of steam enough to boil the nose off your face! And *mud!* Such gouts of mud as were flung into the air! High as the Scars the mud flew!"

The mood of the village had turned ugly. Whisperings traveled faster than shouts, and imaginings faster than whispers. Certain youngers had run away, it was said. No, it was disputed, all the youngers of a certain age had been *taken* away. Or *spirited* away. And Ott was confined to his bed with grief. No, with stout ropes to prevent further scallywagging. And Joke Eye. . . .

But nobody missed Chipstone, whose morose aura lent him a certain invisibility in any case. The guard Zook, posted at the thicket, let him pass on his way to and from, and back again to the thatching ground without wondering why he had need of his stone-carving tools to cut thatch.

Chipstone himself lumbered patiently after Trueline without protest, even after they had rounded the Spewing's tip and started up the slanty path to the Aha. To protest had never been his way. He was one, rather, to oblige. The habit of gloom had grown on him since the day he hadn't protested the taking away of his hapless son. He hadn't meant never to smile again, any more than he had meant for Hulin to be made into a Morsel for Belcher's hunger. Sometimes he thought of these two things and how they had happened to him. It was because folk had expected him to give up Hulin, and he had obliged. Then they had expected him to be sad, and he had obliged.

Hammers and chisels jangling in the bag over his shoulder, he followed Trueline up the path and into the stone gallery. Surprisingly, his own daughter Life appeared briefly on the Spewing above them, called out something that Trueline seemed to grasp—a whispering brill? A blue thumb?—and disappeared again. Shaking his head in wonderment, Chipstone turned his attention to the work he had come to do. Chiseling Milk out of a rock was something he *did* understand. Further, it was a thing expected of him. He was nothing if not obliging.

Skarra had had no intention of going anywhere until he found the last bead on the Spewing, no matter what Tacky said through the brill or how much Life argued. He would find the last bead and string it with the rest on the goatstring and then he would go back to the Brow and up the grit path to find MudLar on Belcher's Throat. He should never have come here at all, but now that he had, he would certainly not set one foot upward on the Spewing toward that thing called a Thumb. He would not. Nothing could make him. He would not, would not, would not . . .

Skarra gave a deep sigh as he toiled behind Life up the Spewing, with the beads—except for the last one—jangling in his pocket instead of against his chest. He couldn't sort out how it had happened. All he knew was that when Life started determinedly up the corsa to where Tacky waited, he was powerless to do anything but follow. He feared her scorn and her flashing eye, but there was strength in her. There was strength and there was something else that he didn't have a name for. It was a something that made him want to pour out the secret thinkings closed in the back of his head. He wanted her to know how it was on the Brow with no one to talk to beyond MudLar and Belcher, neither of whom ever listened. He would tell her how MudLar pulled and yanked at the short hairs on his neck to teach him singleness of thought and to close out the imaginings and dreamings and bad thoughts that try to creep in where the eye can't see them.

It came to Skarra as they climbed up the wind of the Spewing that all of MudLar's pullings and tuggings at that patch of his head had not so much kept imaginings out as trapped them inside, where they continually bumped against the thoughts in the other patches of his mind.

"Hurry up, Turtle," Life yelled crossly from above.

Skarra hurried.

And he would tell her about the gawk with the crumpled wing; about the goat that chewed up MudLar's best Seth-gown while MudLar was inside it, with MudLar helpless to stop it because he was sitting over the mudpots, and how MudLar whacked *his* feet for not chasing the goat away; and, maybe, about the dream that kept coming back and back . . . He would tell her all these things, and she might scoff at him, but she wouldn't yank at his back hair or smack his legs.

Twice they sheltered from the wind behind upthrust rocks, and Life let him gnaw the juice from a parsnap out of the food wallet. After the first stop she said, "If you had any politeness about you, you would offer to carry the wallet for a while."

It had never occurred to him. When MudLar wanted something done, he simply said so.

"I . . . I . . . May I carry the wallet for you, Life?"

"No thank you," she said with deep scorn. "You would sour the milk, the way you stumble about. But you should have offered." She added more kindly, "Still, I'm glad you came along. It's lonely on the Spewing." Then, "You're better than nothing."

"I suppose so," he said humbly.

At the second stop, as they sucked at their parsnaps, Life said suddenly, "I know what you remind me of! The mask I made one festival time. It had a terrible frown, and no matter what folk said to me, the mask just went on frowning. After a while nobody wanted to talk to me. That's the way you are! Not frowny, but cringy, as though you expected somebody to hit you all the time. So of course that's what I feel like doing. I don't want to, but I *want* to!"

"But I . . ." Skarra felt helpless before her flashing eyes. "What's a mask?"

She gaped at him. "You really are *ignorant,* Blue. A mask is . . . a mask is made of clay and you shape it to go over your head, with holes for your eyes and nose and mouth; and you paint faces on it, however you feel like *being* when you wear it . . . funny, you see, or ugly, or frightful . . ."

He thought about masks as they continued their scramble to the top. If he were to make a mask, it would be a strong, brave face, full-cheeked, with lips curved into a smile, and everybody would want to talk to such a face, and the words that would come from those smiling lips would be strong and sure and wise, and everybody would listen in wonderment to the marvelous things he would tell. They would call him "Wonderling" or "Tall Mind" or . . . or "Friend."

"Hurry up, Witless," came Life's voice on the wind.

How could she move so surely on the rough rocks, while he fumbled and slipped and turned his ankles and jammed his toes? MudLar would have switched his feet five-times-five by this time. MudLar . . . Uneasily, he thrust his hand into his pocket and clutched the beads.

"There's Tacky!" Life shouted.

160

He was standing beside the tall thumb of rock that glinted in the sun, his red garben tattering in the wind.

Skarra stumbled again and stopped to rub his hurt toe, but Life went on climbing, jumping, skipping like a goat up the corsa. Skarra hobbled to his feet and limped after her. The next time he looked up, she was standing at the top with the wind whipping her hair and her bright pinover into splendid wings. Suddenly she flung her arms to the sky, her head thrown back, as though she was calling with the wind.

Skarra felt his throat ache from the sight, and he bent to the slow, painful climb again. As he crept up the last few lengths, Tacky was there to hold out a hand and pull him along the top to the Thumb.

The wind almost toppled him. Through a blur he saw a terrifying expanse of dead corsa sweeping down to the sea. A trembling seized his legs and he shrank against the base of the Thumb. He was hunched on the edge of nowhere, for the ground fell sharply away behind the sentinel rock to form a small cupped palm in the immensity of the Spewing. In the center of the smoothed surface there was a long bundle of clothes, but the wind lashed his hair so furiously over his eyes that he couldn't see properly.

Hands pulled at him; he was dragged and pushed until the wind no longer scoured the hair from his head, and he could even hear snatches of Tacky's voice shouting above the wind's whistle: ". . . sun-crazed . . . goat . . ."

When he could get his stinging eyes all the way open, he saw that he was being led down alongside the cupped palm below the Thumb. ". . . must have been at the Thumb . . . fell or slid down . . . too weak to get out of the brill . . ."

A goat? Here?

Life yanked at his arm and jumped down. Skarra teetered on the lip of the corsa, but then Tacky took his other arm and together they jumped onto the smooth palm of the hand.

Suddenly there was no wind. His ears felt deadened, the way they were when the gusher stopped its spouting every morning.

They let go of him and he stumbled after them.

The bundle of clothing he had seen from above turned out to be an old wadding draped over a long shape.

"Is that the goat?" he asked.

They looked at him blankly.

"Goat?"

"But I thought . . ." In his confusion, Skarra plucked the wadding off the form. "I thought you said . . ."

He was staring down at the ancient features, so very still; and the earth seemed to tremble beneath him.

Life caught at him. "It's all right, Blue. He's just a poor old solitary . . . a thing of the corsa. Didn't you hear Tacky say so?"

Skarra shook off her hand and knelt beside the collapsed bones and flesh. Through him there washed the old fear and dread and awe, to spill at last into a slowly eddying pool of lost loneliness. Tears ran wet down his face.

"What *are* you bawling on about?" Life demanded. "It's just a poor old thing . . ."

Skarra shook his head. "No," he said, and looked bleakly up at her. "It's MudLar."

Overhead, Belcher gave a bellow of grief.

17

"Standing tall and mighty above the ordinary
must be a grand thing, though surely
troublesome when going through low
doorways."

—*Legends of Murkle*

There was but one slender strand, thin as a distant scream, still holding MudLar to his frayed body. When the time came he would slip from that last loop, but not yet. In his deep sleep he drifted in and out of the whispers that went on around him, but he was no longer of the Now. He could feel the splash of his poor Skarra's tears, but not their dampness.

The one called Life, she of the sharp tongue, said he couldn't possibly be MudLar, that MudLar should smell of the sun and wind, not of old wet goat. Skarra said fiercely through his tears: "He didn't *like* not bathing in the pool. It was a *trial* he put on himself long ago."

But Life didn't lightly give pardons. "Disgusting! He couldn't have *wanted* anybody to get close to him!"

This one would have made a good Skarra. MudLar allowed himself a twinge of regret for what had not been. More tears were dripping on him. Skarra had loosed the neck of his Sethgown to look for a sign in the lumpish beads strung on the rank goatstring. There was fright and sorrow and uncertainty in the head bent over him, and MudLar turned away from the burdensome grief. The other two were disputing farther away; he had to strain his powers to understand what they were saying.

". . . imagine crying over somebody who did nothing

but kick you and call you bad names and make you count stupid beads all day, and starve you to the bare bones."

"But MudLar was all he *had*. He was better than nothing."

"Better than nothing . . . That's what I told Blue on the Spewing. 'You're better than nothing,' I told him, and he said, 'I suppose so,' as though he never expected anything better. But of course I didn't mean it, Tacky. It's just that he *makes* me say things like that. Anyway, I would never kick him or call him bad names—at least I would never kick him!"

Perhaps. MudLar smiled inwardly. But she might find that the space between a bad name and a kick was no more than a toe's length, after all.

". . . didn't just happen to wander onto the Spewing. I think he came to look for the way out. The . . . the Way of the Goat."

"That's daft! MudLars keep Firelings in: they don't lead them out!"

"I don't know. He kept talking about a shadow, or a cross, or across the Thumb, or . . . I couldn't really tell, and I thought he was touched by the sun. But he kept saying 'Cross . . . cross!' and then he said everybody should get out. 'Doom!' he said. But I thought . . ."

"Tacky . . . ! Suppose he did find it! The Way of the Goat! Here!"

"But I looked. While I was waiting for you. There's nothing on the Thumb, no shadow or cross that I could see. I went a little way down the other side, too— he might have meant the shadow *of* the Thumb, on the corsa, you know. I couldn't find anything. Just corsa. But Life, he was warning me . . . us. I'm sure of that."

"I wish I had been here. I would have known what he meant!"

"And Friendly One ran away. I forgot about him for a while, and then he was gone."

"Then we'll have to find him again. And I know how. Food! *That* will bring him." There were brisk sounds of rummaging.

"Life . . . wait. Listen to me. I think MudLar was saying we had to get out. Now! Today!"

"But Tacky . . ."

"That means we've got to get them up here. Your dardomma . . . Potter Ott . . . everybody! Get them up here because . . . because, Life . . . somewhere from this spot—from the Thumb! I *know* it—the Way of the Goat begins! And we have to find it before it's too late, because we're the only ones to do it!"

There was a short silence, broken suddenly by the din of rattling, chunking, bouncing sounds all mixed together with Life's matter-of-fact voice. "Food, that's what we need. Then we'll think. Look what I've brought—black honey cakes and chukkaberries and beancurd and milk and chortles . . . It's going to be all right, Tacky. We'll look for the shadow or the whatever-it-is, and we'll plan, and I know we'll find Friendly One, and we'll decide what to do with Dirty Toenail there . . ."

"Life! He's MudLar and he's *dead!* You shouldn't . . ."

Dirty Toenail . . . ! Deep inside himself, MudLar chuckled.

"But he's not." Skarra's voice was flatly triumphant.

"What!"

"He's *not* dead. The star bead just moved. He's still breathing."

MudLar heard the other two come scrambling close to lean above him. He could feel their suppressed breathing and a drip of chortle juice fell on his neck. The one called Life was a messy eater.

"It's called deep sleep," Skarra was gravely explaining. "Only a MudLar knows how. . . . If you watch the star bead. . . ."

Faithful little ill-used Skarra! And would he have watched here forever if his MudLar hadn't given himself away?

"But Blue's right. MudLar *said* that!" cried Tacky, wonderingly. " 'Look . . . chest,' he said to me. He must have meant me to see that he was still breathing, still alive!"

"Funny way of talking." Life sniffed.

Dirty Toenail. . . . MudLar felt the laughter start again. It bubbled up and up through his deep sleep until—this time he could feel it bounce on his chest—the pointed star gave another tiny bobble.

18

☀ : Sunbob or Sundrop; to be born; to wake up; to go to sleep

⋈ : Goat; Horns; Goat Festival

⋈ : Dead goat; Goat fallen over the cliff upside down into the sea; Broken horn; Lost goat; A mistake for

◁ : New-born goat; Slaughtered goat; Half a goat; Horncup; Sometimes a badly drawn

△ : Belcher; Hollow window; A flat copper token for hanging on doors to invite good fortune.

⋇ : The number five; Lucky sign; Rain; Spotted or splotched; Juicy chortles for eating; Cherrychoke not for eating; The number six (if the writer can't count)

∽ : The number one; Short way of writing

≡≡≡ : Coming; Going; Being sent; Dancing; A well-worn path to somewhere.

Thus, the following message may easily be read by applying the above meanings with a modicum of common sense: ☀ ⋇ ⋈ ≡≡≡ ⋈ ☀

—from Windlestraw's *Wordgames*

Once the goatstring was broken and the blue lump of a Hollow Day left behind in an unknown crevice, the strength of the blue beads had begun to leach away. Skarra kept his fingers curled tightly around the jumble of seasons-and-days in his pocket, but he now put more trust in Life than in beads as they picked a way across the Spewing towards the tangle of forest . . . and the Brow. They walked just below the crest of Belcher's arm, out of the wind's sweep. Behind them, in the cupped hand from which the Thumb grew, they had left Tacky to watch over MudLar in his deep sleep.

It was a Skarra's duty to stay by his MudLar, but Life and Tacky wouldn't have it so. There was nobody else to give the Seth, and the Seth, they said, was the only way to get Firelings out of the village. "I can't," he'd kept on saying, but "You can!" Life said. "You must!" Tacky said. "You will," Life said.

"But I can't just make up a Seth!" he had cried. "Belcher has to say it . . . in the Mud!"

"You can," said Life, and, "He will," said Tacky.

They were so sure of everything; Chipstone and Trueline would rescue Milk and Mole Star, they said. MudLar *hadn't* gone to Belcher's Throat before he came to the Thumb, they said, no matter what he had told Skarra. There wasn't time, they argued, between the hour he left the Brow two nights before and the first groans from the brill that Tacky heard the next morning. No, they said, MudLar had gone up the grit path above the Brow and then struck across the upper Empty Forest to the Spewing.

Skarra's mind faltered. There were all those other times MudLar had been away from the Brow—to cultivate loneliness, he had explained, or to smooth his wrinkled thoughts, or other excuses. Skarra had thought to know everything there was to know of MudLar—his small meannesses, his refusal to lift a hand at chores, the selfishness of him. And all the while there had been another MudLar he knew nothing of: a seeker of the ancient Way of the Goat.

They had come to the edge of the Spewing. Bordering it was the upper part of the Empty Forest, but it was more tangle than forest, a snarl of tree and vine and thorn that stretched from this side of the Spewing to the Brow, and upward to the sharp rim of Belcher's neck. Skarra stared in dismay.

"The wind has stopped." Life had come up beside him.

Now she caught her breath and, like Skarra, stared at the forest run wild.

"He couldn't have come through that," Skarra said.

"Then how?"

Skarra abandoned the bead-lumps in his pocket to motion despondently upward where a solid collar of rock lined the edge of Belcher's shoulder. Within the collar, the big corsa flow came sweeping down to spill over the arm as the Spewing; without, below the rim of rock, the Tangle took over. There was no break to be seen in the collar, and above it rose the Rift. Even as they looked, Belcher gave a rumble and billowed black smoke.

"Impossible," Life said flatly, and turned her back on the collar and the warning smoke. "If he went up the grit path and he didn't come back to the Brow, the only way he could have got to the Thumb in time for Tacky to hear him was to come through . . . through *that*." She waved at the green tangle. "All we have to do is find his path."

Skarra shook his head. She didn't understand about the Tangle—how the thorn bushes grew thicker than a stout arm—how every season of Bursting Pods MudLar sent him to chop out the vines on the path to the Long Slip—and how it took a full season of days to fight them back with his small chopper . . .

Chopper . . .

He plunged his hand into his pocket and scrabbled the loose beads together.

"What now?" asked Life, as from a great distance. "You look pale."

He closed his eyes and closed out her voice. Chopper. A chopper. MudLar setting off up the grit path. A faded long far-off time, but the picture sprang as bright as the chopper's blade shining in the sun. MudLar swinging a chopper in his hand . . . He had gone off up the grit path with the dread chopper in his hand—and Skarra had never seen it again.

He clutched the beads tighter. *Up or Down?*

He opened his eyes to see Life peering curiously into his face.

"What do you *do* when you do that?" she asked.

"We go up," he said, moving around her.

"Why? What told you to go up?" She looked down at his pocket. It bulged from his hand fisted around the beads. "Do you ask those . . . those *beads?*"

He felt scorn in her words and didn't answer, but started slowly up along the edge of the Spewing, watching the bordering Tangle for signs of a path.

"He asks the beads," Life muttered, and fell in behind him. "Did the beads say there *is* a path?" she called out after a moment.

He nodded.

"Then it had better be soon, or we'll have to go all the way up to the Rift. Look, we're already at the collar!"

He nodded again. The rim of solid rock they had seen from below loomed even larger now that they were alongside, but it wasn't solid. There were cracks and fissures in plenty to slip through—for lizards.

"There's no way to get down to the Tangle," said Life, catching him up.

Stubbornly Skarra kept going. There had to be a way. He felt it in the beads, weakened though they were. He felt it deep inside. Life dropped behind him again.

"We're wasting valuable time!" she grumbled loudly. "You know we'll have to go down again."

He suddenly turned on her. "Then you go! I'll find it my—" In the corner of his eye he saw a sharp shower of sparks—there by the rock, gone the next instant.

"What? What is it?"

Skarra pointed at the rock beside her, and she jumped away from it. He stared fixedly at the place. There was nothing, only a shallow cleft.

He moved his head slightly forward, and suddenly the sparks appeared again, like a small thin lightning streak.

It was the sun's glint on the chopper leaning upright against a stone, just inside the cleft.

Life thought they should take the chopper with them as they squeezed through the crevice that it marked, but Blue insisted they leave it stuck in the ground just as MudLar had left it.

"I don't want to touch it," he said obstinately.

"Why? It's only a chopper. You said so yourself. 'It's MudLar's chopper,' you said."

"I don't know why," said Blue. "I just don't."

Life rolled her eyes and followed him. There was a certain set of Blue's chin she was beginning to learn. They half-tumbled down a rocky path of sorts and landed at the entrance to a cool green tunnel that had been cut through the living tangle of growth. Stepping softly, they entered it and the rest of the world was blotted out. There were little scuttling sounds all round them as their feet ruckled the spongy leaf mold.

"Blue," Life started, and then dropped her voice to a whisper to match the deep quiet. "Blue, how could MudLar have done all this? Cut this tunnel?"

He didn't answer. Exasperating creature! Thinking was not a bad thing, but it was annoying when you were trying to talk to someone to have him go off into a silent world of his own.

They had tramped along for some little distance before Blue said, "He didn't."

"Didn't what? Who didn't what?"

He looked at her in amazement. "MudLar. He didn't. You just asked me."

"Oh." She thought back to her question. "How do you know? And who did if he didn't?"

Blue shrugged. "Other MudLars before him. It's a very

old path. You can see where new branches and vines have been cut off at the sides, but there hasn't been anything growing *on* this path for . . . oh, years and years. The chest . . ."

She waited for the rest, but Blue had retreated into his thoughts again.

"The chest what?" she finally prompted him.

"What?"

"The chest *what?*" You said 'The chest,' and I asked 'The chest *what?*' "

"Oh. It's . . . just an old chest. With skins in it. I wonder . . ." His voice trailed off.

"Skins! What do skins have to do with anything?"

But whatever Blue was wondering, he wondered to himself.

The path seemed to go on forever, but when they came to the thick hanging screen of vines at the end and pushed through to the glare of light on barren pink ground, the sun had scarcely moved in the sky. They stood blinking in the brightness. The bulge of ground sloped up toward Belcher's Throat, but it ended abruptly at a rock face. Across from them, in the distance, the Scars of Cherrychoke rose above the trees.

"Where are we?" Life asked uneasily.

Blue led the way slowly along the pink mound until they came to a shallowness like a wide-lipped funnel. In the center a bulky rock half-covered the smoothed entrance to what might have been an underground cave. A curl of steam floated lazily into the air.

Blue put out a restraining hand. As though she might go nearer!

"The Long Slip," he said.

She finally found her voice. "But it's only a little slot in the ground! It doesn't look like . . ."

"It is, though," Blue drew her back. "Once, a long time

172

ago . . ." He hesitated, then went on in a matter-of-fact voice ". . . . MudLar hung me by the heels down the hole until . . . until I got used to it."

Life stared at him. Her back felt cold. "That's *horrible!*"

"It was MudLar's way of teaching," Blue said simply. He turned and went down the slope. The pink ground narrowed into a gritty path that went winding on down through the Tangle; soon the Long Slip was out of sight, but still it clung to Life's mind, a long, cold shiver of a memory.

"Blue," she said after a while. "Hulin Blue . . ." And then she said it very fast. "Hulin Blue, I'm sorry I called you names, and if you would like really to be . . . my brother . . . sort of . . . well I really almost rather sort of like you now that I've got used to you, you see."

He gave an absent nod and kept on going down the path. When, finally, they came out behind the mean stone hut on the Brow, Blue led the way around to the doorway and ducked inside. "Wait there," he said. "I've just remembered. Venerable will be coming."

She waited, and thought of Milk waiting in the slot to be chiseled out by her dar; and Mole Star waiting inside the meadow, if he wasn't . . . and Tacky waiting with Mud-Lar at the Thumb; and everybody waiting for Belcher to . . .

The sudden clamor of the bell was a shock.

"Inside, quick!" Blue hissed from the hut.

She stumbled into the gloom and caught her breath sharply against the smell of mold and old parsnaps. Blue was fumbling at his clothes, and when she could begin to distinguish things in the dim light, she could see that he had put on a long white gown that dribbled about his feet. The sleeves hung far down over his hands, and he was pulling a pointed hood over his head.

"Do I . . . do I look a proper Skarra?" His voice came in a muffled squeak through the folds of the hood.

173

A proper Skarra! He looked like a very small chidling dressed up in its mother's overgown. No wonder Blue had been worried when they talked about this moment at the Thumb. How could Venerable take him seriously?

"Take it off," she said.

"I can't do *that!* I have to wear it . . . it's a Sethgown!"

"It's a Sethgown that's too big for you. You look ridiculous. Take it off and find me a knife. Hurry up, now."

He kept protesting but he stripped off the gown and fetched a knife and watched Life spread the cloth on the floor. She took the blade to the hem and the sleeves and the flare of the hood and cut off a goodly length from each.

There was a second clanging of the bell, impatiently louder.

"Hurry," Blue whispered. "He doesn't like to be kept waiting."

Life swooped the altered gown off the floor and pulled it over Skarra's head.

"It fits," he said in wonderment. "I won't trip over it."

"Of course it does. And you won't." Life took him by the shoulders and looked into the dimness under the hood. "Remember now, you're a proper Skarra and you're going to say what MudLar would say if he could be here. Venerable will believe your words because they're *true* words. Keep your shoulders straight and your head up and don't *shuffle.*"

"All right," Blue said meekly. The bell started its third clappering. He bowed his head to go through the doorway, but outside he paused. His shoulders straightened, his head went up, and after only the smallest stumble he strode across the grass to the bubbling mud.

Standing well back inside the doorway, Life watched the bell rock. When Blue was halfway to the mudpots, the bell died in the middle of a fierce pull, and Venerable stumped out from behind the shielding rock, hauling a big basket.

His other arm was raised like a threat and his face set in a terrible frown, but as his eyes followed Blue's progress, the arm fell and his set mouth dropped into a slack pouch of amazement.

Life smiled. She . . . almost . . . felt proud of Blue.

Now, looking out of the doorway for the fifth time, she was beginning to fume. Blue had been sitting on that rock staring into mud for so long he surely must have gone to sleep! Even Venerable, crouching beside him, was twitching, but Blue was a white rock in the sun. Couldn't he feel the . . . the urgency all around them? Like a soft pounding inside the head. No matter that Belcher had settled down again to just an occasional puff of smoke. The beat was there.

She had already looked at everything there was to see in the hut twice over, but she made the rounds of the four walls again, took another peep at Blue and Venerable, and then sat down on the hard lumps of one of the sleeping-mats. The other mat was softer and had a fleece spread over it, but it reeked of MudLar. In a moment she sprang up to peep out of the doorway again. Blue hadn't moved; Venerable was hitching his shoulders impatiently. Why didn't Blue hurry! There were five-times-five things to do and it was already well past sun-high.

She lay down on the sleeping-mat, got up, and pulled the mat away to see what made it so lumpy.

Stones! Big stones, little stones, sharp stones, all embedded in the hard floor of the hut, as though deliberately put there just to scar a poor Skarra's back. Scar: Skarra! Indignantly, she pushed the mat back and turned to examine MudLar's soft bed against the opposite wall.

Of course! The floor beneath it wasn't even the lumpy clay of the rest of the room. It was a sheet of hammered ore, as long and as wide as the mat. Puzzled, Life stood staring down at it, and then she yanked the mat fully away and knelt for a better look. There was a small notched place and she wiggled her hand in and pulled; the sheet lifted away a fraction. Careless of the rasping sound of hinges, she got both hands into the notch and raised the lid of a gigantic chest. It was full to the brim with rolls of goatskin.

"The chest," Blue had started to say, and then stopped. It was when they were talking about the age-old path through the Tangle. Older than MudLar? Older than the MudLar before him? Older than the MudLar before the MudLar before . . . ?

She chilled, as though a hand had reached out of the past to touch her. If what she was thinking was right, then she was looking at the story of Firelings right back to when the Very First MudLar crawled out of the ashes!

I must close the chest, she thought. But she didn't. *I must not touch these things,* she told herself. But she did. Gingerly, she ran her fingertips along the top row of rolled skins. She sat back on her heels with a shiver of apprehension. Nothing happened. She peeped out of the doorway and saw Skarra and Venerable still sitting. Sting bees encircled Skarra's head—a swarm of them—but he didn't move.

I walked on the Spewing, she told herself, *and I touched MudLar, and I went through the Tangle on the secret path, and I saw the Long Slip, and I'm here on the Brow, and I even took a knife to a Sethgown. And besides all that, I not only touched the blue beads—I broke the string!*

Still she hesitated. Then another thought flew into her head. *When MudLar told Tacky to look at his chest, he meant this chest, not the one under his chin!* Conscience at rest, she reached in, picked out the newest-looking roll, and spread it open on MudLar's mat.

Her anticipation turned to dismay. She didn't know what she had expected, but it certainly wasn't this childish sprawl of inkings. Was it supposed to be a story? The fat cone at the bottom was surely Belcher, for all its crooked tip, but why were there tracks? Belcher couldn't *go* anywhere—he could only spit out fire and ashes.

Life stared at the sets of word-signs across the top.

"Sun-up (or sun-down?), Sky, Season of the Long Dark,"
the first set read. And the second was "Sun-up (sun-down?),
Sky, Season of White Tears." Then, "Cloudy day, Sky, Bitter
Ice." Days and seasons! Each track went to the first day—
the day of the Sky—of a new season; and sometimes the sun
shone and other times it was cloudy. She looked at the rest
of the seasons: Chiseling Winds, Shivery Rains, and Singing
Grass, all in order. Singing Grass had a cloud over its sun.

And what did the slashes mean? There weren't any over
the cloudy days . . . She pulled out the next roll, but it was
the same, except that it was filled to the edges with tracks,
and all of the seasons were there. A third and a fourth and
a fifth were the same story told over again, but now there
was a mix of days instead of the Sky signs: Thunder, Rain,
Wind, Seed . . . It was very mysterious.

She glanced through the doorway again. Venerable, his
head cocked to one side, appeared to be listening. Blue must
be saying the Seth at last!

Quickly she rolled up the skins and put them back in the

chest. It was one thing to confess what you had done, and quite another to be caught doing it.

It was then she saw the tiny roll tucked unimportantly in with the rest. She snatched it out before she could think not to and unrolled it. There were two skins, not one. Picture stories, like the Story Stones! She held the skins to the light to see better. One was a story about—it looked like a domma and chidling, or dar and chidling, going on a journey. Then there were some strange markings rather like two bowls of stirabit, over a lopsided mouth. And a pool.

She looked at the other story: the pool again and somebody running . . . many tears. The last picture was unmistakable. It was the Long Slip, and a shape very like a long bag of wool was slipping down it.

She stared fixedly at the markings, willing them to give up the story. *Like a long bag of wool,* domma Joke Eye had said, and *whuuuuushsh* . . . ! The goatskins rippled under Life's suddenly shaking fingers.

Hulin? She looked up at the brightness of the doorway without seeing it. *Drowned?* And by accident? Where was the sense to it?

The small clatter of the bell brought her to her feet. Venerable had gone, the bell's tremor a whisper of his departure; but Blue sat on, a white lump sagging over the mudpots.

Life moved towards the chest to put the tiny scrolls back and then changed her mind. With a sudden crumpling of her hand, she thrust the small pieces of goatskin-story deep into her pocket.

19

"The only thing that keeps me brave," said Windlestraw, "is being frightened that folk will find out what a coward I am."

—from the *Windlestraw Legends*.

"Have a bite," Joke Eye said, poking the spoon at her son's set mouth, "and then I'll tell you a story." But she felt distracted. Her mind didn't want to stay on the adventures of Windlestraw or Murkle.

Her misgivings grew stronger as the hours wore along. Life hadn't come back and no more had Chipstone. Strangely, too, there hadn't been a single caller since early morning to tell her what went forth on the Pillow. Not one body had come—except for Flaw and Overshot. They, without so much as a may-I-please, had marched past her into her house where they noisily thumped about; then came out with sour looks and stomped off as rudely as they had arrived, with a slam of the gate and no reason given for their visit. They hadn't even glanced towards Hulin, hidden as he was under an old cloak she had thrown over his head.

And still Chipstone didn't come home. Life didn't come home. Nobody came.

Joke Eye's worry deepened. The air was heavy with threat. That other time—the bad time—nobody had thrown a shadow on her doorstep either; nobody, that is, until they came for *him*. She wished she had gone to the thatching ground with Chipstone this morning after he came home to fetch his tools. He hadn't been back since, not even after Belcher gave that peculiar snort. It wasn't like Chipstone not to come back. Chipstone always came back.

When she heard footsteps near her gate she looked up, but it was only to see the tiptops of Flaw's and Overshot's heads bob along the other side of the wall. A few minutes later she saw Yoe the Beekeep's webbed hat going by in the opposite direction. The story of Windlestraw dried in her throat. Flaw and Oversot had taken over Yoe's guard on the pucker.

Suddenly she knew what her dread was. Flaw and Overshot weren't interested in taking a small stone image. That was Ven Ida's idea. No. Flaw and Overshot wouldn't be content with stone—they wanted a living creature. A life.

Joke Eye jumped up, her mind stung. Life . . . !

Without knowing how she got there, she was standing outside her gate in Puddingstone Lane. Starm and Frail—no, no, they were long ago gone. She must not dream now. It was a time for reality. A time for *deeds*.

She took a few uncertain steps into the lane. Grey Gammer? Ven Ida? Venerable? No, no. Anner? Thin Yukie? Names surged through her head, to be discarded as soon as they were thought of, except for . . .

He would have to do.

If, of course, he wasn't sodden from one of his eternal pipes.

Somewhere deep under her feet—did she imagine it?—there was a change in the heartbeat of the earth. For a moment longer Joke Eye stood there, feeling the throb of it through the soles of her feet.

Then she struck out along the Crossback.

Tacky's tongue was so dry it rasped against his teeth. "Think!" Life had commanded him as she and Blue set off across the Spewing. "We'll do the rest!"

Think . . . ! It was all he could do to draw breath in the roasting heat of the pit. Friendly One was gone, and Mud-Lar lay as deathlike as when Blue spread the wadding over him again. Blue . . . Skarra . . . Tacky suddenly took fright at the enormity of their daring—Life's and Blue's, not his. He had already used up every pore of courage in his skin. But, "Think!" Life had said. He jerked his mind back to the problems she had set. One: How did MudLar get into the brill? Two: What did he mean by the Shadow and the Cross? Three: Where was the Way of the Goat? Tacky couldn't remember Four and Five. His head felt boiled.

Nothing came to mind, nothing at all. He stared into space, ready to welcome thoughts, but instead his eyes came to focus on a small cranny just beneath the base of the great golden Thumb. It was a cranny full of mouth-watering clumps of rootbite. They were out of reach from below, but if he were at the Thumb . . . ? His tongue tingled.

The wind snatched at him when he stepped out of the palm, but he pushed against it to the top of the arm, and leaned against it along to the Thumb, where he let it plaster him against the rock. There was no shade; the sun was at its middle. Shade . . . shadow. Shadow . . . A shadow moved with the sun. Later the shadow of the Thumb would move back over the pit. Was there any meaning in that?

Or did the secret lie in front of him, in the valley of corsa that swept down to the Swollen Sea? Or in the looming ridge of Belcher's leg across the big flow, in the trees that angled from the mountainside, in the high waterfall that glinted in the sun, or perhaps in the jumble of rocks near the top of the falls?

He turned a despairing back on the black valley. Better that he put his mind to harvesting rootbite! By stretching out beside the Thumb and wriggling forward, he could almost reach the nearest clump. He wriggled more, precariously balanced now, found a knob of rock to steady himself and with the other hand was just closing round the rootbite when something scuttled from under it . . . a furry, pink-eared . . .

Tacky let go of the knobby rock and grabbed. Friendly

One squaacked; the rootbite came out of its cranny; and Tacky, Friendly One, and rootbite went somersaulting down the steep bank. They all came to a tangled stop, with Tacky's head halfway down the neck of the brill. Friendly One took a big chaw on his finger, and Tacky almost dropped him the rest of the way.

He had a dozen new bruises and scrapes, but he pulled himself upright and sat back with a smile wreathing his face.

"Now that bit of thinking wasn't so hard as I thought it would be," he told Friendly One, stroking the ruffled fur on his neck. "Question One: How did MudLar get into the brill? Answer One: He fell in."

Searching about for the rootbite, Tacky found it oozing juice onto the ground. "Have a bite, Friendly One," he said, "and we'll think about Question Two."

Question Two . . . The Shadow and the Cross . . . He frowned in the effort of concentration. Time crawled. MudLar remained lapped in his deep sleep. Friendly One finished the clump of rootbite, gave a gentle *burrrrp,* and began to snore. Tacky closed his eyes for a trickle of time to help along his thinking . . . thinking . . . think . . .

Slowly, as Tacky roused himself, he became aware of a small jiggle in the bottom of his stomach, the suggestion of a throb. He looked to Belcher . . . Black smoke billowed from the Rift, as it had been doing off and on since the queer hiccup Belcher gave earlier, but that was all.

The jittering in his stomach persisted. Tacky moved over to MudLar and lifted the coverlid. The gawklike face hadn't changed. Nothing had changed.

Question Two . . . Tacky suddenly realized he was staring at the point of shadow that was moving snaillike toward him. It was a shadow of the Thumb, and soon, very soon—he twisted to see—it would fall directly across the mouth of the brill!

Excitement wiped out the jittering. What if MudLar

hadn't fallen into the brill, but had gone in purposely, in order to . . . because . . .

"Friendly One," he announced, "we are going to answer another question."

Gingerly, he lowered himself feet first into the brill's maw. He expected a ledge to put his feet on, a ledge and a branching-off place, with the brill going two ways—down to the Aha and up to the top of the arm, and then . . . He frowned. Did brills run sideways or only up and down? There were brills a-plenty in old stories, but how did they behave outside of stories? Questions within questions! Once started, there was no end to thinking!

Just now he was beginning to think there was no end to this narrow tube. Swinging his feet around to find a foothold, he let himself slip several spans farther into the brill; felt again with his feet, slipped; felt, slipped. And then he slipped farther than he meant and at the same time he felt a sharp bite on his nose, a warning. It came too late. The brill had closed snugly about him, leaving his feet dangling in some lower space.

Friendly One dived for his other shoulder and chittered urgently in his ear.

Tacky groaned. Even MudLar, bone-bag that he was, could not have wriggled through this small space that fed into the brill. So he couldn't have found the Way of the Goat down here. He must have fallen from the Thumb after all, just as Tacky had fallen earlier; but being old and feeble, he hadn't been able to pull himself out.

Tacky, young and strong, dug his fingers into the rough stone and pulled. Nothing happened. The brill had him clasped by the middle and wouldn't let go. He sent his dangling feet exploring frantically for something they could push against; they touched nothing but space. He strung himself out thin and pulled again with all the might in his arms. It was no use. He was stuck like a grass wad in a narrow-necked pitcher.

The jiggle came back, but now it was a deep throb-bing . . .

He felt the *Booooommmm!* before he heard it. It pounded against his ears and shook the brill around him. He dug his fingertips into the corsa.

There was another *boom,* and another, but the echo that filled his ears whispered *Doom . . . Doom . . . Doom . . .*

Chipstone didn't flinch when the sudden *boom* of Belcher's explosion bounced from one end of the Aha to the other. Long before Belcher gave voice, Chipstone had been striking the chisel in time to a new inner throb of the earth. No more did Trueline's hand falter as she chipped at the rock on the other side of the slot. Only Milk gave a start, and yelped as he scraped his head between the slabs of rock that had him locked between them.

"Best hold still there, younger," said Chipstone. Seeing the tears of pain standing in Milk's eyes, he tried to think of something comforting to add. "Reminds me of a time . . ." he started, and then stuck. He wasn't reminded of any time at all, that was the sorry truth of it. Frowning, he went on with his steady tapping, and the clean-cut shards dropped away from his chisel in orderly succession. Nobody could cut stone better; nonetheless, he wished he had a story or two to tell the younger. Happy, cheering memories like other folks', not the lumps of sadness that sat in his head like stones set into a homing wall.

"It reminds *me* of an old song," said Trueline with a laugh. "Listen:

> Where the goat rears up
> And his whiskers fall,
> It's quick through the wet
> And up through the wall!

"Only," she added, "you're one goat that didn't get all the way through!"

Milk's usual good humor had been squeezed out of him. "You changed the words," he accused her. "It's a *mouse* and it goes *past the net,* not through the wet. And up *to* the wall. How could anyone go *through* a wall!"

"*You* tried." Trueline smiled into the slot at him. "But I wasn't singing the game-chant. This is the way the song went in the beginning, before it was made into a game. Dar Toothacher learned it from his dar, and *his* dar from *his* dar, and . . ."

But Milk had stopped listening. He had an intent look, as though straining to hear another voice, far away, indistinct through Belcher's measured throb . . .

Milk . . . ? Milk! Hoi there! Mole Star was feeling, just the tiniest bit, frantic. He was stuck, badly stuck. Spread-eagled against Belcher's arm, he clung to two holds: a niche for one foot and a crevice for one hand, with no way of reaching another hold for his extra hand and foot. Climbing out of the meadow up and across the wall-face to the Spewing had looked easy from the ground. But now he was stuck, and he couldn't raise a response from Milk.

When the split rock jammed shut just short of his nose, Mole Star had stood in front of the hairline crack saying *Whew!* over and over. If he hadn't run back for a last look at the meadow before following Milk into the Aha . . . *Whew!* He only began to worry about Milk when he realized that the closed rock had severed the . . . the *hearing* that ran between them. Sometimes, though, he reminded himself, Milk needed prodding. Sometimes he forgot to listen.

He reminded himself, but he didn't stop worrying. That's why he had started to climb out . . . to find Milk. And now he was stretched against the wall-face like a curing goatskin, unable to go up or down. He could only cling to

185

his two holds until somebody came to help, or . . . *Whew.*
Milk! I need help! Milk! Help! A last imploring cry.
Faintly, oh very faintly, he seemed to hear a sound, like a
thick rustle, in his head.
He hung on.

20

"It takes the sun to see the shadow."

—MudLar

Potter Ott sat by the dead firepit staring at the cracked slagstone. His head felt muddled, his wits out of line; he couldn't get hold of what Joke Eye had been saying. Something about life and death . . . no, just life. Life! Joke Eye's younger, Life. And Joke Eye expected him—him!— to do something with Flaw and Overshot. What?

He lumbered to his feet. Danger, that was it. He had promised to remove Flaw and Overshot from . . . because . . . he couldn't remember. No matter. Remove Flaw and Overshot. Joke Eye had been very clear about that. Into the muddle of his wits wandered the Stony Bib. Was that where he was to remove them from?

He was halfway out of the door before he thought of arming himself. A stick? Spade? His eye fell on the birding net hanging on the wall and he snatched it down. Before he could stop to reconsider, he was around the house and storming up the puckered ridge behind it, waving the birding net like a banner.

"Here you, stop!" Flaw's startled face loomed before him.

Without a thought, Ott brought the net down squarely over Flaw's head. It made a very good thunking sound as it settled round his shoulders and arms.

"Here *you!*" Flaw spluttered through the webbing, his eyes beady as any bird's, his nose drawn down to his chin like a beak.

Seeing him like that, Ott realized that he didn't like Flaw. Never had. There was unexpected joy in finding out.

With a jerk on the handle of the net, he hauled Flaw up over the pucker and marched him around the house and through the door and down onto a tipstool by the firepit.

"Ott," Flaw pleaded. "You don't know what you are doing. Overshot, he's the Chief Steward now, and I'm his Second. Ott, what are you *doing?*"

"Why as to that," said Ott, busy at his biggest pipe, "I've just remembered how fond you are of a good smoke, Flaw. This is my treat." Suddenly he thrust the mouthpiece through the netting and lodged it in Flaw's gaping mouth. "For old times' sake." He pulled down his brows in a horrible frown. "Draw!" he thundered.

And Flaw drew until the cherrychoke glowed red—and so did Flaw's face. Tears streamed down his craven cheeks; his eyes began to glaze. Only then did Ott remove the birding net and let Flaw's head droop against his skinny chest.

Overshot was another matter.

Ott paused uncertainly on the mud-caked loosestones of the Bib. Overshot couldn't have seen the netting of Flaw, else he would already be here.

"Ho-la!" The shout rang along the Stony Bib, and Ott licked his lips with anticipation. He suddenly realized that he didn't like Overshot any more than he liked Flaw.

"Ho-la! Flaw! Where are you?"

Ott paid no attention. He bent over and stared fixedly at a large rock lying beside the pucker—one that must have been part of his own wall before it was swallowed and then regurgitated when the split earth closed up again. He stared at it in the hope that Overshot would turn curious and come running.

Overshot didn't. "Ho-la! You! Ott! I see you by that rock! Come here!"

With a sigh, Ott straightened. Shouldering the net, he set off at a lumbering trot before he noticed that Overshot was flourishing a stick wildly in the air.

His courage ebbed. He was having hasty thoughts about retreat, and then he saw Life. She was running down the path from the Brow, her face flushed and set.

Overshot heard her at the same time and turned, his own face flushing up with a rude pleasure. "Well then, Ott, I had you wrong," he said. "I thought that you were coming after *me*. Now don't let her get past you! I promised her faithfully to Venerable for the Summoning today."

Ott gave a strangled warning shout, but Life was upon them before she looked up. She was running straight into Overshot's grasping hands.

With a wild flail Ott brought the net down, but Overshot moved and it bounced harmlessly off his shoulder to fall to the stones. Overshot half-turned to glare at him.

"Have a care, Ott! You bungle everything!"

Ott fetched up a great sigh. "Well *then*," he said, and flung his arms round Overshot's shoulders in a sudden clinching hug.

Overshot's eyes and mouth made three great round O's of astonishment as he sagged to his knees. "What are you *doing!* What is this, Ott?"

"A friendly warning," said Ott with a terrible smile, "to keep you from your unfriendly self." He gave Life his pleasantest glower over the Chief Steward's head. "Now then, younger, domma Joke Eye will want to see you. Er . . . would you mind, before you go, handing me that net? I don't want this bird to fly away."

There was a particularly sharp stone under Skarra's pallet that prodded his shoulder every time he moved. It goaded him into wakefulness now. Such dreams he had had! Not the old nighttime horror, but a floating calm, like drifting clouds. A soft swirling, like . . . like . . .

He sat up and looked round him. The doorway framed a late sun. But where was—he had trouble finding her name —Life? Where was Life? She was in the hut before he went out to the mudpots to meet Venerable, but now she was gone. He felt oddly disjointed. Time was a fuzziness; place was nowhere. He had been on a journey into the swirling mud, and words had come to him. Words. A Seth. From Belcher. Yes.

Then had come a time when he no longer swirled with the mud, and someone—Life—drew him along to the hut, her voice washing over him in great waves: . . . goatskins . . . a chest . . . be sure to look . . . and did he give the Seth the way they had planned. They? But the Seth had been in the mud! Hadn't it? A Seth from Belcher.

The next thing he remembered was the going-away of the disturbing voice and the sinking into perfect quiet at last.

Except for the buzzing sounds, or were they just in his ears? And the booming . . . Was this what happened when you had a true Seth?

Or was he still asleep?

He struggled to his feet and almost went headlong over MudLar's mat. He started to push it back into place and then he saw, beyond it, the chest yawning open. Horrified, he scrambled to close the lid quickly, before . . . before what? Memory came filtering back. Look in the chest, Mud-Lar had told Tacky. Life must have already looked! Skarra forgot about closing the lid. He sat down on MudLar's fleece and unrolled a skin from the top layer. It was a skin he remembered well; he remembered even better MudLar's anger at the bad job of scraping he had done on it.

He stared at the unexpected design for long moments before he realized that it must be a chart. Excitedly, he traced one of the sweeps from the horn sign at the bottom: *Slaughter a goat, go to (or look at?) something (or as far as possible?) at sun-bob (or sun-drop) in the season of Singing Grass on the day of the Sky, which is cloudy . . .* In dismay he followed a second sweep; it read the same except that the season was Shivery Rains, and there was no cloud circling the sun. But there were two slashes through it. Mud-Lar hadn't taught him anything like this.

Leaving the skin flat, he picked out another roll, and another until he had ten of them, all crammed to the edges with the same sweeps, over and over. There were years of seasons marked out on the goatskins. Why? He delved into the chest again.

Now there were charts not of MudLar's hand. On some the tracking signs sprouted from a smoking Belcher cone, and there were no seasons or days or time marked, just tracks spraying out like the fronds of a jimcally plant; on others there was no figure at the bottom at all, but the travel signs tracked endlessly up skin after skin, always, always ending in either a cloud or two slashes.

How many MudLars . . . how many years? Back, back in time they traveled, MudLar before MudLar before Mud-Lar. And each MudLar left the tracks of . . . of his journeyings? . . . on a piece of goatskin . . .

Finally, there was only one roll left—so brittle and fragile and dark, as though charred, that he was almost afraid to unroll it. The markings on the big skins had been in countless hands, some fancy and careful, some plain and simple, but this was crude, dashed-off. A browsing goat? More likely a butting goat, with long wisps of grass still streaming from its mouth. The body was a few sketchy lines, the legs half-finished, and there was only one horn. It was a goat such as a chidling might scratch on the ground with a stick.

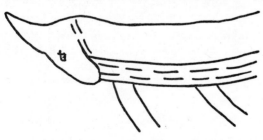

It occurred to Skara that this might be the most important roll of all.

He sat back and stared at the stack of goatskins. There must be a chart from every MudLar since the first one had crawled out of the ashes. Had all of them spent their lifetimes searching for a way out? And when *he* became Mud-Lar, is that how he would spend *his* lifetime? And he would then have a Skarra, too, to raise and teach, and when his own time was up, that Skarra would take up the search?

Not if today's Seth . . . Uneasily, he began to roll up the skins and place them in the chest, but when he came to the one on the bottom he stared at it for a long time.

Slaughtered goat . . . what could that mean? Or half-a-goat. One horn? All of the journeyings stemmed from it. Half-a-goat. One horn. One . . . what else could the word sign mean? One-something, and on the first day of every season, at sun-up—or sun-down?—Mudlar had gone out from that one-something until he was stopped! Until he discovered that the Way did not lie in that direction? In that place? One horn . . . One—Skarra fastened his gaze on the chart and opened the back of his mind to anything that would enter.

But it was the shape and substance of Mudlar that formed in his thoughts. Not the MudLar who snapped his feet and pulled his hair, but the MudLar lying in the pit in his deep sleep. The vision widened and heightened as Skarra drew back from it, and now he saw MudLar as a smaller figure in the midst of the Spewing, his size diminished by the towering . . .

Fingers shaking, Skarra took up the last goatskin and stared at the bottom word sign. But it wasn't a word. It was a picture.

It was the Thumb!

21

"We can no more understand the troubled heart
of a MudLar than we can divine the mystery
lurking in the barred eyes of the goat."

—Arkive, *True Tales*

Skarra took time only to haul off the Sethgown and get into
his blue plaingown before leaving the Brow. He had to find
Life!

Taking the Venerable Path at full tilt, he came down
head before heels onto the hardened mud of the Stony Bib.
Righting himself with a groan, he looked up and down
the Bib—empty—and scuttered across to climb the puckered ridge that masked the village. There he clung open-
mouthed.

There were houses and houses, big, daunting houses, and
in them there would be big, daunting people like Venerable,
demanding to know who he was, why he was there. He
wished he had one of the masks Life had talked about, a
fierce mask to hide behind! When he found her . . . A
new thought struck him. He didn't know which of all those
roofs belonged to Life!

In sudden panic, he clutched at his chest. But the beads
weren't there! Remembering, he plunged his hand into his
pocket. Nothing. He had changed the beads to the Sethgown and forgotten them. He had to have something to hold
even if it was only . . . only pebbles. Pebbles! Moments
later he had pried a handful of smooth loosestones from the
dried mud of the Bib and was ready once more to go into
the village, when he saw figures coming up the lane. His
assurance fled. Turning abruptly, he ducked behind the

houses that backed onto the pucker and set off at a run.

When he finally nerved himself to leave the safety of the housebacks, he came out at the top of a lane that bustled with sound—and almost retreated again. He was bound to meet someone. Nervously, he rattled the loosestones in his sweating palm and mumbled over the words he had been practicing: "I am Blue. Hulin Blue," he would say, "and I come from the upland farmings . . ."

He suddenly felt eyes on him and broke off his mumbling. A domma, her arms full of pots and jars, was staring full at him from her doorway. Her eyes were wide and startled, her mouth a circle of surprise.

"You're a new one! How did you get here? They're saying the farmings are cut off now, so how did you come? You weren't here this morning!"

"I am . . . I am . . ." Skarra backed away from her. "I am . . ."

The domma put the pots down all a-haggle and advanced on him. "Have you seen Mole Star? And Milk? Don't you know it's dangerous for one of your age to be here?"

Skarra's mouth opened and closed. His hand froze around the loosestones in his pocket. "Run," something whispered inside his head. "Run!"

When his feet finally started to move, they didn't stop until they had carried him down the lane and round a bend to a great open circle. Toothy Maw! Everything was there that the others had talked about, and more. Carts, people, noise, confusion. Skarra bowed his head to the Belcher Mound and then suddenly jerked it up. Voices close to him. Somebody coming from the binhouse. He ducked into the cleft between the legs of the Mound and raised his head just enough to peer over the left leg.

They were two olders, and they were staring straight at him, their chins dropped.

Skarra took to his heels. He went over Belcher's other leg and was off in a limping run, following the lane that curved away from the Maw. Footsteps pounded behind him. Voices shouted. More footsteps pounded. People popped out of doors, gasped and shouted and came running to their gates. What was it about him that made everybody want to chase him—like one of the old dreams come back?

His eyes swam with tears until he could scarcely see the roadway, and there was a thundering in his head, but still he ran. The thundering grew louder; his head was full of crackles and booms and hissings, so loud that they drowned out the shouts and the pounding of pursuing feet. He couldn't bring himself to look back at his pursuers, and then he dared not.

He came to a stumbling halt against a gate in a homing wall.

Nobody was chasing him. Nobody at all. Along the lane he had run just now, folk stood and stared . . . but not at him.

Above the village, appearing smaller from here than from the Brow, the Scars of Cherrychoke reared; but where one of the pinnacles had stood moments before, there rose a column of dust. It kept the familiar shape of Toplady for several moments, and then began to fuzz at the edges.

Skarra leaned weakly against the gate as the motes that had been Toplady drifted away, leaving Sadiron bowing and scraping to empty air.

The gate slowly sagged open from his weight, and Skarra all but fell into the courtyard beyond. For a wonder nobody shouted at him, and he stood up, hesitant, looking around. It was a place of stones he had stumbled into: stones carved into stools and tables and wondrous things he knew nothing of. It was a cluttery, clustery place, but welcoming. Safe. He poked his head out of the gate, as quickly pulled it in again. Down the lane the figures stood still as stones, too. He liked it better here where the stone was real and not people turned into it.

He shouldn't have come to the village. On the Brow,

when he'd found the drawing and the charts, he had felt strong, even powerful; but once on the Pillow he had shrivelled, dwindled. He had run from the first person who spoke to him; then he had imagined himself chased by the whole village, when it was the falling Toplady they were shouting about.

A warning! Suddenly he knew. Toplady's fall was a warning. He had gone too far, just as MudLar had done, for hadn't *he* been struck down at the moment of seeing the Way of the Goat! And now Belcher was telling him, the Skarra, to get back to the Brow where he belonged. Tears started to his eyes. He would have to forget Life and Tacky and the others, become a proper MudLar. Even were he to find the Way of the Goat, just as surely as MudLar had found it, Belcher would never never never let Firelings go. The tears spilled over and ran down his cheeks.

He saw the door of the house open, and turned blindly to flee.

The voice stopped him. "I'm so glad you've come to call," it said.

For a slice of a moment he thought it was Life, but of course it wasn't. She was full-grown, a domma she must be, and she was staring at him as though there was something amiss about him. He pulled nervously at his plaingown.

"H-hallo," he managed.

She became completely still when he spoke, like a bird in the poised moment before flight. Then she drew a deep breath and held out her hand to him, a smile lightening her face. "I expect you're from the farmings, by your blue smock," she said. "Won't you come and have something to eat? I had just laid the table for . . . why, it must have been for *you!*" and she laughed.

It was like a dream. He let her draw him along to a small retreat shaded by a candletree. A stone image of a chidling stood smiling at them by a stone table that was set with a steaming bowl, a round crusty loaf, and thick golden cheese.

"Now sit and eat," the domma invited him.

Skarra struggled for words as he sank down on the bench beside the smiling stone boy. Finding none, he lifted a spoonful of the steaming pudding, first to Belcher and then to his mouth. It exploded with a sweetness he had never tasted before, and he forgot to offer the second spoonful to Belcher. The domma watched him eagerly, and he nodded his head with his mouth full.

He should ask about Life—where she lived—and whether Venerable had yet delivered the Seth, and about . . . No, no, that was over and done with! He had to go back to the Brow. The moment he had eaten the rest of the creamy pudding, he would go. Even though the domma brought another pudding, he would go.

A waver of wind brought a sudden small sprinkling of ash down through the candletree. The domma's smile flew off her face, to be replaced by a withering look that reminded Skarra of Life in one of her moods.

"Feeble-wit!" The domma's voice was scathing. "Idiot!"

Skarra choked on a mouthful of pudding. "Wh-what?"

"Belcher. Stupid. Worse than stupid. A dolt, a fool. He lets his firepit burn up his house. An evil neighbor, too. His sparks burn up other houses."

Hastily Skarra lifted the next spoonful high to mollify Belcher. "But he . . . But in the Story Stones . . ."

She gave him a scornful glance. "Oh yes, the vaunted Story Stones. And when there are none left on this fated land to read them, of what use will Story Stones be?"

"But you really shouldn't say things." Skarra dared not look up at Belcher's smoke. "He will hear you!"

The domma's smile was back, but the scorn was still there. "How can he hear if he has no ears?"

"Has no . . . ?"

"No ears. Have some of the bread."

His tongue is the flame, his eyes the gusher, his mouth the mudpots through which he speaks. Skarra groped for the

197

bread. Why had he never wondered where dwelt Belcher's ears? *It is not for us to question,* MudLar liked to say. Skarra suddenly had a terrible suspicion that MudLar didn't know the answers. Sternly he recalled himself. Where had such thoughts come from!

As though waking from a dream, he began to hear the sounds around him: the underlying throb; the distant thundering and hissing that had started when he was running up the lane; and, faintly, shoutings and running about, bangings of gates, footsteps near at hand . . .

He jumped up.

The footsteps stopped, and the gate was flung open.

I should have gone, Skarra thought, despairing. He shut his eyes and waited for a hand to fall on his shoulder.

Instead there was a voice, squeezed out between gasps. "Overshot . . . he got away! After all that dragging and pulling of him, too. He promised not to escape and then . . . and then he tripped me. In my own house he tripped me!"

"Sit down and collect your breath," the domma said. Her voice was calm and soothing, but there was a shake in it.

Skarra dared open his eyes. He was looking at the biggest, roundest, angriest Fireling possible to believe. Every lap and fold of his face was a-twitch with rage. Skarra got lost in the welter of words that clacked back and forth between the two. One picked up at the toe where the other left off at the heel, and Skarra stumbled five paces behind. Familiar names popped out like currants from a spotty-bun, but there was no weaving them into sense until, at last, the newcomer ran out of words and only the domma went on talking.

Her voice was hushed. ". . . and she left the pictures with me, but I don't understand. They show my poor chidling drowning in the steaming pool, but I don't . . . and what I *saw* that day . . . I kept hoping a domma's hope . . ." She pulled a creased roll of skins from her pocket and spread them on the stone table.

"See on this first one how the little one is taken from the village up to . . . the Brow, but on the second—I don't understand—he is bathing in the steaming pool, and then the gusher—the boiling water—and the little one drowned . . ." her voice broke . . . "And all these years I dreamed another dream."

Skarra stared, horrorstruck, at the skins lying under the domma's hands. They had to have come from MudLar's chest. Life! And this domma, then . . . Joke Eye! And the round one? Snatches of their talk shuffled together in his mind like parts of a riddle. The round one was Potter Ott and he had got Flaw and Overshot to his house, but Overshot had escaped . . . and was a danger to Life. And Life had gone to see Grey Gammer or someone . . .

Potter Ott was lumberingly patting Joke Eye's shoulder and mumbling heartening words while he examined the skins one after the other. Skarra itched to snatch them away. It was faithless of Life to take them from the chest! He must put them back the moment he could escape from here.

The moment came sooner than expected with the insistent ringing of a bell. Joke Eye gave Potter Ott a frightened look and suddenly turned to Skarra. "We must go to this Summoning. If my daughter Life comes back, on no account let her go out again. Tell her that Overshot is looking for her. Will you do that?"

Skarra nodded dumbly. He was used to being told what to do.

"And . . ." The domma smiled. "You will find more pudding inside. Make my home your home. You might say a word to Hulin now and then. He gets lonely." She nodded toward the stone boy, smiled again, and went out of the gate with Potter Ott, who was looking fatly fierce.

Hulin, she had said! But of course! Life had given him the name of her brother. The pieces of the puzzle shuffled closer together. Skarra reached for the skins.

They were pictures, like drawings meant for a Story Stone. In the corner of the second one were writing signs in MudLar's hand: "Day of the Sky, Season of New Life, Second Year of the Gawk." The same as yesterday! Except for the year. Never at his best while counting, Skarra waggled his fingers to figure the years since MudLar made the drawings. Ten of them. Ten . . . ? But he had more than ten years in his own life! Wouldn't he have known about this happening . . . the water jet spurting twice in the same day, Hulin helpless in the pool?

Skarra scrabbled through his memory for scraps of information about the Morsel of the Twelfth Story Stone. Belcher had demanded a Morsel, and Hulin had been given to Mud-Lar to put down the Long Slip as the offering: that's all there was.

He bent over the first skin again, perplexed by the picture of—bowls?—drawn above . . . a mouth? It was more like a . . . He stared fixedly at it, and something stirred at the back of his mind. His head began to prickle, the way it had for the Seth.

With shaking fingers he rearranged the skins. Now the year-day writing appeared at the top. Ten years ago, a child had drowned in the blue pool when the gusher jetted a second time and MudLar wasn't there to pull him from the steaming water. Ten years ago that child had been put down the Long Slip, and bitter tears had fallen. Ten years ago, another child was taken to the Brow and there . . . Those weren't bowls and a mouth in the picture. They were the webbed feet of a gawk and a chopper.

With a cry of pain and fear, Skarra jumped up from the table. Stone Hulin wobbled, and Skarra thrust out an awkward hand to right him, but the statue tottered twice and fell from its pedestal with a fearful smash. Splinters flew. A stone shard landed on the bench where Skarra had been sitting. He stared at it for long moments before he saw what it was.

It was part of a stone foot. Cunningly carved toes peeped out of open sandals. They were webbed like a gawk's.

High above on the Scars, Sadiron, still obsequiously bowing to the vanished Toplady, slid into dusty oblivion.

22

One day Murkle sat down on a sunny rock before he saw that a snake was already curled there. In great panic he fled, falling downhill and knocking the breath from his body and the teeth from his mouth.

The snake, awakened by the clatter of teeth, nodded sleepily at Murkle where he lay. "Thank you for waking me up," it said, curling its dainty tongue into a two-part yawn, "for I was getting much too hot in the sun." And it wriggled into the cool grass, where it went back to sleep.

When Murkle came to his senses and saw what damage had been wrought in his fall, he knew how right he had been to fear snakes.

—*Legends of Murkle*

By some strange quirk of the wind, the sound of the summoning bell was borne up the Spewing to Belcher's arm. Mole Star was trying once again to lower himself on the cliff wall, but he couldn't reach a foothold without losing his handhold.

Milk! He was beginning to grow frantic. *I . . . need . . . help! . . . help!*

"Steady now," Chipstone was saying to Milk in the Aha below. "Won't be long. The hard part by your head is done. It's your chest that still won't slip through."

"Leave it!" Milk yelled. "Go get Mole Star. He's going to *fall!*"

Trueline glanced up sharply. "Where is he? Milk, where *is* he?"

Milk looked confused, then motioned slightly with his head. "Up. Somewhere. A steep place. But you've got to hurry!"

"Well, this can't be hurried, you know, Milk," Chipstone said mildly. "All in good time. Then we'll chisel through that other rock you talked about and find your friend."

Trueline had stepped back to scan the mountain wall rising behind the Aha; she suddenly clutched Chipstone's arm. "I see him! It's Mole Star! There, dar Chipstone, straight up and to the left!" She brought her eyes down to Milk's agonized face peering from the slot. "Don't worry, Milk. Dar Chipstone will get him down!"

The face that Chipstone turned to hers was utterly confounded. *"I?* I don't know anything about cliff walls and such!"

"They're stone, aren't they?" Trueline's voice was positive. "I'll finish here while you go up the Spewing. You'll think of a way, dar Chipstone. I know you will. Milk and I'll come as soon as we can." She went back to her tapping, and when Chipstone still hadn't moved, she threw over her shoulder. "Don't forget your tools!"

Toothy Maw was crammed with Firelings gathered for the Summoning, but they stood about in close family clusters. Even the chidlings had no heart for playing together but stood dumbly by their dardommas, their rounded eyes raised to the ash-coughings from Belcher's Rift. Beyond the Scars, heavy black smoke billowed the length of Belcher's chest; occasionally it lifted for a moment to reveal tongues of flame licking out of a new spewing.

When Venerable's voice quavered to a stop at the end of the Seth that Skarra had given him, there was a long, shocked silence as Firelings sought out the meaning.

"Are you sure you said it rightly?" Witlatch finally dared to ask.

"Tell it again!" cried Anner.

Venerable repeated the Seth:

> "The day grows dim—
> The Rat is near;
> Leave the firepit,
> Outrun the fear!
> O follow life and seek the wind.
>
> "In fiery pain
> And shrieking mud,
> I send a doom
> Of fire and flood!
> O follow life and seek the wind.
>
> "Seek the Brow
> And then the Spew;
> By Way of Goat
> Begin anew!
> So follow life from night to day—
> And with the windsong fly away!"

A long, ragged sigh went through the listeners, like wind rustling through tussock grass.

Oldest Gar finally got enough spittle together to make his voice work. "But just what exactly does it say? What's that about following and seeking?"

"Ehh," said Venerable. "Ehh. The way I see it, the wind dwells, ehh, dwells up high, and life is, ehh, ehh, the opposite of death! In simple, the Seth tells us to, ehh, go up to the Brow for safety. Tomorrow dawn will suit admirably. Then when the wind has blown out Belcher's fires, ehh, we can come back to the Pillow."

"But it says the Spewing!" cried domma Kirtle. "And the Way of the Goat!"

"Belcher means to bury us!" Thin Yukie shouted.

A new cry erupted. "The Morsel! That's what Belcher wants!"

"The youngers! They've done the hurt to us! Give the youngers to Belcher!"

Suddenly Grey Gammer was staunchly in front of Venerable's speaking bench, her hair ruffed out by her passage through the crowd. "My ears hear differently!" she cried. "My ears hear that we go to the Brow and then to the Spewing, and after that through the Way of the Goat. And my feet tell me not to wait for dawn. The Seth says to follow Life and seek the windsong bird, and I for one intend to do exactly that, for surely Life knows where to find him!"

Oldest Gar began to clap, his thin hands like weeper branches whispering together. Another and another joined in, pattering raindrops of sound. A trickle of voices swelled into a gurgling stream, and again the Maw overflowed with words. The pleasant shower ended with a thunderclap.

"Hold!"

A ripple of movement started at the edge of the crowd. Heads turned, folk fell back, a way was made; and Overshot strode to the speaking bench, where he stepped up beside Venerable. The engorged purple of his face was enough to silence the crowd.

"What nonsense is this!" he roared. "Are you going to be led by old cracked pots and little jugs too small to hold a swallow of milk? I'll tell you what the Seth says: *Follow Life*, it says! You will do just that! For I am taking that child of Joke Eye and Chipstone to the Brow and then to the Long Slip, for *that* is what Belcher demands. *That* is what the Seth tells us. I call on Venerable to witness!"

"No." The small scritch of a voice carried unexpectedly clear above the heads of the hushed throng. "No!"

A new ripple started in the crowd, but it stopped well

short of the speaking bench. Firelings watched in astonishment as the scrawny, blue-smocked younger climbed up on a high cart.

"That's *not* what the Seth says!" The scritch had turned into a scratch.

"Who is that?" demanded Oldest Gar.

"It's the stranger," Mole Star's domma cried. "The one I was telling you . . ."

"The Seth," the voice went on, growing stronger, "says to follow Life to find Tacky-obbie on the Spewing. He is watching over MudLar at the golden Thumb!"

Out of the groan of disbelief, voices stood out.

"How does he know! Golden Thumb, did you ever hear!"

"Nothing but a daft chidling from the farmings."

"Not so!" an indignant farmer bridled. "From the minings, more like."

But Overshot shouted above them all. *"It's only one small life for all your lives!"*

And now another ripple, a wave—a tide—stirred the crowd, all the way to the bench. Potter Ott's eyes blazed with rage. His hair was on end. His cheeks joggled. With a roar he fell upon Overshot and bore him to the ground. They rolled over and over.

Venerable was rendered speechless, but not Ven Ida. "Disgraceful! For very shame!"

The chorus was quick to follow. "Disgraceful! Disgusting!"

"Overshot is right! Follow Overshot!"

"Overshot will save us!"

Voices swelled louder and louder, until Venerable fought his way to the bell and gave it two sharp jerks.

Skarra, on top of the high cart, watched dumbfounded the spineless shuttle from one belief to another and back. He wanted to run—run as fast as his scarred feet would carry him back to the Brow where he belonged. He had had enough of these quarrelsome, shouting Firelings. He was no part of them, or they of him . . . A wistful little pang of regret for the stone courtyard stole into his mind, and the domma Joke Eye's soft smile and touch . . .

Then suddenly that same domma had stepped out of his mind and climbed up to stand beside him. Her eyes were shining-deep.

"You are not of the uplands," she said, her voice soft under the clapper and clatter of the crowd. Confused, he shook his head and then nodded it.

"Then who are you?" A smile hovered at the corners of her mouth as though fearful of being banished.

Out of long habit, Skarra looked to Belcher for an answer, but as his eyes slid past the Scars, he forgot Belcher and Joke Eye and the noisy crowd.

A small puff of dust showed at the top of Ashlar's head. As it slowly cleared, Skarra could see that the long-tailed rat was missing a part of its long tail.

"Never mind, then," domma Joke Eye was saying, and an old grief tinged her voice. "But I fear for *her*. For Life. Overshot will have his way, unless somebody raises a voice against him. Ott's temper has undone him. Venerable is weak . . . and Chipstone is gone . . ." She fell silent for a space; then, her voice quickening, "What is it? What are you staring at?"

He pointed. Another piece of the long tail broke away.

Joke Eye caught her breath. ". . . The Scars," she whispered.

"Domma," Skarra said urgently, "can you get to the bell and ring it?"

She looked oddly at him, but she nodded.

"And go on ringing it until . . . until you see me raise my hand?"

"Yes," she said. She gave him a long searching look. "I beg you not to vanish," she said hurriedly, and jumped to the ground where she became part of the crowd in a moment.

Skarra tried to put her shining eyes out of his mind. He had to go back to the Brow. Hadn't he . . . ?

The rest of the rat's tail came away; and then Ashlar's head, with the rat still riding it, toppled. If there was any sound of its smashing, it was drowned in the noises of Belcher and the squabblings of Firelings. The dust slowly settled and still Skarra watched, oblivious to hands pulling at him now, oblivious at first to the voice jabbing at him from below the cart . . .

"Blue! Hulin Blue! Blue! Answer me!"

To his dismay he saw Life standing below, tugging at his plaingown.

"You shouldn't be here!" he hissed. "I thought Overshot had you!"

"He did, he did. But he left me with Flaw, and Flaw kept snoring off to sleep." Her voice sank lower. "Didn't the Seth work? What happened? What are you going to do?"

He didn't know. The folk pressing closer around the cart were looking curiously at Life and whispering to each other. Was he only imagining that they were trying to close her in, cut her off from escape? He could see Overshot back on the bench now, and no sign of Potter Ott. Anxiously he looked to the Scars, wondering if he was also imagining a rumble above the other noises battering at his ears . . .

The summoning bell began to toll.

The hubble-bubble of voices stopped. Mouths hung open in the middle of a word.

Like a small shimmer of heat the shadows of Old Crank and Wotkin wavered on the shoulder wall . . . Skarra strained to see, but he was distracted by the restless surge around the cart as suspicious scatterlings strove to get a better look at Life . . . Yes!

He threw his hand into the air. The tolling stopped. Bewildered faces looked from the hushed bell to Skarra's hand. It was pointing to the Scars.

Skarra opened his mouth, but only a whisper came out. A hand slapped his ankle. "Yell!"

"The Scars will sink," he faltered, and heads turned now to follow his pointing finger. Skarra's voice strengthened.

> "The Scars will sink
> In crumbling dust;
> To Joke Eye's young
> Give now your trust!
> O follow Life and seek the wind!"

A long *Ahhhhhhh* swelled from the Maw as slowly, slowly, Old Crank and Wotkin went down together. And only Skopple Guy remained.

Skarra could feel Life's eyes staring at him. All the other eyes that had turned to the Scars were now fastened avidly upon him, waiting, expecting more.

He groped for words, but the end of them had come. The end had come . . . The end has come . . . ? High above the Pillow, Skopple Guy gave a jiggle.

Words came in a rush:

> "The End has come!
> And Skopple Guy
> Now drops his arm
> In sad good-bye . . ."

The jiggle grew into a tremor, the tremor into a tremble, and Skopple Guy's arm, that across the years had protected the Firelings of Belcher's Body, became a waver of dust that hung in the air. In a moment Skopple Guy too began to slump and shiver apart and fold into itself.

Over the wailing that burst forth, Overshot made one last demand, his voice tremulous. "Who are you? What do you want!"

Skarra's voice rose strong and heartening over the wailing, the furious pounding of the sea, and Belcher himself.

"I am Hulin, the son of Joke Eye and Chipstone." His voice rang out clearer than the summoning bell, triumphant. "And I am your Skarra!"

The wailing hung quivering in the air as long as it took Fireling mouths to shape disbelief and then dawning wonderment. A slow rumble of excitement took hold and grew louder and finally erupted into a halting cheer that was taken up by this villager and that scatterling until even Flaw and Overshot were swept into giving voice, and the entire Summoning exploded into celebration of the returned Fireling son.

But underneath the noisy merrymaking, like an accompanying drum, the slow steady beat of Belcher's wrath marked ominous time.

23

When the fearworm takes gobbling big bites, it is in danger of expiring from its own greed; for if there is nothing left to feed on and no more space to swell into, it begins to devour itself.

—Attributed to Tacky-obbie

The land of Belcher's Body was alive with movement. Inside the Rift a molten lake boiled and sloshed and steamed and spattered and spilled over. Outside, animals fled and cowered, and fled again over the uncertain ground; birds twittered and shifted and clung to their nests. The day was waning.

On Belcher's arm, Mole Star's hand had gone numb from holding onto the crevice. It was hours since Chipstone had appeared on the Spewing and started his sidling advance across the cliff face. *Hurry! Hurry!* Mole Star had urged, but there was no hurrying the stonecarver. Painstakingly he stopped every few lengths to hack out a new niche or enlarge an old one; then on he would come, a poking side-creeping thumbworm. Mole Star had closed his eyes against the agonizing crawl, and when now he dared look again, he was astonished to see Chipstone only a few lengths away.

"Almost there," Chipstone grunted, and with care extracted the small axe from his belt. Five deliberate strokes he laid into the rock face, and a niche appeared. Another five strokes: another niche blossomed. He replaced the axe, moved to the new holds, reached for the axe again. In methodical succession, he laid a patterned track over to Mole Star and then, tucking his axe away, he slowly began to move back toward the Spewing. As Mole Star felt for the first notch with his foot, he caught a glimpse, beyond Chipstone, of Milk and Trueline waving encouragement from the Spewing. Relief washed over him, leaving him weak for a moment, and then strong. He reached for the next handhold.

It was a long, trembly journey, but Chipstone's notches were true and wide and deep, and the climbers reached the Spewing before the light had quite gone. After the first excitement, Trueline briskly set about making everybody rest for a while; and very shortly, just as briskly, she set about making them bestir themselves.

Mole Star punched Milk to get his attention. *Hoi, are you all right?*

"What?" Milk took his gaze from Trueline. "Oh, yes. Trueline thinks we should go on up the Spewing. She says the others expect us. She says they must have found Tacky all right. She says we can't go back to the Pillow yet, anyway. She . . ."

Mole Star slowly turned to face him. *What's all this she says, she says, she says . . . !*

But Milk had scrambled to his feet in answer to Trueline's beckoning, and forgot to answer.

From the Pillow a slow stream of bundled figures trickled up the Venerable Path to the Brow, on up the grit path past the Long Slip, through the Hollowed way choppered out of the Tangle, and so toward the top of the Spewing.

Venerable was the last to leave his homing. Ven Ida, complaining bitterly, had gone on ahead in Overshot's care. Now he banked the firepit, closed the lattices, shut the door, and latched the gate behind him. He walked to Toothy Maw to make sure the binhouse door was fast, though nothing remained within. He gave the summoning bell one last pull, but its peal was drowned in the roar of the sea below and a louder roar that came from the direction of the yammy patch. Red fire lit the night from Belcher's Rift down to the upland farmings and down along the Pubbly Way.

It was time to go. Weariness dragged at his legs. He thought of the long, unknown journey ahead, following youngers, mere chidlings. He would fall a care upon their shoulders, an extra bundle on their backs. On the Pillow he could have ended his days in dignity: advising, teaching. But a bundle on the back, carried far away to nothing-that-is-known?

Thoughtfully, he retraced his steps to his homing, opened the gate and shut it after him, opened the door of his house, and stopped in astonishment. Flames snapped brightly in the firepit, and the room was filled with a bittersweet aroma that made his mouth water.

Ven Ida came out of the shadows. "It simply isn't respectable toiling up a steep path in the middle of the night with strangers," she said. "It's a time for being inside, around one's own firepit. I've set out the old pipes, you see. I didn't think there could be any harm in cherrychoke just this once."

"But I sent you on!"

"Just like you!" she sniffed. "Making me trundle about with smelly torches and all those gruntings in my ears. That Flaw and Overshot are low, very low. Often enough I've told their goodwives they should be taken in hand. Still, others have done that now, and a good thing! So we'll sit by our fire, we two old venerables, and remember the good things." She ended firmly, "And then we shall leave here in a dignified fashion." Her nose always quivered when she felt deeply, and it was quivering now. "It doesn't matter if you lead or follow, so long as you go with dignity."

Venerable nodded. A pipe would be good. He never would have thought of it for himself. And they would talk awhile of long-ago sunlight on the Scars and the dusty grass sweet-smelling and running after goats, laughing and laughing . . .

"Here you, Flaw!" called Overshot, coming up to where his fellow Steward was resting against a tree on the Venerable Path. "It's your turn to carry Ven Ida's truckle." He dropped the heavy satchel of provisions on the path.

Flaw coughed delicately. "Not my affair," he said.

"Oh ho, and it wasn't your affair to let Life get away from you, was it!"

"*It* was not," said Flaw. "I was a victim."

"A victim, were you? Flaw, you'll carry this truckle or I'll show you a proper victim." Overshot jutted his chin close to Flaw's face. But a sudden slap on his back knocked his nose into Flaw's teeth. Flaw bit it.

"Now then," said a voice behind him, "as sure as Flaw is my goodhusband, you shall cease your bullying of him, or your answer will be to *me*. So hoist up that satchel and get along up the path!"

Nursing his throbbing nose, Overshot fumbled for the satchel and hoisted it to his shoulder.

Life glared at Hulin over the open chest in the stone hut on the Brow. It was no wonder MudLar kicked his Skarra's feet and beat him with bad words. Ever since their first meeting at the rock pool, she had felt like kicking the shrinking, weepy child he was into something strong and brave, somebody who would kick back.

And now he *was* kicking back. There he stood, pinch-faced and scrawny, defying her even as he flinched under the words she hurled at him. No, they could not take the ancient drawing of the butting goat out of the hut. No, they could not make a copy of it, for there was nothing to copy it on that could be taken from the hut.

"We *have* to take it!" Life flourished the brittle roll under his nose. "It's too important. How can we remember it exactly if we leave it here in the chest?"

"I can remember," he said in the scringy voice she hated.

"But what if you fall down the Long Slip on the way?" She regretted the words as soon as they were said and rushed on. "Of course you won't, but Tacky should see it too. Besides, what good will the picture do lying in that old chest if there's nobody still here to find it?"

"I . . . It . . . What if . . . if those other Firelings, the ones who found the Way in the beginning, hadn't left it behind? *We* never would have seen it!"

She felt a prickling under her hair.

"That's true," she said finally. A faint rumbling grew under her feet, and the light flickered. Outside, there were frightened calls as Firelings passed over the Brow. Life looked at Hulin's closed face. "I'll tell you what I'll do," she said. "We'll take the picture, and after sun-up tomorrow I'll bring it back and put it in the chest. I promise!"

His face looked a shade less stubborn, and she pressed on.

"Good, then." Briskly she rolled the crackling skin into a scroll and blew out the oilwick light. "And Blue . . . Hulin . . . don't *worry!* As soon as we get to Tacky, I'll make an oath on our Oathstone to bring the picture back the very exact *moment* we've seen the shadow!"

"If the sun doesn't shine," Hulin said lugubriously, "there won't be a shadow."

Her toes ached with a fierce urge to kick him thoroughly and for a long time. "Listen to me," she said fiercely. "You listen, Skarra-Hulin-Blue! Tomorrow the sun is going to shine brighter than it has shone in your whole life. That is a Stone-Solemn Promise!"

Grey Gammer lagged behind no one on the grit path. In her heart there was a singing, louder than any song that had ever welled out of her throat. Her voice might be quavery and cracked from long use, but the heart's song was as fresh and light as the ancient time she had once dared to put a foot on the Spewing—the merest mischief of a chidling—and promised the wind that one day she would go beyond the Spewing, beyond the arm flung against the sky and sea, beyond Belcher himself. It was her Song of the Wind.

> The wind blows free
> From the star-tipped sky,
> To roam the land,
> And so shall I!

She chuckled to herself and shifted her granson's youngest higher on her back. She was scarcely moving free as the wind, but she was roaming—that she certainly was!

Stuck fast in the brill, Tacky-obbie had resigned himself to waiting for help when another possibility dropped into his head: nobody was coming at all!

Panic laid hold of him. He kicked out with his feet and flailed with his arms, but the brill only gripped him tighter, and he collapsed into despair. Sweat poured down his face, prickling his chin. He brushed at it . . . and felt, huddled close against his neck, a soft, breathing-in-and-out, re-turned-home Friendly One! The tickle was a stem of root-bite still hanging from his sleepy mouth.

"You've come back," Tacky said wonderingly. He managed an unsteady laugh. "And you've brought me dinner!" Dislodging the stem, he put it in his own mouth and sucked the juice. Friendly One gave a friendly snore and snugged closer under his chin. Trustingly. *He* thought they were going to get out of this hole. The sweat began to dry on Tacky's face, and the mite of warmth under his chin gave him a curious feeling of strength.

The hole they were in was long and narrow, Tacky thought. If he could string himself out to be even longer and narrower and then urge himself upward with his elbows . . . *Trying is better than sighing,* folk were always telling youngsters. *Or dying,* Tacky thought.

The brill begrudged his going every hand's-breadth of the way, but Tacky edged up and up and up until his legs were no longer swinging in emptiness. After that it was short work pushing against the sides of the brill with his feet.

They emerged into a night of flame. Red tinted the sky and the moon glowed red; red tinged the black corsa around them. Bright fire coursed down Belcher's farther shoulder, turning with the tilt of the land. The world of Firelings was swept with flame. But the Firelings themselves—where were they?

And what of MudLar . . . ? Tacky pulled the limp coverlid back. MudLar's face was all shadowy pits and sharp angles, the skin stretched tight across the bones. There was a . . . a drawing-in, a going-far-away-and-beyond-ness, a *departing* look to him. He was not coming out of his deep slumber . . . he was sinking ever deeper into it.

But they *needed* him! All they had was a garble of words about a shadow and a cross . . . or a shadow across . . . Across *what?* The Thumb?

Tacky looked up at the massive rock towering over the pit. That was where MudLar must have stood before he fell into the brill. MudLar was at the Thumb while he, Tacky, was in the hide-hole under the Sky Stone that first night.

He squinted his eyes in the effort to remember just how it had been: there was the groaning, the *Ar-rarh* . . . Tacky gave a start. *Ar-rarh . . . Arrarh . . . Arrah . . .* Skarra! Mud-Lar had been calling Skarra! Why hadn't he realized that before! What else had he missed? He thought back to the groans that had frightened him out of the hide-hole into the Aha . . . and the sun was casting its first long shadows . . .

Its first long shadows. Across . . .

218

Tacky jolted to his feet, and started up the corsa. Friendly One gave a *squaack* and scrambled for a hold on his shoulder. When they came into the wild wind at the top, he burrowed under Tacky's gowns, a shivering lump of distress.

Tacky stared out over the red-black emptiness of the night. Somewhere across the sweep of corsa, high on Belcher's leg, must lie the Way of the Goat. And when the sun first rose, they would see it, just as MudLar had seen it before he fell into the brill. He turned to look across the Spewing to the collar of rocks where Life and Hulin Blue had disappeared from sight and his heart jumped. The spark he saw looked no bigger than a glowfly.

First one light, then another, flickered into view. Tacky gave a shout, and Friendly One started to dig in. "It's all right, Friendly One, it's all right!"

From the collar of rocks rimming Belcher's shoulder came marching, now, a line of flaring torches. The Firelings had arrived at last!

Skarra was the last to step through the stone cleft from the Tangle onto the Spewing. Before him the torches strung out across the corsa to the Thumb, their flames like long ribbons snapping in the wind. Domma Joke Eye waited for him to pass the sentinel chopper and join her, but still he hesitated.

"Bring the chopper," Life had ordered. "And don't forget."

Still he hesitated. The old terrifying dream hovered between him and the blade. He looked at the chopper quivering there in the red night and felt the sharp pain.

He could say he forgot. Or that it was too heavy. Or that the point was buried so deep he couldn't get it out of the earth. But then Life would pour her scorn over him.

The torches were moving farther away; his domma was beckoning.

Suddenly his arm shot out and his hand closed over the

hilt of the chopper. It was unexpectedly warm to his touch. He pulled, and it came springing out of the ground into his hand. The blade shone bright and beautiful in the red glow of the night. Wonderingly, Skarra looked at it, and he forgot the pain. He looked at it and felt its strength surge into his arm, his shoulder, and spread all through him.

He held the chopper out before him, and his feet began to follow it.

It was on the way up the Spewing from the rescue of Milk and Mole Star that Chipstone began to talk, and once started, words fell about him in sprinkles and showers. Beside him Mole Star nodded absently, the while he glowered at the backs of Milk and Trueline, who were leading the way to the Thumb rock standing against the red-tinged sky.

Chipstone was vaguely aware of their pointing to a waver of lights—torches, were they?—crossing the skyline toward the rock, but he had other matters on his mind. "I'll tell you this," he went on. "I'm not ever going to let folk *expect* me into anything ever again. And I'll tell you this more: folk make a picture of you in their minds and they make you fit into it. They'll whikker your head this way a bit, crook your neck th'other way, skewer your shoulders and crick your back, and before you can say 'You've got me all twisted!' they'll turn you into a sideways sort of creature to suit themselves . . ."

The line of torches had gathered into a cluster of light at the rock rearing directly overhead now, but Chipstone talked on, the words spilling out of his silence of twice-five years. He was still talking as they came up to the tail-end of the torch procession. "There's one thing more," he said, cramming in his last bit of truth. "I can't say I'm not to blame for the picture folk got into their minds at the beginning. I let MudLar take Hulin to Belcher without a plaint. I did that.

Ott hid Tacky away, but I let MudLar have Hulin. And that's the truth of it."

He heard cries and shouts of "Blue! Hulin Blue! We're here!" and bewilderedly looked at his companions. They were the ones shouting, and they were crying out to a frail-looking younger carrying a long broad knife before him, the last in the procession. He turned, this younger, and a bright smile flashed across his solemn face.

"You've come!" he cried. "Domma Joke Eye, they've come!"

For some reason, the voice raked him with pleasure. And there was Joke Eye, her eyes beaming in the light of the torch she carried as she turned to greet him.

Chipstone could feel tears pushing into his eyes, but he pushed an answering smile through them.

As the straggling procession of Firelings gathered around the Thumb and in the palm below it, the long slow sleep of the MudLar was deepening. Soon he must decide whether to come back or to sink deeper, and yet deeper, until the last scantling of breath was spent and he could become the earth and the wind and the sun and the stars. He had a longing to let go the thread now, a longing to know the sweep of the wind down the Spewing, the flight of the gawks, the waves plunging against the cliffs . . . all these things he would know when he let loose the woven thread that held him.

And Skarra—no, Hulin now—would forgive him for trying to make a MudLar of him. It had been too late, the getting of Hulin; a mistake born of grief over the loss of the real Skarra. *Wisdom comes not with grief, but after grief. And pain never goes.* Even now, in his deep slumber, he could hear the shrill scream over the sound of the gusher, could feel his feet pounding the earth, covering the impossibly long stretch between hut and pool, could see the second spout of the gusher pour its steaming flood over the helpless little dab of a Skarra, and his feet still pounding, pounding until he reached the flooded pool . . . the little Skarra at the bottom . . . the scald of water on his own arms and legs as he drew him forth. And then the Seth, born of his own grief and longing, bubbling up through the mudpots . . . *Send me a child of Skarra's years* . . . But the villagers had cheated him with Hulin, for his feet were webbed like the gawk's. Then the severing with the chopper and the binding of the poor toes to help the child walk and run and to keep him from flying away with the other gawks. And Hulin's thin screams, like that other thin scream . . . He longed for the time of wind and stars when he would no longer hear the scream.

But not yet awhile. Not until the Promise of MudLars was fulfilled and Firelings were at last gone from the mountain that was trying to devour them and safe in another land. Better that those Five-left-behind of old had pinned their trust to the sun or the stars than to a smoking mountain whose warmth of body they had mistaken for heart's core.

No, not yet. He heard voices, now, calling out to each other: Life and the Hulin Skarra greeting Tacky. With the shrinking of his body his mind was clearer than it had ever been. He knew all that had happened since the Tackity one had so ungently pulled him from the brill, even to the scamperings of the Friendly One, and now he felt Skarra's hovering presence and the flood of his anxious thoughts. He gave an inward sigh.

You must go, Hulin. Go with your dardomma. He could sense the turmoil in the mind bending over him and made his message sterner. *I release you from the duties of Skarra. I command you to take the chopper that is in your hand to a safe place, for it is a precious thing and must not be lost. I charge you to learn its secret, for one day* . . . The confusion again. *Just go. Take the chopper and go with the others. And now cover my face and look on me no more. I would be alone. So I command you.*

For a long moment nothing happened. Then Hulin spoke.

"The bead no longer moves on your chest, so I know you are not coming back. I don't know what to do except to leave you here, so I shall cover your face now against sun and rain, and . . . and wish-you-well. I . . ." His voice trailed away and then came back, stronger. "I found your chopper, and Life said we should take it with us. I . . . I don't know about that, but there is something strange in the chopper that makes me feel . . . I hope you don't mind that I take it. And I found the goat-picture. Life has it, but she has oathed to put it back in the chest. And . . . and my beads are broken and one lost, and I forgot to take them out of the Sethgown, so that I'm not even a proper Skarra any more. But . . . I wish you well, MudLar."

Another long moment passed, and then MudLar felt the soft folds of the wadding gently covering his face.

24

. . . and the fear-worm had eaten so deep inside Firelings that they put bundles on their backs and made ready to follow the Way of the Goat. Through fire and water and rock they must go . . .

—Stone the Eighth: The Back-Bundle Stone

Firelings crouched miserably on the red-lit corsa wherever they could find some slight shelter from the wind and fed from their sacks and satchels, or fell into an exhausted doze. Twice the wind choked them with ash and fume, and twice it had as abruptly blown the ash and fume off down the Spewing. Belchers' Throat boomed and throbbed like the beat of a troubled heart.

Shivering in the wind, six of the Firelings huddled at the Thumb to await the coming of the sun. Twice-five times Life had unrolled the ancient picture and held it against the whipping wind while Tacky and the others studied it over her shoulder. They memorized its lines and then looked across at Belcher's leg, searching every ledge and stone for a likeness. They found none. Nowhere on the cliff face was there anything like the butting goat of the picture. There were outthrusts of rock that stood in a line just below the Brow; there was a long waterfall lacing down from the top; but there was no goat. They searched until their eyes burned. The goat was not there.

"It's the *shadow* we have to see," Tacky said. "The shadow of the Thumb—the horn—against the cliff. It's no use . . ."

"The sun will tell us." Hulin's voice was confident. "It told MudLar and it will tell us."

"MudLar should have told *you* what he was looking for,"
Life grumbled.

"See there!" Trueline flung out her hand.

Gold tipped the highest point of Belcher's leg. The sun
had bobbed out of the sea at last.

They scanned the cliff—six pairs of eyes straining to see
whatever it was they must seek. Out on the corsa, figures
stirred, sat up. The wind faltered for a moment and a flurry
of ashes came sweeping over them, but the next moment it
took up its steady course and wiped the air clean again.

Slowly the gold crept down the cliff, glinting on bare rock,
limning the scattered trees springing out of the rock.

"Does anybody see the shadow?" Tacky shouted into the
wind.

"There!" Trueline pointed across the valley of corsa.
"Above the waterfall . . . to one side!"

"But . . . but . . ." Life sputtered. "It's so little! Just a
skinny little shadow. And it's not sharp and clear. It doesn't
look like a thumb *or* a horn!"

"Yes it does! It does! It's a goat horn!" Hulin jumped up
and down, his chopper clanging against the rocks.

"But where's the goat?"

"Keep watching!"

They were all shouting and pointing, and then suddenly
they fell silent as they strained to discover a magic trans-
formation of rock and shadow and waterfall into goat.

"Do you see it?" Tacky asked urgently.

Mole Star and Milk shook their heads. Hulin stood mute.
Tears threatened to spill down his cheeks.

They stared so hard that the cliff wavered before their
eyes, and still the shadow of the Thumb crept downward as
the sun rose higher out of the sea behind them, but it
touched on nothing that could be called a goat.

"The sun has moved in the sky since MudLar saw it,"
said Trueline. "It's been two whole days . . ."

225

"Maybe he didn't see it after all," Tacky said slowly.

"He saw it!" Hulin cried. "I know he saw it! He wouldn't have gone into sleep if he hadn't found it! It's there! We just have to find it!"

Life was unrolling the picture once more.

"No use doing that," said Tacky. "We all know it by heart."

Life paid no attention. She was squinting at the picture of the butting goat, her brows wrinkled into a terrible frown. "There's something . . ." She turned the picture this way and that. Suddenly she laughed, a peal that rang through the wind's howl and Belcher's insistent boom.

"Here!" She thrust the picture sideways under Tacky's nose. "We were looking at it the wrong way around. It's not a *butting* goat—it's a *prancing* goat! And he's not eating grass—those are his whiskers! It's the . . ." She stared with narrowed eyes across the corsa to the Leg. "There!" Her hand shot out, pointing. "The waterfall!"

For a breathless time they watched as slowly the shadow of the Thumb touched down on the curved head of the goat above and to the right of the cascade—the goat that was only a meaningless collection of rocks and waterfall until the sun was just right in the sky and sent the shadow of the Thumb to form its horn.

Hulin drew a long shuddering breath. "And all the seasons through the ages, MudLars have searched for this. But *our* MudLar found the secret!" He smiled in pride. "He knew the ancient ones started to leave at sun-bob on the first day of a new season—that's in the Story Stones—and he thought of the sun casting a shadow. And all those years, every new season, he came here, and when it was cloudy there was no shadow at all . . ."

"Whew," said Mole Star, "then if it had rained on *this* year's Day of the Morsel . . ."

Hulin nodded soberly. ". . . he would have to try again next year." Tears washed down his face. "He was a great and clever MudLar!"

Life slanted one of her disparaging looks at him. "If you're going to grow up and make speeches, you'll have to carry mopping cloths in your belt."

"But those are tracks on the picture!" Tacky turned his back on a new gust of wind and took the roll from Life. "See? Aren't those going-to signs? They go straight up the waterfall! How can that be?"

With a new despair clutching at them, they looked from leg to picture and back again. Unmistakably, the tracks marched up the middle of the waterfall.

Milk suddenly gave a great shout. "The Mouseway Song! The way Trueline sings it—with goat instead of mouse! 'Where the goat rears up, and his whiskers fall!' That's it! That's it!" He grabbed Mole Star with a whoop and they beat on each other's backs.

Trueline stood stockstill. "Yes," she said. "Yes! Just the

way it was passed down. Listen: 'It's quick through the wet, And up through the wall!' "

"That's right!" Hulin's voice shrilled with excitement. "It's *through fire and water and rock*—that's what the Story Stones tell!" He raised the chopper and pointed across the wasted land. "We're to go *through* the waterfall!"

"Hoi," Milk breathed. "Hoi!"

"Hoi!" Milk and Mole Star shouted together.

Roused, the Firelings on the corsa took up the cry. "Hoi! Hoi!" With a surge they were on their feet, facing into the wind.

Life gave Tacky a push on to the corsa.

Belcher gave a warning hiccup. A column of orange flame shot into the sky and hovered a moment before fanning into myriad splashes like golden birds in wild flight. Burning gobbets of stuff fell *szzz, szzz* all round the Thumb. Suddenly the air was filled with hot ashes as the wayward wind changed, and the new day turned to night. Wailing cries rose through the hissing blackness.

Tacky fell back to the shelter of the Thumb. "We'll have to wait!"

"No!" Life screamed into his ear. "Go! Go now! Through fire and water and rock! Look! Look at Hulin! The chopper!"

It hung there in Hulin's grasp, still pointing at the waterfall, and in the blackness it had somehow gathered light to its blade. Like a long glowing torch it pointed to the Way of the Goat.

They set out side by side, Tacky and Hulin; and from the pits and crevices of the corsa Firelings roused to follow them.

As the procession moved off through the spitting ashes, they were soon lost to sight but there floated back to the Thumb a snatch of a singing voice, a little off-key.

". . . with a shining blade and a tackity song!"

25

... and so it was that the number Five became a Good number.

—Stone the Tenth. The Story Stones

Life didn't know that Mole Star had followed her across the top of the Spewing until she reached the Hollowed path choppered out of the living Tangle. Now they ran along together, without words. The thickly laced trees dulled the sound of Belcher, but they could hear the patter of ash sifting down the branches, and sometimes a hot cinder sputtered through the leaves.

Life had the goat-picture in her pocket, but she kept her fingers curled round the Oathstone that held her secret oath to Hulin. It was warm in her hand, and on her arm there was a remembered warmth—where Hulin had grasped it to pull her along with him across the corsa. He wanted to excuse her from her oath to return the goatskin to MudLar's chest on the Brow. Then why had she not gone with him? She didn't know, any more than she knew why she wanted to kick and embrace her brother all at the same time. It was no matter. She was bound to the oath. It was an oath promised in exasperation and anger, but it was an oath made well and truly over MudLar's slumbering body, and Mole Star's finger had stopped the third hole for the witnessing of her word.

Thick blackness gave way to dark gray tinged with red as they came out of the Hollowed way onto the bare ground of the Long Slip. Steam billowed from the slotted passage, and Life hurried Mole Star past the treacherous hole. Down the grit path to the Brow they went with linked hands. Fire swept the land in a great half-circle, wherever the burning melt had run . . . from belching Rift to Mudsock. Flames licked the sky above the village and flared, a vast torch, from the Thicket.

There was a sudden sharp crackling, and a flame shot out of the Empty Forest high into the air. A tree . . . a tall tree. The wind had veered! Another great flaming sparked the sky, and Life suddenly felt the hand of fear. If the wind didn't change back, the fire would eat up the Empty Forest —and the Tangle—in one great gulp, long before they could climb back up to the Hollowed way.

The wind will change. She gripped Mole Star's hand tighter. *The wind* must *change.* They reached the Brow, rounded the hut, and stopped.

Desolation lay before them, the mudpots gone mad. Mud spurted from the earth in twice-five places, spouting and spraying over the grass with sickening plops. The air was fumed with Belcher's noxious breath.

Life jerked at Mole Star. "Come *on!*"

Inside the hut she fumbled in the dark for the chest. It was so *like* Hulin to close it and put MudLar's mat over it, even though he knew she was coming back. She tore at the mat, and felt Mole Star take it from her. The lid of the chest resisted her frantic pull, and Mole Star raised it for her.

Gouging the rumpled goatskin from her pocket, she flung it inside the chest, banged down the lid. There was a soft thunking, and she wanted to laugh. Mole Star had replaced the mat.

They ran out of the hut, careless of the hissing mud from a new gout that split the earth at their feet. The fire had swirled up the Empty Forest almost to the Brow. Tops of trees blazed overhead.

The fire kept pace with them as they stumbled up the last few lengths to the Long Slip, torn by brambles, bruised from falling, their throats burning from the fumes.

Steam boiled out at them. The great barren mound was

alive with it. They stood awestruck, feeling their faces blister in the heat.

Life felt herself jerked off her feet. "What . . ." She flailed her arms and legs, but Mole Star's grip on her waist was stubborn. *Stupid! They would be boiled like parsnaps in a pot!* She could feel the skin wilting on her face, her eyes burning through the lids. *Stupid! Stupid! Stupid! To die like this! Boiled parsnaps!* Her arms and legs were going limp . . .

When Mole Star put her down, she almost fell, but her anger flowed into her legs and kept her standing. "Stupid!" she hissed at him. "Stuuuuupid!"

For answer he turned her around and pointed. They were standing just inside the Hollowed way, clear of the steam except for a few wisps that wandered in. But the Long Slip —the whole of the barren mound—had split apart. It was a great gash from which vomited a sea of boiling water.

"Oh." In the darkness of the Hollowed way, Life tried to look into Mole Star's face. "I see," she said lamely. "I'm sorry. Mmh . . . thank you."

Mole Star fumbled in his pocket and brought out a handful of tart gillydore berries. Gravely, he popped one into her mouth and one into his own, then another for each, until his hand was empty. Still without a word, he grasped her hand and started trotting along the Hollowed way.

The crackle of burning trees grew louder. Burnt crisps of twig leaked through into their path. On they ran until Life felt that there was nothing in the world but running. They would never reach the Spewing.

And then they did. Behind them the forest blazed; ahead of them was a world of swirling ash, and through it Belcher's leg was only a darker mass against a dark sky.

Mole Star stopped, searching Belcher's leg for direction. He pointed.

"No," she said. She pushed his arm aside to point the way

she knew was right. He shook his head and pointed again, higher. She saw it, then, a beam of light in all the darkness —far, far above their heads and moving along the cliff mass. The Firelings had got up the waterfall. They had found the Way of the Goat!

"I'm sorry. You're right," she said. *Twice sorry in the same hour.* That's what Grey Gammer would say. She laughed suddenly. "Let's go, then."

The corsa had changed. Where there had been rough cutting rocks that scraped flesh raw, there was now a bed of crunchy ash to do the same work. Cinders filled the pits and crevices; their heat burned through sandals and sent Life and Mole Star flying onward. Belcher flung chunks of flame and blasted them with fumes, but they dodged the hurtling rocks and held their sleeves across their faces and ran.

The waterfall was a broad curtain of rainmist foaming into a wide channel that ran along the side of the leg. There was no way across the channel.

"Has to be!" Life mouthed—she couldn't hear her own voice between the thunder-thrum of the waterfall and the boom and hiss of Belcher. She yanked at Mole Star's arm and started down the corsa alongside the channel. The chilling spray of the falls drenched them; they licked the sweet fresh water from their lips and scrambled onward. Where was the crossing!

They saw the glimmering at the same moment—a starlike light beckoning them through the water curtain.

A hump of rock reared out of the foaming channel.

Belcher gave a great bellow. Life leaped on the humped rock and leaped again, blindly, through the water curtain. Mole Star was at her heels. Behind them, beyond the water curtain, a sheet of flame erased the night in one blinding blast. Searing heat thrust at them; boiling water splashed against their legs.

"Hurry!" an urgent voice shouted into Life's ear. "Almost gave you up! This way!"

One more moment and we surely would have died, Life thought dazedly. *Cooked.* She stumbled along after the grotesque bundle-backed shadow that moved under the light of a sputtery torch and was aware of another shadow or two. One of them had a voice that bounced round her ears . . . "Dignity, I said to him . . . we must proceed with dignity . . . and that is what we did . . ." *Ven Ida!*

They were in a cavern of stone, glistening wet from the spray. A runnel of water snaked along the floor, a miniature channel cut deep into the rock. They began to climb. Through narrowing walls, up and up they went for a weary long time, when suddenly the guiding torch stopped moving. Life heard an exclamation of dismay.

Behind her, Ven Ida went on ". . . so dignified that we almost didn't get here. If *he* hadn't been waiting for you two youngers, I just don't know . . ."

The bundle-backed shadow lowered the torch, and Life was looking into the face of Potter Ott, sagging bleak in the flaring yellow light.

"The rock has shifted," he said steadily. "There is still enough space, but you must go carefully. It's a stream bed you'll be walking through. Just follow your noses, and you'll come up with the others."

Numbly, Life took the torch he handed her and edged past him. The gentle path, wide enough for two Potter Otts, went on for several lengths, and then she saw why he had stopped. One great slab of wall had moved inward, as though a monstrous hand had half-closed a gigantic door. Water seeped beneath the slab and spurted angrily through the long narrow opening left at the side—a crevice no wider than her head. She had to squeeze sideways through the tiny space. Like Milk in the slot, she thought with a shudder.

Beyond the crevice was the red-hot sky, paler now. The wind must have changed and was blowing the ash away from them. In a few moments they would all be free, and they would hurry to catch up with Tacky and Hulin and

Milk and her dardomma and, yes, Trueline. But it was a near thing, she thought as she sucked in her breath to edge through a narrower bit and felt the scrape of rock against her ears. Two arm's-lengths to go now . . . If she was one mite bigger, or if Mole Star wasn't stringy as a longbean; if the others weren't scrawny as winter trees; if Potter . . .

She went hot and then cold.

Potter Ott! Potter Ott was twice as big as this crevice. He was twice-*five* times bigger! A great rage swelled through her, and she struck at the rock with her fists. That . . . that fat *glob!* Squatting over his everlasting cherrychoke, lopping over his bed with his fat snores, of no use to anyone . . . to *anyone*. She sobbed aloud.

Why did *he* have to wait for them! Why not somebody skinny! Why anybody!

But he had waited. Of all the Firelings who had escaped from this place, he alone had waited for them, to guide them through the water curtain to safety. It was his torch she was holding now, the same that had showed them the stepping stone and saved them from Belcher's explosion of fire. Maybe he had fallen behind the others in his lazy fatness and that's why he had waited. But he *had* waited. He had been there, just as earlier he had been on the Stony Bib to save her from Overshot, and he had handed the torch over to her without a second thought . . .

"What's the matter?" Mole Star's voice was hollow in the stone passage.

She clung a moment longer to the rock door, breathing freedom, then slowly began to edge back.

"Try again!" urged Potter Ott. "Draw in your breath!"

She tried to shake her head, but only banged it against the rock. At last she was free and turned toward the anxious faces. Belcher exploded again, and she had to shout over the noise. "You should go first, Mole Star. Then the Venerables, and I'll help shove them through. Besides," she said hastily, "it's too scary for me, going first."

Mole Star looked puzzled. "You?" There was a change in his eyes as he looked past her. "Hoi!" he yelled.

Life turned to look back, but she was suddenly yanked off her feet and went stumbling down, banging against the sides of the passage.

"Stop! Stop!" she cried, beating against Mole Star's arm. "Let me go!" She broke free and twisted her head to look up the Way.

The rock door was moving, settling. Grinding and showering rock splinters, it shuddered to a rest against the wall. The crevice was gone. *For Belcher never opens a door that he does not close again* . . .

Outside, Belcher's relentless *Doom* . . . *Doom* . . . *Doom!* had finally stopped.

26

"Where are you going?"
"I don't know."
"Then how will you know when you get there?"
"I'll ask."

—Legends of Murkle

The Way of the Goat led in a steep climb from the water-fall's source to the top of Belcher's Leg, or nearly, then along a gallery like a dozen Ahas stretched end to end, and finally through a break in the cliff face that took the Fire-lings round to the far side of Belcher's Leg. It was from this sheltered ledge that they heard Belcher's final roar. His fires leaped to the sky-crack and thundered to be let in, while Firelings cowered against the cliff. Whirling winds pinned them to the narrow ledge, sooting them with ashes until their garbens were all of one color. Rain squalled.

The wind changed at last, and the sky slowly grew lighter as the ash was whipped away. They were in a gray world of peaks and crags and ragged shapes. Stark bald mountains tumbled into the distance without end.

Grey Gammer was the first to recover her voice. "Hoh!" she said to the sprawled shape beside her. "So Belcher's legs lie in the sea, do they! To think I might have passed down the Long Slip without ever knowing the truth of it!"

Flaw groaned and sat up. "I wish I had," he said. "I wish I had."

"Nonsense. There are places to go and wonders to see out there. So pull out that punkshell of yours and give us a tune. Where's Overshot? He can thump his drum." She lifted her quavering voice and began to sing:

"The wind blows free
From the star-tipped sky . . ."

Flaw's punkshell wavered uncertainly into the tune, and
all along the cliff face Firelings stirred. From somewhere
amongst the bodies came the *thum-thum* of Overshot's
hand drum and, unexpectedly, the piping notes of several
thistlewhistles.

". . . to roam the land,
And so shall I!
And so shall I!"

Firelings trundled to their feet, shifted bundles and
babies, and when the line began to move, they followed
after Tacky and Hulin, one step and then another.

Only Milk, the last in line, went the other way. Trueline
caught up with him before he had gone far on the way back
to the water curtain. The outer rim of rocks was broken
here and there where chunks had torn and gone hurtling far
down to the corsa, or had fallen across the path itself.
Together they skirted and scrambled and slid. When they
heard the waterfall they knew they were near . . . and
then they came to a spreading pool of water.

Milk stared at the pool where there should be no pool,
where there should be a small runnel of water welling out
of the cliff face and dipping down the slope to the cavern
behind the water curtain. He turned and looked out over
the corsa, a lifeless expanse of drifted ash, to the flaming
forest beyond the Spewing, to the pall of smoke and ash
that hid Belcher's Rift, to the pouring fire that rimmed the
land. Nothing stirred.

Mole Star? Mole Star? He stood motionless, waiting.
MOLE STAR . . . ?

He felt Trueline's touch on his arm, but still he waited,
while time grew heavy. A fitful wind brought Belcher's
fumes sweeping down at them. Trueline touched his arm
again and turned to go.

Mole Star? he pleaded.

Mole Star? Hope died in him.

He stood a moment longer, and a feeling of sadness welled up in him like the spreading of the water pool at his feet.

Wish-you-well, Mole Star. He sent his farewell down through the swelling pool, through the rock, into the cavern, for if Mole Star still lived, it could only be there. All the rest of the land was dead.

There was no answer. There would be no answer ever again. And yet . . . And yet . . .

So faint in his head that he couldn't be sure he was hearing it, came a whispered something.

Wish-you-well, Milk. But it might be only his own wishing.

He turned and followed Trueline along the Way of the Goat.

The long trail of bundled Firelings wound wearily behind Tacky and Hulin—along terrifyingly narrow ledges, through crawl spaces beneath tilted stones, over dizzying heights, down steep slants and up again and down again. Behind them Belcher still flamed the sky. The wind blew at them from this way and that way, bringing rain to wet their parched mouths and ash to dry them again. It was never quite dark, nor was it ever light. They plodded through a world of gray.

Tacky found paths where there were no paths, pushed boulders aside as though they were straw balls, but the tightness remained in his chest. He could not have stopped Life from going back to the Brow; he could not have guessed why she asked him for the Oathstone. But the tightness remained all the same. He stumbled on the path, and Friendly One, clinging to his shoulder, woke up and gave him a reminding nip. Life and Friendly One: goaders and prodders.

He steadied himself against the rock wall and frowned. Until now there had been only one way to go, but here, suddenly, was a choice. One way led up; the other down. He glanced at Hulin, who stood at his shoulder, but Hulin shook his head. The chopper in his hand gathered light to its blade as always, but it gave no sign of liking one way better than another.

He had to decide. He was the leader of the Firelings, and he had to decide. Life would have looked about and found some sign, and it would turn out to be right. Even if it was only the stone he had stumbled over, she would have found a meaning in it. He looked down. It wasn't much of a stone, just a rock embedded in ancient dust that lay weathering on the ledge. He nudged it idly with his toe.

"Bad luck to kick a Belcher stone," Hulin said with disapproval.

A Belcher stone . . . ? It was more like a horn—or the Thumb. Its curved point was directed toward the upper path.

"This way," said Tacky.

They went up and up, and the air grew colder and colder. Tacky wished he had taken the other path. It must have been a bad-luck Belcher stone instead of a good-luck Thumb stone . . .

"Look," said Hulin, pointing with the chopper.

They had wound around the bowl of a valley far enough to see the place where Tacky had chosen the upper path. Below it, the other path plunged in a steep slide and ended abruptly in space.

Tacky drew in his breath sharply. It had been a good-luck Thumb stone.

On the second gray day they saw another Thumb stone and followed it to the rim of the bowl, but they only faced another bowl like the one they had come from. A cold rain set in. When they rested, they chewed on dry grain and rock-cheese from their stores and opened their mouths to

239

let the rain in. The sky behind them was still black with Belcher's smoke and they no longer looked anywhere but ahead.

On the third day they followed the pointing of a Thumb stone through a cleft in the mountains. It rained again. On the fourth day they came upon a valley of rancid weed and black-tongued snakes—and it rained. On the fifth day they wandered a high desolate land.

They lost count of the days after that and only struggled on through the hours until gray turned to black. Sometimes it rained, and always the wind blew. Once they tasted Belcher's fumes again and felt his stinging ash in their eyes.

There came a day when they went straggling up what had to be their last mountainside, their strength almost gone, millen bags sagging empty over their shoulders. Even Grey Gammer no longer raised her voice in song. The stringed punkshell was silent; there was no *thum-thum* of the hand drum; no thistlewhistle sounded. Far in the rear Trueline and Milk coaxed and drove the forlorn stragglers into line to mount the path.

Tacky walked alone, for Hulin had dropped back to help Chipstone support domma Joke Eye. This was the end. There was no strength left in Firelings to go on. Even if there was a Thumb stone at the top to point the way, it was of no use. Even Life would see that. Life . . .

He paused between one step and the next and looked with blurred eyes to the top of the mountain. He was beginning to see things that weren't there. Earlier that day it had been a goat, but there had been no goat—only a senseless pile of rocks. And now it was the Thumb of the Spewing he saw standing at the top of this mountain—the horn of the goat.

He blinked his eyes against the dazzle of a sun's ray that pierced the grayness. The Thumb didn't go away. It was very odd—the Thumb at the beginning, and now a Thumb at the end. Was this Belcher's mocking answer to their escape?

He took another five steps and looked again. The sunray was shining on the Thumb, sending off a golden shower of light. Something moved beside it. Two things, and then more. And more. They glittered and flashed in the sun's rays. They were like . . . like . . . they were like Firelings!

It was a mock, of course, a mock of his eyes and of his tired brain and of his dragging body.

And now there was a further mock—of joyous voices ringing down the slope. Not the sad soft sighing of Ancient Shadows buried in the Spewing so long ago, but of Firelings alive and welcoming, their voices stretched over the years from one to another, remembering through countless generations, remembering and waiting, always waiting, for the Five Firelings who had not bundled their backs in time.

"They've come! They've come!"

"They followed the Way!"

"The Way of the Goat!"

"They've come at last!"

And now in a wave of sun-sparkles the keepers of the memory came flashing down the mountainside to enfold their kin.

And After That . . .

27

"If you would go where the sun goes,
you must rise early and travel late."

—Life

Belcher had spent himself. The fires that had tormented
him over the ages now lay smoking deep in new spewings
across the Brow and the Pillow. They buried the mudpots
and the gusher and the Long Slip; they piled high over
Stone Hulin's fragments and Toothy Maw and the summoning bell; they obliterated the remnants of the Scars and
the Pubbly Way and the place where Toothacher watched
the Swollen Sea cover Hungerbite Rock; they lay, a vast
black barren field, over the upland farmings and minings.

All that had been inside Belcher was now outside, and
the Rift lay open and drained, a vast bowl of dismal rock.
Squalls of rain sizzled against the hot bed and floated off as
steam; seedgrass, coming on the wind, turned to cinder.

There was a thick settling of ash in the deep cleft between
Belcher's arm and leg, thinning out as it approached the
lapping sea. Along the bottom the trees had shaken themselves free of ash; wildroot and sourgrass and the good
sweet linberries struggled up through the nourishing black
coverlid. Brooklets trickled here and there.

At last the water curtain parted and five wan Firelings
crept, blinking, into the new sunlight and looked with
wonder at the land they had inherited. Spellbound they
walked beneath the trees and heard the scuttling of small
animals come back to life. A browse of piggers wobbled out
of a ticktoffer patch and stared at them in surprise; they

stared back. They wandered down to the edge of the lapping sea.

Venerable and Ven Ida, steadying each other, stood straight and gaunt and looked about as though deciding where to start organizing the sandspit they stood on.

"There's grain in that satchel of mine," said Ven Ida. "We'll have to clear land somewhere for planting it."

Venerable gave an absent-minded "Yes," and went on with a deep-thinking frown, "We might try to get to that secret meadow Life spoke of. There is every possibility that the split rock has moved again. Why, I can remember a place—it was on the Scars—that opened and closed several times when we were very young."

The Venerables' voices cut sharply through the blur in Potter Ott's head. All the long days and nights of crouching in the cavern while ash sifted over the land and they pieced out their meager stores of food, there had been nothing but rememberings to cheer them. The others had memories in plenty, but his own were no more than a fuddled snatch here and there. He wanted to remember happy, busy days in shade and sun; joyful meals with a table full of rollicking chatter; cosy gatherings around the firepit with stories and games that led evening into nighttime . . .

It was no use. He had only a long waste of days, a clutter of misshapen pots, the glutting of his stomach, fuzzy nights of bad dreams, ill-tempered flounderings out of bed in the morning, bootless complainings against MudLar and Belcher . . . and all of it laced together with futile, empty talk . . . talk . . . talk.

A gawk hovered above the sparkling blue of the sea. As Potter Ott idly watched, it swooped down to the water and then up, up it soared, its beak stuffed with a big, flopping fish. Ott's mouth watered.

Fish. To fish a fish from the sea was a wondrous thing.

If he were a gawk . . . But he wasn't. He was only fat
Potter Ott, as awkward and useless as a gawk waddling on
land; and, he thought with a wry smile, destined to become
thin Potter Ott of the watering mouth when their food was
finally gone, unless . . .

A picture took shape in his mind: walking up the sandy
shore with a basket full of flopping silvery fish . . . a blaz-
ing fire, and fish roasting . . . and afterwards the stories
and the teachings and the games until the stars fell . . .
eyes glistening with wonder in the firelight . . .

But first he must think out how to catch that basket of
silvery fish . . .

Mole Star turned from the sea and looked back across the
ash-covered land that swept to Belcher's broken Rift. Venerable and Ven Ida were talking earnestly about Venerable
things, and Potter Ott . . . Suddenly fish flopped into Mole
Star's mind. A basket of fish, and firelight, and stories.
Startled, he watched Potter Ott pat his shrunken middle
and make little sucking sounds with his teeth.

There was a strange thing! He had never thought to listen
to anybody but Milk. He wondered if Ott could hear *him*
. . . and if Life . . . ?

But Life was staring out to sea, and what she was thinking was closed inside her own mind for nobody to hear until
she chose to tell.

Mole Star stood very still, then, but there was only Potter
Ott's vision of fish. Or was there something else? Something
far away, so faint that he couldn't be sure it was there at
all . . . and yet . . . and yet . . . A feeling of . . . Or
was it even a feeling? A something. A little bit of a something it was that came stealing over him.

Life felt Mole Star's look, but her mind was taken up with
what-had-gone-before. Somewhere beyond the mountain

247

that was Belcher's leg walked Tacky-obbie, named for the windsong bird that swoops and soars, and she would never see him more.

And Hulin and domma Joke Eye and dar Chipstone—they were a part of each other in a way that always kept her outside. Or had she ever wanted to be inside? Had she stood alone because she wanted to stand alone? Because the standing made her strong? *And one day,* she whispered inside herself, *I too shall go where the sun goes.* She looked up at the sun brushing the top of the waterfall on its journey toward wherever-it-was-the-Firelings-had-gone, and she sent a silent message from the Five-of-them-left-behind. It was an age-old promise, said to have been made by those earlier Five-left-behind when Firelings first found the Way of the Goat.

"I too shall go where the sun goes,
And if it be not today that I start,
It will surely be tomorrow.
But until that morrow comes, there is life to be lived!"

Life to be lived . . .
But SHE was Life, and . . .

Just beyond the waterfall a huge knob of rock parted from the cliff face and came plunging down to the bottom in a shower of dust. A moment later more pieces stuttered down. If they only waited long enough, she thought wryly, the mountain would come down of its own will, and they could walk over it. If they waited long enough . . . If . . . She almost forgot to breathe. *If* . . . !

Suddenly she laughed, a great ringing shout of a laugh, and the others looked at her, shocked and startled. She was Life!

Still laughing, she pointed at the cloud of dust where the rock had fallen. As they looked, another great chunk broke away and came tumbling down into the valley of corsa.

"It's all right," Potter Ott spoke comfortingly. "If we stay away from that part, we can't be hurt."

"Can't be *hurt!*" Life realized that she was shouting. "Of course we can't be hurt! That's our way out—*our* Way of the Goat! Don't you *see?*"

"No-o-o," said Potter Ott.

"No," said Mole Star.

Ven Ida and Venerable looked dubious.

"Then watch!" Life went running up the corsa flow to the waterfall and beyond, where the fallen rock lay. The others followed. Scarcely pausing, she picked up one of the far-flung shards and running on, threw it down at the base of the leg. "Come on!" she ordered. "Pick up rocks, stones, anything, any size. We're going to pile them right up the side of the cliff. To the top of the waterfall!"

"But what good . . . ?" Potter Ott left his mouth open.

Mole Star's eyes gleamed. "It will take a lot of rocks, a lot of time."

Life nodded. "And aren't those the two things we have most of?" She flung up her arms with a joyous laugh. "We're going to build a road of stone up the side of Belcher's leg, and if the Way of the Goat is still there, we'll *walk* up to it!"

Tacky-obbie stood beside the Golden Horn, Friendly One riding his shoulder, and looked out at the mountains and valleys they had crossed to safety. The smudge of black smoke had long been gone from the far horizon, but still he came every day to this place just as, through the ages since the first Firelings left Belcher's Body, a sentinel had kept watch for their own Five who had been left behind so long ago.

From the slope behind him came sounds of a cheerful bustle as Gold Mountain celebrated a declared Hollow Day —Holiday, they called it here—to commemorate the coming of the new Firelings. The descendants of the Earlier

Five had been showered with gifts of clothing and food and any number of things they didn't even know the use of, and part of today's Holiday was the completion of the new houses built to shelter them.

But Tacky had no need of a new house. In the midst of the early ceremonies after their arrival he had been adopted into the House called Gam. His new family had given him a finely wrought gold chain to wear around his waist, and he had presented them with the only thing he had of value —the cup with the windsong bird etched on its side. It had been placed with honor in the Great Meeting Hall where all might see the gleaming perfection of this new treasure.

In time he might grow used to being Tacky-obbie of the House called Gam; he might even feel completely comfortable in the gold-spun garben he wore; he would master the craft of gold-shaping and his life would meld into the happy workaday world of Gold Mountain; and that other life—of running, and hiding, and the gnawing of the fear-worm— would finally fade into an old dream. And yet . . . And yet . . .

Hulin and Milk came to find Tacky as they usually did, and all three stood by the Thumb—the Golden Horn—and looked along the way they had traveled. Then Trueline came and silently joined them in their watch.

"They think the chopper is magic," Hulin said after a while. "The Earls—you know, the ones that have the forge . . . they say it might even be the real Balefire. They say likely it *was* taller than a small candletree at the beginning, but the tree went on growing. And the stories about the chopper got bigger too. More magical."

"And what is magic?" Often, when he'd stared hard enough at the bit of path winding into view from behind a far mound, Tacky could imagine people on it. There were days when he could actually count five of them. But when he blinked, they always disappeared.

"I'm not sure. I think it's believing in something so much that it comes true."

"Oh." Tacky went on staring at the bit of path shimmering in the sunlight. "If . . . if we believed hard enough that we saw . . . *them* . . . coming up the path, would it come true?"

"No-o-o. I don't know. They talk about things I don't understand. About possible and impossible. They say . . . oh, I can't remember. But they want me to help study the magic of the chopper. They call it a sword."

"Mmmm," said Tacky. *Possible* . . .

"And I've finished telling them all our stories and legends," Trueline offered, "and they're going to put my 'Song-chant of the Twelve Story Stones' into the History Chamber. Only of course I . . . don't have the last verse. Yet . . ." Her voice drifted softly away. Then, "Milk . . . ? What is it . . . ?"

He stood frozen, his mouth a little open, his gaze fixed on the middle distance. Still as the Golden Horn he stood, listening, listening . . .

Hulin reached out to take Trueline's hand. Tacky dared not let go his breath. This time he would *not* blink if he saw them . . .

And then they came.

Wavering into view like a heat shimmer on the bit of path where Tacky had so many times imagined them, they came slowly, step after step, and now they were looking up toward the Horn. And there were five of them. Five gaunt travelers through a strange and terrible land, coming home at last.

Venerable and Ven Ida. Potter Ott. Mole Star.

And Life.

High on the Spewing, back where it all began, the golden thumb of rock glinted across the ash-filled corsa, its fastness sheltering the bit of cupped land that cradled MudLar in his ever-deepening sleep. And now, released at last from the age-old Promise, his charges safe in another land, Mud-Lar loosed the thin twist of thread still binding him and, smiling in the deepest slumber of all, passed into the wind and the earth and the stars and the sun. He went sweeping down the Spewing and whirling into the sky, and he no longer heard the scream.